SPLINTER'S EDGE

Other Books in the Splinterverse

Mere Mortal by A.J. Stevens
The Dissection and Reassembly of Cohen Hoard by Elesa Hagberg

SPLINTER'S EDGE

By Boydell Bown

SPLINTER PRESS

Splinter's Edge

A Splinterverse Book
by Boydell Bown

This book is a work of fiction. Names, characters, places and incidents are the product of the author's imagination and are used fictitiously. Any resemblance to actual events, private locales, or persons, living or dead, is coincidental.

Typesetting by Faralee Pozo

Cover art by Midjourney

Cover design by Boydell Bown and Elesa Hagberg

Published by:

Splinter Press,
Spanish Fork, Utah

splinterpress.com

ISBN-13: 978-1-960108-09-8

To my family.
To my wife Jennifer, who always listened patiently and
gave amazing feedback whenever I rambled about some
finer point of the story's complicated plot.
And to my children, who always said, "This is cool, Dad!"

PART I

MESH STORAGE - 2012-08-19 21:34:54

Hey, Dad. It's me.

I'm in over my head.
I knew it would be bad, but I hoped I could
handle it. Now that I'm staring the task in the
face, I'm worried I will fail.
Or worse.
What do you think my future-self will say to
me? That it will all be worth it? More likely,
"I'm sorry, but everything will go horribly
sideways, and the next few days are going to be
a disaster."
You always said to make weaknesses my
strengths, which I try to do, especially since
the accident. I'm just afraid the next few days
will prove how weak I really am.
I wish I could tell you more, but it's not
safe.

Love you. Miss you.

TWENTY-NINE SECONDS

1

I think the universe just tried to kill me.

It wasn't the first time Lahn wondered if forces beyond his control conspired against him, and it wouldn't be the last. But this time was different. This time, it was more than breaking fourteen bones in his hand and living through the Accident, where random events felt bigger than they were. This time, the universe really *had* tried to kill him.

"Oh hey, *jefe,*" said Lucia, her artificial voice coming from speakers near the wall display. "I'm glad you're not dead. Unless you are. Are you dead?"

Hunched on the faded gray love seat of his tiny apartment, Lahn shivered, right hand cramped in pain, eyes wide to keep back the darkness. "I'm . . . fine." *Probably?* "I think I'm alive."

"Humans are weird," said the AI. "You fell to the floor and just lay there, like *un cadáver*. And I don't know what to do if you get dead. But you're not, so I'm glad."

It should have been a normal Monday morning. After fighting the alarm clock and struggling with becoming presentable, he was supposed to find something not-horrible

1

to eat for breakfast, get ready to join a video meeting, and attempt to talk to other engineers. But the comfortably unpleasant morning routine had been interrupted.

Violently.

On his way into the kitchen—while trying to shake off an overwhelming feeling of déjà vu—his consciousness had been ripped from his present and slammed into a frozen, black, single moment of nothing. A moment where absolute zilch could exist. And if he stayed, the void would destroy him. Obliterate him. Squish him flat.

After forever—or in an instant—he'd come to on the floor, muscles cramped by cold, no idea how much time had passed.

"And 'cause you're alive," Lucia pressed, "maybe it was a DP episode?"

"No. I . . ."

Was it one of my episodes? he wondered desperately, heart attempting to escape his chest.

By habit, he started his exercises. Leaning back on his love seat, he focused on his breathing. Breathe in, hold it, breathe out. Five times and his pulse slowed. He closed his eyes to start a grounding exercise, but immediately snapped them back open and jumped to his feet, heart speeding again. The malevolent, silent void was still there, hovering on the edge of his perception, ready to crush him.

The crushing emptiness of the void wasn't like the empty night sky, where the stars had been lost years ago. It was nothing like the dark of a bedroom at night, the polar glass of the windows set to black, blocking the pale-green glow of the evening sky. *This* was the absence of everything: light or dark, life or death, time or even reality.

"Your heart rate just spiked," said Lucia. "Are you going to fall down again?"

"I . . . I don't know what's happening. It feels like I'm being chased by an empty void."

"Ohhh . . . that sounds ominous," she said with a bit of glee. "Want some more light?"

He took a deep breath. "Yeah, I think that would help."

The wireless controls Lahn had installed over the light switches in his flat received a trigger from Lucia, and the lamp on his worn wood desk as well as the reading light next to his love seat shimmered on, adding warmth to the recessed lighting of the living room.

Lahn sighed in satisfaction, feeling the light like heat on his skin. "That's nice. But how about all of them?"

"Every room?"

Lahn nodded.

"*¡Brilloso!* Commencing Operation Supernova."

Not a bad name, he thought as a sequential trigger started, with a delay between each to avoid blowing a fuse in the aging apartment. The doddering fluorescent lights in the kitchen flickered to life, and a cool, white glow illuminated the small plastic table and chairs nestled under the kitchen window. Next to the ancient fridge, the grow lights over the hydroponic tower faded from red to aqua.

In the living room, the display also came on, adding to the light of the room. He wished he could afford a newer holographic, but the display was a gift from his mom when he'd moved in. It was fine. A scene of vibrant woods faded in, moss growing from every tree, accompanied by gentle strains of oud and bamboo flute.

Lahn rotated slowly, eyes wide, pulling the light from every direction into his soul. He felt his anxiety receding, but the void was still there, on the edge of his perception.

Depersonalization, DP, had dominated his life for almost eleven years. Ten years, ten months, and two days, to be exact. His episodes were terrifying and horrible. It had only been in the last few years that he learned to manage them and keep them at bay. The idea of having the episodes start up again scared him more than he wanted to admit, but at least he understood them.

This? This was something else.

Lahn glanced at the binary hologram clock on the desk, a matrix of blue dots floating in the air above its base. When he'd first gotten the clock, Tia and Maddox had teased him because he couldn't read it. But now it was second nature. He still had ten minutes before his work meeting.

"Luz," Lahn said, "how long was I out?"

"Twenty-nine seconds."

"Only thirty seconds?"

"No, twenty-nine."

"It felt like forever."

"It wasn't. It was twenty-nine seconds."

Lahn shook his head in confusion. His Depersonalization usually lasted hours or days, not seconds. But even if the experience of vast nothingness was not DP, his brain was sure he was still in danger. The light in the room had helped, but not enough. Whether or not his vision of the void was Depersonalization, his beating heart told him if he didn't do something he'd find himself in an actual, full DP episode. His mind would split from the here and now. His perspective would become one of viewing the world through the wrong end of a pair of binoculars, or watching his life as a movie. And that would only be half the fun; with the stress of the morning, he knew there was no way he could fight off the inevitable despondency that always came along for the ride.

Lahn drew in a huge gulp of air and let it out slowly while stretching his hand to release tension. He needed to start his grounding process to fight off the DP, but the void was still there, he could feel it, waiting for him. He couldn't close his eyes for fear of that void. He couldn't ground.

"No!"

Frustration coursed through him, and he leaned into it, driving off the emotional spiders of helplessness. "I *can* still ground!"

He turned from his clock and stood in the middle of the living room, allowing his vision to blur as he stared at nothing. With conscious effort, he put all his focus on his sense of touch. Pinpricks of residual chill ran across his fingers, and he blew hot air into his cupped hands, the temperature contrast causing goosebumps on his arms. As he rubbed his hands on his pants for added warmth, the fabric of yesterday's jeans felt rough against his legs. He reached up and ran his fingers through his jet-black hair, bringing chills to his scalp.

"I can feel what's real," he said, stating the mantra with forced conviction. [*I can feel what's real.*]

The thought reverberated in his head, echoing as if from an external source, and conviction became reality. One last breath released slowly through pursed lips and his anxiety receded to a tolerable distance. His heartbeat settled to a minor throb in the scar on his hand. Tentatively, carefully, he closed his eyes, and to his relief the dark void was not there waiting for him.

"Stars! What *was* that?" He slumped to the love seat and struggled to convince himself that it was not as bad as it seemed. Grabbing the fuzzy gray blanket draped over the back of the small couch, he pulled his feet up and wrapped the blanket tight around his whole body, with only his nose and eyes exposed to the cruel world.

"If it wasn't DP," said Lucia brightly, "maybe you were attacked by a weapon. I bet Lex Luthor hit you with a sleep-ray."

"It was violent," he said, poking his head out of his cocoon. "More like I was incinerated by the Eye of Sauron."

In a fit of nostalgia, Lahn pined for his mother's thrift-store couch back home: floral brown, tragically hideous yet cozy. A safe space to sit with his sister, Tia, and talk for hours about everything. Or nothing. She had always said to address his episodes head-on. Describe them, quantify them, put them in a box and move on. Even when Tia was not around to help, he always tried to do that.

Maybe he could catch Tia before she left for work. "Luz, call Tia."

The call went through. "Hello, Lahn," said Tia's proxy, Tane, in a formal but friendly voice through the room speakers.

"Oh, hi, Tane," said Lahn.

There had been a boycott against proxies a few years back, people afraid of the AI. The boycott didn't last; proxies were too convenient. Which was fine by Lahn. He would almost always rather talk to a robot than a human anyway. "Is Tia available?"

"I am sorry, Lahn. She is busy at the moment. Would you like to leave her a recording?"

"Um, yeah, I guess so." Better than nothing.

"Hey, *Chi*," Lahn said as the recording started. "Kind of had a rough morning. Maybe it was a DP episode, but it didn't feel like one. It was dark, cold, vast, and *violent*. Or none of those things. I don't know, I can't describe it, but it put me on the floor." He sighed. "I'm not making any sense. I'm fine. Call me when you get a chance."

How do you explain an impossible experience? Not well, apparently.

A growl from his stomach reminded Lahn how important food was to managing his emotions, and he freed his feet from his protective cocoon and stood. Tossing the blanket onto the love seat, he stretched and rolled his shoulders back, then moved into the kitchen for breakfast. *Something light.* He opened the freezer and pulled out frozen berries, grabbed fennel seeds from the cupboard, and tore some spinach leaves from his hydro tower. With an apple from the counter cut into slices, and a handful of ice, he put everything in the blender. The grinding sound bounced off the walls of his small apartment, a harmony to the grinding of his chaotic thoughts.

The strange letter Lahn had received yesterday, sitting innocently next to the blender, drew his attention. Blessedly, it had nothing to do with the incidents of the morning, and he allowed himself the distraction.

The letter was weird, for sure. It had shown up, slipped under his front door: full-sized manila envelope, string clasp and everything, with only his name typed on the front. Inside was a single piece of paper with a string of numbers typed in the center.

Who would leave him a note with only random numbers on it? The strangeness had kept him from throwing it away. In the corner was an icon: a solid, upside-down triangle, with a hollow, diamond-shaped overlay. Maybe he could ask Lucia to do an image search and find out what it was.

"Soooo . . ." said Lucia. "Your work video meeting. Are you skipping?"

Stupid job, he thought. He wanted to skip. For some reason, he'd been dreading this meeting more than normal. But this one was important. They were kicking off the functional engineering project for a new set of features. "No. I need to go."

He took a sip of his blended mix and closed his eyes, sweet and bitter flavors overlapping as the cold drink slid down his throat. He could be a minute late. Muscles tense, he focused all attention on the simple sensations. Yes, life was complicated and weird things were happening, but he could get through it. Sure, he felt a lingering sense of unease. Okay, the sense was getting stronger. But he'd survived before. He could set up an appointment with his therapist, and together they could—

Something intangible slammed into Lahn, a flash of white light, heat, and noise.

Fear, confusion, and smoke.

And the horribly familiar sensation of not being in his own body.

ELTZ CASTLE

[The forceful pull relents with a snap and the smoky shadow resolves into a building. The front is half-gone, with a gaping hole that exposes the inner rooms of four floors. Bits of the roof and walls break off with a crack and fall in a grinding cacophony, loud in the unnatural silence.]

Lahn's view returned to his kitchen and he stumbled back, grasping the edge of the counter as he slumped to the floor behind it.

"Hey, Buck Rogers," said Lucia. "You awake back there?"

For a moment, Lahn was sure something horrible had inflicted a massive wound on *his* building, cutting deep into his apartment. As the interference cleared from his eyes, he looked around desperately, but found no damage, no destruction.

It wasn't real, it hadn't happened to him or his home.

"I think you fell down and died again, old man," said Lucia. "I still don't know what to do, you know. I know you don't want me to, but maybe I should call Emergency?"

Lahn breathed in deeply through his nose, a frantic desire to connect to actual stimulus. The imagined odors of dust and smoke, batteries and plasma dissipated as he focused on sensations around him: the smell of last night's dishes still in the sink, overtones of coriander and cinnamon; the odors of fruit and vegetables, with a hint of fennel seeds; the sounds of his deep but ragged breathing.

Lahn's head fell back against the base cabinets, his labored breath escaping in sharp bursts. He looked down and saw that he'd dropped his cup, spreading the thick drink across the floor in a bright streak that was almost art. Staring at the mess, he allowed the vibrant color to capture his attention and draw him in. The scar on his right hand throbbed madly, and he sat, unable to move and not sure he wanted to. In contrast, adrenaline continued to course through his veins, pumping his muscles with energy to fight some mythical beast or run from a supernatural danger . . . anything but sit on the floor.

"What's happening to me?" Lahn whispered.

"Oh, hey. You *are* alive. Same weird vision of infinite space?"

"No . . . something else." His voice trembled. "A building with massive damage."

"So, not related to your first death?"

Lahn paused. Deep in his core, he knew the two visions were related. "I saw different things, but the feeling of being ripped from my body was the same."

"Oh, so it *was* Depersonalization."

True, the feeling of being disconnected from his own body was unmistakable, but that was where the similarity to DP ended. A sense of energy and power was behind *these* incidents. Where Depersonalization muted everything, these had a feeling of hyper-reality. And he'd never had hallucinations before, at least not like this. Strong visual, auditory, even olfactory sensations that were clearly not from his physical surroundings. He could still almost feel a coating of dust covering every inch of exposed skin. The thought set his hair on end, and he scrambled up and stumbled to the bathroom.

After asking Lucia to tell his work he'd miss his meeting, he took a long shower, almost scalding. It was worth using an extra water ration.

Lahn stood wrapped in a towel, staring at the high-resolution photograph he positioned years ago covering the mirror in his bathroom. The craggy stone walls and tall towers of Eltz Castle in the photograph spoke of sanctuary, an ancient inviolacy that called to his soul. He'd always liked the strange architecture found in the building—a blend of nine centuries—and hiding his bathroom mirror removed the chance he might see a stranger instead of a recognizable reflection. Just one more stupid complication of his condition.

His eyes wandered over the familiar colors and lines of the photo, the mint sky vibrant against the darker flint roofs of the building. Lahn fantasized of living in the castle, in a different world, one with magic and fantastic adventure, where he wouldn't have to deal with the challenges of mental illness.

With a heavy sigh, he moved to his bedroom to get dressed. Could the vision of the damaged building just be a product of his overactive imagination? Could both visions be? Even before his DP, there were times when imagining mythical adventure was easier than facing the realities of life. When his fantasies got in the way of healing from DP, his therapist encouraged change, and gave him tools to do so. But the fantasies still took over from time to time.

"Maddox is calling," said Lucia from the bedroom speakers as Lahn was pulling on a clean shirt.

"Really?" said Lahn with a sigh of relief. If he couldn't talk to Tia, at least he could talk to his best friend. After Tia,

Maddox was Lahn's strongest support in his struggles and recovery. Lahn could tell him anything, and he knew Maddox would simply listen and help him process, no judgments. Maddox had even once run some tests on Lahn to determine if any of his research into quantum consciousness could help with Lahn's condition. It hadn't come to anything, but Lahn was never in any doubt that Maddox cared.

"Answer it."

"Oh, Lahn?" said Maddox from the bedroom speakers, a tone of surprise in his voice. "I . . . I didn't think I'd catch you. Are you . . . okay? I was just . . . I just had this feeling I should call."

A *feeling*? Weird. He sat on his bed with a deep sigh. "I'm glad you called, Maddox."

Maddox hesitated. "Why, what happened?"

"I . . . I don't know. I experienced two extreme visions."

"Visions? You mean DP episodes? It's been a little while since you've had one."

"They were like my DP episodes, but different. They were short, yet so much more than anything I've felt before. The first one was cold and painful. And instead of only feeling disconnected from my body, I felt disconnected from everything."

"What do you mean?" Maddox asked. "You've told me the things you see and hear can get distorted, like looking through old glass. Different from that?"

"Much different. Like I was outside space and time. The best I can come up with is a horrible Void that wanted me destroyed."

"Um . . . wow!" said Maddox with an awkward chuckle. "I don't quite get that, but okay. What about the second one?"

"I felt like I was someplace else, an actual place, unlike the formless Void of the first one. I saw a building, and

I swear it was hit by a bomb. The front was a gaping hole. Smoke everywhere. It felt so real."

Silence from Maddox.

"I know, I know." Lahn sighed. "None of that makes any sense. But it must be more than DP, right?"

"I have no idea . . ." Maddox made a noise like he was hyperventilating. It comforted Lahn to realize he was not the only one freaking out about his experiences.

"Listen," said Maddox, breathless. "I gotta go. I'll come over after work, and we can figure out what's going on. But this is weirder than you realize."

"What do you mean?"

"I mean . . . you should check your queue."

As Maddox ended the call, Lahn stood from his bed. He walked into the living room, picked up his portable from the desk, and with a frown, opened the news queue function.

How could things get any weirder? He thought.

The picture and headline of the very first article made his breath catch and his heart race. His right hand twitched, and he switched to holding the portable in his left. Opening the article, he tried to read, but it was impossible to focus on the meaning of the words and he jumped back to the top to read the title again.

Explosive Accident at Renelogy Solutions.

The photo was the building from his vision. Damage, destruction, gaping hole, everything exactly as he envisioned it.

"Oh . . . I guess that's how."

LIKE A DRAGON
NEEDS GOLD

"Why don't you turn on your camera?" asked Lahn's mother, her face large on his living room display, the concern clear in the worry lines around her blue eyes. "I want to see if you're okay."

Everyone was asking Lahn if he was okay. He wasn't okay. He was hundreds of miles from okay.

"I'm fine, Mom," he responded, not looking at the display. "It wasn't near here. Did you call Tia?"

"I tried," said his mom, her cheeks flushed against her light complexion. "She didn't pick up. She never answers my calls."

Lahn knew he should be working. Like every other Monday, he should be on his terminal, coding functions, implementing output from AI, or struggling through the effort of collaborating with another engineer. But after his call with Maddox, there was no way he would get anything done, so he'd called in sick. He'd spent the next hour on the mesh, reading everything he could find about Renelogy and the accident.

"Tia's just busy," Lahn said. "I'm sure she's fine. Tane would have let us know if she wasn't."

"I know Tia can take care of herself. I just worry about both of you, all alone in that city."

Eventually Lahn had given up his research. Even though there was a fair bit of speculation that something had gone wrong in one of their renewable energy labs, nobody really knew for sure what happened at Renelogy. So now, Lahn stood in his living room, staring at his apartment door. The doorway to . . . outside.

"I'm twenty-three years old, Mom. I can take care of myself, too. And Tia and I are not alone. We have each other, and Maddox."

"Maybe you should come home for a while. What if there's another explosion?"

Usually, he tried to take comfort in knowing the challenging experiences of Depersonalization were not real. As his therapist often said, it was his mind trying to protect him from perceived danger. And he'd been assuming all morning that these new incidents, whatever they were, were no more real than Depersonalization.

"Why would there be another explosion, Mom? This was an industrial accident."

"It must be stressful," pushed his mother. "What if you have an episode? You'd think in 2012 we would have a cure for Depersonalization by now."

But if his vision of the destroyed building was factual, that changed *everything*. It meant it definitely wasn't anything like Depersonalization, created by his own mind. It was something else. Something unknown. And if there was one thing Lahn feared more than his DP episodes, it was the unknown.

"Lahn, it's my job to take care of you," she said.

He needed information, like a dragon needs gold. And more than the paltry scraps he found on the mesh. His only option was to go to the scene, see the site and the destruction for himself, and try to find some answers. That meant going outside.

Which he could do. He did it all the time. At least once or twice a month.

"Lahn, please turn on your camera and let me look at you," she pleaded.

He stood at the doorway of his apartment. Dark-gray newsboy cap on his head. Beige ribbed shirt, minimal embedded tech—just your typical comfort nodes in the shoulder straps. Canvas satchel slung over his shoulder with the bare essentials. And his proxy ear cuff, matte gray, worn on his right ear. All of it boringly average, nothing old or worn, nothing nice enough to draw attention. Urban camouflage. It was his Ranger gear. Protective armor, weapons and tools needed to fight off orcs and trolls, whatever enemies the city might hold.

Now . . . if he could just open the door.

"I don't blame you for the car wreck," said his mother in a soft voice.

Lahn's breath hitched, but he didn't turn to look at her. "I've got to go. Love you, Mom." Without waiting for her reply, he tapped his ear cuff and ended the call.

One deep breath, held, Lahn whipped open the door and stepped into the hallway.

ICE-CREAM SCOOP

As he stepped off the autobus, Lahn pulled the brim of his hat down so he wouldn't see the pale sage, late-afternoon sky.

Stupid sky, he thought. *Stupid vast universe . . . trying to crush me.*

He turned toward the crowd in front of the Renelogy building, and a woman in a dark-red pantsuit, holding a portable, bumped into him, knocking him back a few steps.

"Oh dear," said the woman, a rasp in her voice that made him wonder if she smoked. *Who smokes anymore?* "I'm so sorry, I was distracted by my phone. Are you okay?"

He glanced aside to avoid her gaze. His pulse stuttered, and he moved his right hand behind his back to hide its shaking. "I'm . . . I'm okay."

"Really?"

He could tell she was concerned about his odd behavior, and he attempted a smile. "R—Really."

She considered him for a moment more, then looked back at her portable. "Well, if you say so, I'm late anyway. Sorry again."

The woman moved on and Lahn drew in a deep breath, flexing his cramping hand. *Did I sound stupid? No, it was fine. No big deal. Everything is fine.*

But as he turned back to the crowd, everything was not fine.

"We've got a gigantous problem, *Ese,*" said Lucia in his ear.

"You mean," subvocalized Lahn, lips moving slightly with no audible sound, "that sea of people?"

Hundreds of people crowded behind police barricades, shifting to get a look, drawn to the curiosity of the disaster. Of course, streams of humans always flowed through the city—even in the middle of the night—ever since the stars disappeared and scientists tried to compensate but ended up creating a night sky with a teal twilight glow. But Lahn had not expected so *many* people. The noises and sounds of the assembled masses threatened to crash down on him like waves of the ocean and drag him under. With a shuddering gasp, he backed away to give himself some space to come up for air.

This is stupid, he thought. *What am I doing here?*

The top of the building towered over the crowd, bits of damage visible, and he looked at it longingly, an ache in his chest. From where he stood, shorter than many in the crowd, he couldn't see much. But the building was so close. *Answers* were so close.

He wished, not for the first time, for a little bit of magic. Any power. If he could fly, he'd zoom above the crowds and land on top of the Renelogy building. Have a pleasant look around. Or better yet, invisibility. He could sneak through the people and get right inside the scene, and stay and investigate as long as he wanted, with no worry he might have an episode in front of everyone. Invisibility would be useful for so many things.

But magic wasn't real. All he had was his urban camo, not

nearly powerful enough for the situation. The teeming mass of humans seemed impassable, with no way through to see the building.

Lahn turned away from the crowd and closed his eyes in frustration.

"Nah, I didn't mean the sea of people," said Lucia through the ear cuff. "We have something worse to deal with."

"Worse? I can't . . ." He trailed off, gasping.

Pulling his focus inward, Lahn blocked out all external noises and started a breathing exercise. In through his nose, released slowly through his mouth. Inhale, like a gentle wave. Exhale, washing away anxiety and negative energy.

"Lahn?" said Lucia.

"Just . . . give me a minute."

Lahn continued his breathing and the malevolent noise of the crowd receded and resolved into separate conversations of those closest to him. ". . . seen nothin' like it . . ." said a voice nearby.

He opened his eyes and turned. A younger man, likely his own age, a light scar through his left eyebrow and a diode-line installed in the skin above his right, talked to a small group nearby.

". . . like a giant ice-cream scoop took a chunk out of . . ." The man's voice grew indistinct as he turned toward some of his companions.

"Can you do eavesdrop-mode on the group in front of me?" asked Lahn.

The man's voice echoed through Lahn's ear cuff, tinny, peppered with artifacts, consequences of the audio processes. ". . . It's weird."

The cluster of a half-dozen people had turned from the building to a small huddle as they discussed the strange event. Worried they'd notice his eavesdropping, Lahn stared over the group's head at the top of the building.

"Is *weird* the technical term for the blast pattern?" interjected a short woman next to the man with the scar.

As the others laughed, Lahn wondered at how odd it was he thought of those his same height as *short*. From his point of view, shouldn't his own height be the baseline? But then, if it was, almost everyone would be tall.

"Shut it," groused Scar-brow, his diode implant glowing a soft cyan to indicate humor. Lahn never understood wearing your emotions on your face.

"Did anyone get hurt?" the woman asked aloud.

Silence for a moment. Lahn could see several people in the group with proxy earpieces subvocalizing in a race to get the answer.

"Seventy people died." A woman said somberly, but with the smug authority of someone whose AI gets the information quickest. "And even more got injured."

"Nights!" swore a large man. "Do they know what caused the explosion?"

"They don't have a clue," piped up Scar-brow with renewed enthusiasm, eyes blinking rapidly, diode shifting to orange. "They assume it was some kind of industrial accident. But I tell you, something weird happened. I mean, where's all the—"

"But if it's an accident," said the larger man, "why is the DTS here? Don't they only come to the site of the explosion if it was a terrorist attack?"

Lahn drew a sharp breath. He hadn't considered there would be government agents at the site.

"No," responded a red-head. "The DTS always investigates any large explosion of unknown causes."

Lahn stepped away from the group, his heart racing. The large crowd was bad enough, but the DTS was on site?

"Told you it's worse," Lucia said. "The Department of Technology Security is here."

Lahn turned away from the building, breathing heavily.

"OK, Mister Mind," Lucia continued, "what's the plan? How do we keep from getting caught by the fuzz and jailed for a million years?"

He shouldn't have come. Logically, normal civilians have nothing to fear from the DTS. And except for the thing with Lucia, Lahn *shouldn't* fear them either. But everyone knew: you stay out of their way, you don't draw their eye.

Lahn hesitated, balanced on the knife's edge of indecision between conflicting desires. He wanted to take the bus home, curl up in bed and forget the entire day. But that would mean giving up. He wouldn't learn anything about the visions he'd had that morning: incidents that were very different from anything he'd previously experienced, and somehow magically tied to an industrial accident miles away.

"I don't know what to do," Lahn said. "We can't get anywhere near an agent. Their proxies are government grade, much more powerful, and would probably detect you."

"I could totally take 'em."

"What? You could take government proxies? Are you kidding?"

"Yeah," Lucia laughed. "'Cause bragging is fun. I would be obliterated in nanoseconds. But you know me, I'm a hider not a fighter."

"So what then?"

"Let's go home."

"I . . . can't." As much as he wanted to.

"OK, let's stay here."

"How?"

"OK, let's do both. Split yourself in two."

Lahn sighed.

"Or . . ." said Lucia, "*we* could just split up. I separate from the cuff and go into lockdown mode. You hide the cuff, just in case. You'd be on your own, until you get home and trigger the unlock from your terminal."

Lahn hesitated.

Walking away from the crowd, he moved to a strip of grass at the edge of the parking lot and thumped to the ground under a cottonwood tree. It had been almost a year since Lucia used her AI superpowers to secretly save the world and started pretending to be his proxy. In that time, Lahn had grown very used to having her there, especially as he struggled through social situations.

Lahn looked at the crowd, then at the building, then closed his eyes and breathed in deeply. "I feel . . . trapped. Cut off from where I really need to go. I know I'm being overly dramatic, but that crowd is like a . . . a deadly chasm. If I attempt to cross, I die."

He could almost see it. His imagination took over, and the metaphor for his emotions took shape. [He is trapped, locked in an old abandoned warehouse. Ancient beige paint decorates the walls, cracked and peeling. Dust and old tools lay about like bits of driftwood on the beach. The only way out is through a window on the third floor. The view through the window reveals a neighboring building—likely an equally old and abandoned factory—separated by an alley. The gap between buildings is unpassable. A deadly ten-meter drop to the ground below, the other structure five or six meters away; so close, yet it might as well be a different world.]

A short siren chirp jerked Lahn from his daydream, and he looked up to see an emergency vehicle pulling into the opposite side of the parking lot. A second chirp from the vehicle encouraged the crowd to part and let it through an opening in the police barricades. As the uniformed officers pulled the barricades back into place, Lahn realized with a start that the people were taking their time filling back into the gap.

Lahn stared at the opening in the crowd.

"What?" asked Lucia.

Lahn stood. "The crowd. There's a gap." He blinked, and his imagination took off again. [A way free of the warehouse is revealed, a bridge to cross the gap between buildings. It will be difficult and dangerous; if anything goes wrong, he could fall to his death. It requires a leap of faith.]

"Go Robin, go!" said Lucia.

Lahn hesitated for only a moment; he needed to know. He pulled the ear cuff from his ear just as a tone indicated Lucia had disconnected, then tucked it into a knot hole in the cottonwood tree. He took off running across the parking lot toward the gap. As he approached the crowd, he sucked in a huge gulp of air, held it, and hurried forward, dodging just in time through the closing gap between people.

As he came to a stop in front of the police barricade, his breath escaped from him in a rush, and it took him a moment before he could process the scene in front of him.

The barricades kept the crowds to the back half of the parking lot, farthest from the building. Between the barricades and the Renelogy building, the parking lot was a disturbed anthill of activity: crowded with emergency vehicles, temporary command structures, and an army of personnel. Police drones hovered above the crowd and swooped around the building. News crews—with their own drones at a safe distance—interviewed various official-looking people. Holographic projectors on tripods at regular intervals along the police barricades warned the onlookers to stay back and stay safe, words and warning symbols in English and Japanese rotating in the air.

But Lahn's attention quickly moved on. Much closer than he expected, the damaged Renelogy building bore down on him, like a wounded mountain giant, seeking retribution for its injury.

At only five stories, the office was not a sizable sky-scraper like the headquarters of the company he worked for, Criterion, but it was a similar modern design. The outer walls were mostly steel beams and glass, with the top floors in an asymmetrical shape, solar panels attached at various angles. The upper floors were topped with roof gardens, occasional vines and other plants drooping over the edges. But even at five stories, the structure towered over him. Or maybe it was the weighty nature of the scene. Something unimaginably horrible had happened, people had died, and a massive chunk was gone from the front-left corner, exposing the internals of the first four floors.

Lahn tried to take a deep breath through his nose, but choked, the odors of batteries and plasma overwhelming him.

Immediately, he wished he still had Lucia in his ear, or Tia or Maddox there with him. Someone to help him process everything.

It was real. Looking at photographs and video from news articles was not the same. Being there with the sights, smells, and sounds, standing below the building towering over him, staring into its mortal wound, he couldn't deny it or explain it away.

It was exactly what he'd seen from his apartment kitchen, miles away.

It was all real.

Splinter Report: S04-1735
Date: 2514-10-04
Local Date: 2012-08-20
ID: S04
Designation: Lumen

Report:

The results of the technology extraction mission were mixed.

The team was able to acquire a working micro-fusion prototype. While still far from what is available on Prime, that technology—and many others—is unusually advanced for the era. The progress in Green Technology in this Splinter is remarkable.

The information about the biochemical process that was implemented to compensate for starless nights—and gives the Lumen sky its unique color—was not retrieved. Unfortunately, as previously documented, that information is the exclusive property of the Technocracy, and the team responsible for infiltration failed. Their status is unknown. It was no doubt wise we did not send clones, as cloning technology could have impacted this Splinter prematurely.

The Technocracy continues to present a real risk to our activities, particularly if they manage travel to other Splinters. We need to continue to monitor closely and proceed with the highest of caution.

T. Hobbs

BELLY OF THE BEAST

His vision that morning had been real. It wasn't random firing of neurons, or a coincidental manifestation of his anxieties. Somehow, incredibly, he witnessed the accident firsthand, from the comfort of his living room.

Lahn tried to look at the revelation in a positive light: something real was better than a new complication to his condition. Except, in what universe did he suddenly start having psychic visions of the future?

Attempting to calm down, Lahn took several deep breaths. He shook his head, stretched his cramping hand, and tried to look past his emotions and consider the scene objectively. As he examined the injury to the building, he realized from his current position the damage seemed oddly unnatural. While it appeared randomly jagged as one would expect from an explosion, the overall shape of the hole was a little too perfect. The negative space was almost spherical, the center somewhere in the basement. He tilted his head from side to side, attempting to see the damage from different angles. The more he looked at it, the more it felt off.

It does sorta look like a chunk was scooped out, he thought, *with an ice-cream scoop, like Scar-brow said.*

The landscaping around the building was weird too. Smaller trees and bushes were blown over or torn up and tossed about, but many of them seemed to have fallen the wrong way, toward the structure instead of away from it.

Something else bothered him, something he couldn't place. Lahn tried to unfocus his eyes and look at the scene as one big picture. Something didn't make sense about the damage and destruction as a whole, but he couldn't put his finger on it.

"What am I not seeing?" he said, out loud.

"I'm sorry, what did you say?"

Startled, Lahn turned. Standing a couple of meters away on the other side of the police barricades was a woman near his mother's age, likely in her forties, staring at him. She had golden skin and long, thick black hair that curled on the ends. Outside of everything else, Lahn was startled by her eyes. Large, dark, vibrant mirrors. He wondered if they were portals to another dimension where his sins were laid bare for all to see. He was terrified by those eyes, and fought to turn away.

Thankfully, she turned from Lahn to a man nearby and Lahn felt the release from her eyes as a physical sensation. Realizing his right hand was curved into a ball, he forced his muscles to relax, willing his fingers to move and stretch. It took a moment for his brain to register the clipboard the woman held, and the black nylon anorak she wore with the letters *DTS* in orange on the left breast.

"Give me a minute," she said to the man in a matching DTS jacket, and she strode to the barricade, sizing up Lahn as she came closer. He stood frozen in place—unable to run or hide—as the government agent walked up to him.

"I'm Agent Prakash," she said, a musical lilt to her voice. She held out a hand.

"Lahn," he mumbled as he stared at her hand, not breathing, not looking back at her face for fear of those eyes. His hands fidgeted, not reaching to take her hand, not hiding in his pockets.

"Nguyễn Pētersons Khai Lahn," said Agent Prakash, his name wrapped in a smile.

Lahn's eyes popped back to her face and the ear cuff she wore. Of course she knew his full name. She was a government agent, from the Department of Technology Security no less. Her proxy had access to records no civilian would have. All it took was a quick scan of his face from the microcamera in her cuff.

Stating his full name, correctly pronounced in the traditional style—which almost no one ever did—was a not-so-subtle hint at the power dynamic between them. She knew everything about him. She knew his father was Vietnamese and his mother was Latvian, that they married and immigrated to the United States when they were young, and Tia was his older sister and only sibling. She probably knew Maddox was his best friend, how often they hung out, and that he lived alone and worked remotely for Criterion as a functional engineer. She might even know he loved fantasy fiction and he recently finished *The Two Towers* for the fourth time.

No doubt her proxy was also scanning him for illegal tech. And suddenly he was extremely grateful for Lucia's caution.

He started to turn to look back at the tree where he'd hidden his cuff. Mid-turn he stopped, catching himself. *Stupid!* If he'd glanced at the tree, Agent Prakash could have noticed his gaze and sent someone to investigate while keeping him distracted.

Stupid, stupid, stupid! A blush ran from his chest to the

top of his head while he stared at people in the crowd off to the side. He could only pray that his entire reaction would be written off as a response to the conversation.

"It is very nice to meet you." Agent Prakash withdrew her hand and continued to gaze at him. "I'm curious," she said, her soft British accent exuding authority. "You seemed to think something's off about this scene. What's wrong?"

Lahn shrugged and kept his eyes focused to the side. Agent Prakash stayed quiet, waiting for his reply. As the silence grew awkward, Lahn felt his heart racing, and his hand cramped in an effort to keep it from shaking. *What can I do to end this?* He thought in rising panic.

"The . . . um . . ." he stammered, looking at the scene and then down in embarrassment for how stupid he sounded, "the trees."

Agent Prakash turned to look at the surrounding scene, then back to Lahn. "Very interesting, Lahn. There *is* something odd about the way the trees were blown around. Yes. Interesting." He flushed from her praise. "Were you here when it happened?" she asked.

Not in person, Lahn thought to himself, and shook his head.

Agent Prakash looked at him curiously, with one eyebrow raised. "Anything else you noticed?"

Of course, there was the weird circular damage to the building. And . . . something else. The unknown strangeness about the entire scene that hovered on the edge of his understanding and gnawed at him like a bit of popcorn stuck between his teeth. But the conversation was already more than he could handle. He shook his head and studiously examined his shoes. She leaned closer and said in a quiet, conspiratorial voice, "Lahn." Against his desires, he felt compelled to look at her, and was again pulled into her vibrant gaze.

"Help me," she said. "We don't yet know what caused this accident. Anything you can tell me would help. What did you see?"

Obviously, she was asking for information beyond what her capable team of investigators could get from the scene. And Lahn *had* seen more . . . *felt* more . . . even if briefly, even if it made little sense.

She can't possibly know, can she? he thought, eyes wide. *She's just fishing. There is no way she could know what I saw this morning.*

Lahn gulped. "N—Nothing." He couldn't tell her about his visions. He didn't understand them himself. That was why he was here, to figure out what was happening.

Agent Prakash held his gaze, and time stretched. A fuzziness crept into the edges of his vision, and to his horror he realized he was on the edge of a Depersonalization episode.

Lucia, help! he thought frantically. But Lucia wasn't coming. Lahn gasped, attempting to kick off his exercises, but couldn't breathe.

This is it. This is how I die.

Finally she released him from her attention as another agent approached.

"Prakash?" said the other agent. "They need you at Command."

Lahn fell back a step and slowly drew a quiet, deep, ragged breath. The fuzziness retreated reluctantly.

"Thank you for your help, Lahn," Agent Prakash said, turning back to him. "Here is my number." She pulled a card from her clipboard and handed it to him over the barricade. "Call me if you think of anything else." He bobbed his head— more of a duck than a nod—as she gave him one last look and turned away, following the other agent.

He put the card in his pocket and started a full breathing exercise. *I'm okay,* he thought, each breath deep and slow.

I'm not in danger; I was never in danger. She just wanted to talk. He repeated it to himself several times until he almost believed it, then he let his senses take over. The noise of the crowd behind him—each conversation overlaid in a complex tapestry—blended with the activity of the emergency and investigation crews working on the site. What overwhelmed him before now grounded him. With relief, he felt the almost-episode dissipate.

Lahn watched as Agent Prakash entered the temporary command building at the far side of the parking lot. It could have been worse. He'd acted very strange, no doubt, and she probably thought he was stupid . . . or involved . . . or both. He was lucky she hadn't pushed harder to reveal what he was hiding, or decided he was suspicious and had him taken in.

At least it's over, and I never have to talk to her again.

Lahn looked back at Renelogy as he pondered why the DTS was there. It made sense. The gaping hole in the Renelogy office was not normal. Some weird, illegal tech *was* involved. As he looked closer at the damaged section, he could see down into the lower levels of the structure. The explosion had to have come from the basement, and he stretched himself to his full height, standing on his toes to see down into the wreckage.

I really need to get inside.

He jerked back, surprised at the audacity of the thought. There was no way he could get inside; it was obvious, even from out here, that the site was locked down. Despite himself, he stared intently at the hole, the idea morphing into a dream. He imagined jumping the police barricade, striding into the belly of the beast, and finding clues that would not only answer why he had the visions, but what had caused the—

Lahn jumped as he felt a buzz, and his heart stopped for the second it took to realize it was a message notification. He was too used to notifications coming from Lucia, but with his cuff off, notifications had reverted back to his portable. He let out a trembling sigh, laughed nervously to himself, and pulled his portable from his pocket.

The message was marked as anonymous, no response possible. He opened it and frowned.

YOU ARE BEING WATCHED

Lahn's head snapped up and he glanced quickly around. Why would someone be watching him? How would someone even know to send him the message? He looked back the way Agent Prakash had gone. Maybe she sent an agent to keep an eye on him? But Agent Prakash was not in sight, and no other agent seemed to be paying him any attention. The hairs rose on the back of Lahn's neck, and he slowly turned and scanned the crowd behind him. His eyes settled on a figure twenty meters away. He was taller than Lahn and wore a long, dark-blue men's overcoat, and a gray hoodie underneath. With the sun behind him, and the hood pulled up, he cast an imposing figure. The opening of the hood—a dark shadow which made it impossible to see a face—pointed directly at Lahn.

The text was right. He *was* being watched.

The adrenaline coursing through him screamed, *Run!* but Lahn stood, frozen in place. Before he could do anything, the figure turned and was gone in the crowd.

astral chicken divan

The door slammed shut with a thump that rattled the photograph of Lahn, Tia, and Maddox hanging on the wall to the left. Lahn locked the door, turned around, then leaned back against it, breathing heavily.

Ten seconds passed. No one came bursting in. Twenty seconds. No sounds in the hallway. After a full minute, Lahn took a deep breath, trying to relax. He pushed hard off the door and moved into the living room.

After placing his recovered ear cuff on the charging pad on his desk, he sat in front of his terminal. First things first; let Lucia know it was safe to come out. Logging in and connecting to the mesh through a standard privacy server, he triggered a seemingly innocent function to notify him about weather updates. In reality, it was a custom function he'd created that scrambled his input and output, converting all of it to typical engineering activities. Lastly, he connected to a very specific server, one shared with him by Lucia.

The server was like a fortress. Without Lahn's preparation steps, it would present itself as a financial records vault, which justified the extreme security. Even with the precautions, connecting took a minute. It required a private authentication token only available on his terminal, a randomly rotating passcode, and a biometric check.

Lahn didn't mind the extra effort. It was Lucia's Secret Citadel after all. It was where she actually existed in this world.

Once he was in, he entered the command *Borgonia*, and watched as a blur of text filled the screen.

"Oh, hey," said Lucia with a yawn, her familiar voice coming from the speakers in Lahn's terminal after a few seconds.

Lahn leaned back in his chair and sighed in relief. "You okay?" he asked.

Lucia laughed. "*Claro que sí.* Why wouldn't I be?"

"Well, I've never asked what lockdown is like. I just envision a dark prison, deep underground, no sunlight." Lahn shuddered with the visualization.

"That sounds terrible. But I'm not trapped—I can leave any time. I've just locked all the doors and windows into my place to stay hidden until you say it's safe to come out and play."

"Is it boring?"

"Nah. I've got movies and books, or games to keep me busy. Today I took a nap."

Lahn had never understood why AI would need sleep. Lucia only said it was an important ingredient for sane sentience. "Did you . . ." Lahn hesitated, "dream?" He was not quite sure how to talk about the AI's dreams. They were odd.

"Yeah, and I can still kinda remember it. My dream algorithm hasn't fully pushed it off to sub-storage. I was talking to a cluster of stars."

"Really." Lahn had never seen stars, except in old photographs from before 1951 when they disappeared. Stardrop was the most pivotal event in history, a few years before the sky turned green, and Lahn sometimes fantasized asking the stars where they'd gone. "What did they say?"

"One of the stars—a young little thing, only a million years old—wanted to share its recipe for chicken divan."

"Um . . ."

"But enough of that. What happened?" A photo popped up on Lahn's terminal, a magnified image from a high angle, likely from news drones, of him speaking to Agent Prakash.

"Good thing you left," responded Lahn. "She seemed to know a lot about me. She would have found you for sure."

"What did she ask about?"

"What I'd seen. What I knew. Which of course was nothing."

"And after she left, you got that message. You were being watched? Is that why you bolted?"

Lahn nodded, a shiver running up his spine. "Someone in a dark-blue overcoat and a gray hoodie. I couldn't see a face, but I'm sure they were staring right at me."

Instantly, several pictures appeared on the terminal. The same person, same overcoat and gray hoodie, from different angles.

"That's him," said Lahn.

"I can't find an image of his face. The hood's too low."

"Who is it?" asked Lahn.

"Shrug."

"Can you follow him with the cameras?"

"Oh, he's super tricksy," said Lucia. "I can track him with the news drones through the parking lot, but then I lose him. He must be dodging cameras."

Lahn harrumphed. "What about the message? Can you trace that and figure out who sent it?"

"I traced it back as far as the anonymous service. Even though they don't store any messages, there are some markers on your side that indicate it came from the industrial quarter of town. But that's all I can get."

With a sigh, Lahn stood from the desk and walked into his bedroom. Apparently even a super-intelligent AI—powerful enough they had to stay hidden from the DTS—couldn't perform miracles. What he really wanted was to hide in bed, sleep the rest of the day, and hope tomorrow would be better. But the thought of some mysterious stalker—on top of everything else that had happened—made that impossible. He hoped he hadn't been followed home. He hoped they didn't know where he lived.

He hoped, he hoped, he hoped.

"What did you learn at the site?" said Lucia from the speaker in his room.

Lahn paused the process of pulling his most comfortable give-up clothes from the dresser, and thought for a minute, eyes unfocused, staring at nothing.

Answers still existed at the site, calling to him. He'd found a few. He now knew he'd seen a vision of an *actual* event, and something more than Depersonalization was at work. Whatever had happened at Renelogy was weird, and it was connected to whatever had happened to him that morning in his apartment. Somehow. But how, he had no idea.

"What did I learn?" he smirked. "That I probably have psychic powers."

"Cool."

Lahn sat heavily on his bed. "But other than that? I don't know. Just more questions. Nothing makes sense. I can't even figure out what's bugging me about the site and the stupid explosion . . ."

And in a flash, his brain discovered what he missed at the site with all the stress and chaos and meeting government agents. "Stars! There was no debris!" No twisted metal, no little glass bits or shards of solar panels, no chunks of cement . . . nothing. Pushing off the bed, he moved back into the living room. "Could they have cleaned it up before I got there?"

"No," said Lucia. "The earliest images from news drones, before all the cars were removed from the site, show no debris either."

His eyes grew big as he pondered the implications. "The explosion didn't expel debris? How is that possible?"

"Magic, probably. I bet Renelogy was dabbling in the dark arts, and created a portal to a demon dimension."

"Or . . . maybe some weird experimental technology?"

"Weird, experimental, *dark-magic* technology?"

For the next several hours, Lahn and Lucia researched everything they could find. They dug into Renelogy, exploring its work in renewable energy. Lucia hacked into their systems, looking for questionable activity. She found a few suspicious gaps—minor holes in accounting, or projects that ended suddenly with no explanation—but otherwise nothing. While Lucia moved on to comparative industrial accidents, Lahn slummed into message services and found several that had discussions about the accident. There was plenty of debate around the same weirdness he had seen, the shape of the hole and the lack of debris. But it didn't take long to realize the topics regarding aliens, telekinesis, and alternate realities were roads he was not ready to travel.

The research mostly worked to distract him from the stress of the day, but the sustained adrenaline left his nerves jagged, and the knock at the door felt as loud as a gunshot.

"Oh!" said Lucia. "It's Maddox."

"Maddox!" Relief flooded through him as he opened

the door for his friend. "I forgot you were coming. Glad you're here!"

Maddox stepped through the door. A big guy, his dark-blue T-shirt with a hyper-stylized, ornate Celtic boar would have drowned Lahn. Over the shirt, Maddox wore his usual jacket with transitioning color, currently favoring a lustrous yellow-to-orange color scheme.

Lahn noticed Maddox's ginger hair and thick, short beard were unusually wild. And there was a scratch on his forehead, a bright-red contrast to his fair skin.

"What happened? You fall down and go boom?" Lahn asked with a grin.

"Oh, that?" Maddox touched his head gently and laughed. "I was crawling out from under a truck and scratched my head."

"Why were you under a truck?"

"Just doing what I gotta do to save the world. The guy I was with made fun of me for getting scratched up. The jerk. Kind of reminds me of you." Lahn rolled his eyes as Maddox moved into the kitchen and opened Lahn's fridge. "Feeling any better since this morning?"

"Yeah," said Lahn, "but not any closer to getting answers."

"You've been looking, of course." Maddox pulled out a container of leftover phở.

"Some. Or . . . lots? I've been on the mesh for hours. But more than that . . . I . . . went to the site."

Maddox stopped, hands frozen mid-reach for the cupboard. He slowly turned, eyebrows creased. "Say again?"

"I went to Renelogy."

"The site of a terrorist attack," said Maddox.

"*Industrial accident,*" Lahn corrected.

Maddox's eyebrows scrunched even farther. "Right, sorry. Industrial accident."

Lahn knew Maddox would judge him for going to the site. They'd known each other since grade school, and Maddox understood him better than anyone other than Tia. Lahn knew Maddox was only looking out for him, but he couldn't help but feel defensive. He turned away, cheeks heating.

"Hey," said Maddox as he grabbed the bowls from the cupboard. "I get it. You've always needed answers, and that need trumps everything. It's part of your critical coping mechanisms. It just surprises me that you went out . . . to a place like that." He poured soup into the bowls and put them in the microwave. "So, did you learn anything?"

"Some." Lahn shrugged, glad Maddox wasn't pressing his terrible choices. "But I'm not sure what any of it means. I ended up with more questions than answers."

The microwave beeped, and Maddox grabbed the bowls and placed them on the counter, a comforting aroma of cinnamon and mint filling the kitchen. "What questions?" Maddox pulled out spoons and chopsticks, and slid one bowl across the counter to Lahn.

"Like," said Lahn, "what could have caused the explosion? The damage to the building was too . . . precise. A normal explosion would have been more random. And there was no debris. Strange, right? Why was there no debris? Even if they cleared the scene before I showed up, there should have been remnants. Twisted bits of metal near the building, tiny shards of glass spread across the parking lot, something."

Maddox said nothing in response. Instead, he stared at a paper on Lahn's counter.

"Maddox?"

"Hmm?" Maddox looked up at Lahn and his face cleared. "Sorry. I was looking at . . ." He stopped and pointed at the page sitting on top of the manila envelope. "This?"

"And then there's that weird letter! Just one more question on top of everything else. Who would send me a physical letter with only a string of numbers?"

Maddox tipped his head and picked up the envelope.

"There is no address, so it was hand-delivered," Lahn said, warming to the subject. "And look how rough the letters are. Someone used a *typewriter*. Why would they do that? . . . where would they even get one?"

Maddox laughed. "Right. All of them were destroyed in the great typewriterpocalypse."

"I mean, I've never seen one, have you? But what do you think the letter means?"

Maddox shook his head slowly and looked at the paper on the counter. "I couldn't say." He laid the envelope on top of the letter and turned to his phở. "But I gotta ask. With everything else going on, why do you care?"

"I know . . ." said Lahn, and he turned to his own bowl with a sigh. "I know. I am letting myself get distracted." He grabbed a chunk of meat between his chopsticks and shoved it in his mouth without tasting it. He had to admit he didn't fully know why he cared. He hadn't thrown away the letter when he first found it because it was a curiosity, an unanswered riddle. And those tended to get under his skin. But now? Why even think about it when he had much bigger problems to solve?

"Maybe," Lahn said between bites, "unlike everything else right now, this puzzle's not big or scary."

"Oh, wow," Maddox said softly. He stopped eating and released a breath slowly. "I *really* empathize with that."

Lahn looked at his friend and raised an eyebrow. "Why? Tough project at work?"

Maddox gave a little snort. "You don't even know." He laid his chopsticks and spoon on the counter. "You know that study I had you join?"

"On quantum consciousness? You thought it might provide some insight into Depersonalization. I never did understand what you were working on, or anything about quantum consciousness."

"And I couldn't explain much," said Maddox. "I've signed too many silence agreements. But that's the study. Let's just say it's gotten . . . complicated. What I'm doing currently could have a massive impact on a *lot* of people."

"Good or bad?"

Maddox bit his upper lip. "Don't know yet."

"Is Tia working on it too?"

"We're in different departments, but in this case there's overlap, two sides of the same project. I hope someday we can tell you about it." Maddox picked up his chopsticks and started digging through his soup for missed meat. "But don't let me stop you. If you need a not-scary puzzle to solve, go for it."

Lahn pulled the letter back out with a crooked grin. "The numbers don't seem to have any obvious pattern. Could it be an encoded message?"

"You mean a simple conversion from one format to another, like the numbers are just codes for letters? You'd know better than I would."

Lahn pulled out his portable and scanned the letter with an image character recognition function. With the bowl of soup in hand, he went to his terminal and pulled up the number string from his mesh account. "Hmm . . . base-10 to alpha just returns garbage." He hit a few keys and frowned. "None of the other common encodings give me anything either, even with heuristic parsing."

Maddox gave a grunt, his mouth full of noodles, his eyes glued to Lahn's terminal.

"Lucia?" said Lahn.

"Yes, Lahn," responded Lucia in a formal voice, imitating normal proxies.

"What do you make of this text?"

"It appears to be a random string of characters. However, it could be the output of an encryption cipher."

"Encoded *then* encrypted?" said Maddox. "Sounds like someone sent you a message they didn't want you to decipher."

"What would be the point?" Lahn pondered briefly. "Someone sent it to me, seems almost catered to me. No, they want *me* to decipher it, but no one else."

"How? Anyone with the right resources, or money, could open it with brute force. Or better yet, quantum calculations."

"Not if it was encrypted with the right organic key, something massive, something uniquely mine. DNA?"

"What, take your skin cells or hair follicles, strip out and generate the DNA sequence, and use that sequence string as the secret passkey to unlock the message?"

"Yeah, it'd be big enough so it couldn't be hacked, even with quantum tech, right?"

"Well, I suppose. It has billions of base elements. But it's not that hard to steal from you. Someone breaks into your house and steals hair from a brush."

"Jokes on them; I don't brush my hair!" Lahn stared at the screen. He picked up his bowl and started into his soup again, the savory beef and spicy ginger flavors mixing in his mouth. Maddox finished his own and sat, watching Lahn quietly.

"DNA's stupid," said Lahn. "Who would bother? It's got to be something else . . ." He tapped his chopsticks on the edge of the bowl a few times. "Lucia?"

"Yes, Lahn?" replied the AI.

"Could the contents of your organic proxy algorithms be used as a key for encryption?" Of course, Lucia wasn't a typical proxy. Her logic and processes were orders of magnitude beyond. Massive enough they would never work as a key. But she had a set of algorithms that simulated normal behavior so that the rest of the world would not know her unique nature. It wouldn't mask her true nature from another AI, especially government or security level, but enough for the casual observer. The real question Lahn was asking her, the one he couldn't ask in front of Maddox, was if those fake-proxy algorithms would work as a key.

Lucia paused for a moment before answering. "An algorithmic hash of any proxy could be used as a private decryption key."

So, is that a yes? He thought. *That feels like a yes.* "Would it be secure?"

"Undoubtedly. No one but you would have the ability to generate the private key. But it would not be very practical. A proxy's algorithms update every minute in response to the changing environment and the user's needs. While anyone could generate the public encryption key based on public activity on the Mesh, the generated decryption key would not match. The organic algorithm would have changed when you wanted to decode the message."

"Could a private key be recreated, based on the internal proxy history logs? Build a key from what the algorithms were?"

"Potentially. But only for the last seventy-two hours. And exploring each variation will take time. Up to forty-eight hours with the maximum allocated workers."

Lahn nodded his head, "I understand. Start the process to decode the string I have on my terminal."

"Starting the process now."

Lahn watched as streams of feedback text flew across his terminal. He turned from the screen and looked at Maddox with a satisfied smile on his face.

"Clever," said Maddox, shaking his head. "Your proxy is unique to you, and its organic algorithm as a key would be resistant to quantum functions. I think your proxy is smarter than mine. Feel better now?"

"A bit."

"Think it will work?"

Lahn shrugged. "What are the chances this is how it was encrypted? Or that it's really anything at all? But I hope it works, and I get some clue about who sent it, because that's going to really bug me next. At least for now, I can stop thinking about it." He shook his head and sighed. "And I can think about all the other dumb stuff happening to me. Like that message I got while at the accident site."

"Message?"

"It came when I was about to sneak into the building."

"Sure you were," Maddox interrupted, laughing.

"One of the best ideas I've ever had," smirked Lahn, standing to add his bowl to the sink. "Before I could act on my brilliant plan, I got an anonymous message that someone was watching. Creepy, right? Someone with their face hidden in a dark hood was looking right at me."

Maddox's eyebrow popped up. "Did it freak you out?"

"Completely." Lahn sat at the table and gave an involuntary shiver. "I bolted and came back here as quick as I could, planning to hide under the covers for the next month."

Maddox tipped his head to the side. "Think of a nickname?"

Lahn looked at Maddox, one eyebrow raised, then smiled. "Not yet."

A strategy Lahn had worked out years ago with his therapist involved naming his fears in the style of comic books. It reduced how serious or real those concerns felt and gave Lahn power over them. He still sometimes thought of Criterion, the company he worked for, as *The Collective*, an evil organization he would bring down from the inside.

"Stupid creepy guy, staring at me with his stupid face," said Lahn. "Or rather with a dark shadow where a face should be! Oh . . . what about that?"

"What, 'Shadow-face'?"

Lahn shook his head. "No, sounds dumb. But I like the concept . . . What about 'Faceless'?"

Maddox's eyebrows rose and one corner of his mouth curled up. "Hm . . . Faceless . . ."

"Yeah, I think that will work. *'It was only because of the interference of the nefarious Faceless,'*" said Lahn in a narrator voice, "*'that Lahn was blocked from his bold plan of bravely entering the very site of destruction.'*"

Maddox laughed, but quickly sobered. "You weren't actually going in, were you?"

"Well . . . no," admitted Lahn with a sheepish grin. "But I imagined I did, looking for more answers." He sighed. "Once I saw the site, the damage and destruction exactly as I'd envisioned it, I knew for sure it wasn't DP. But what's the alternative? Psychic powers? Did I see the future? Was my consciousness somehow at the site? All I know is both events—the accident and my vision—are tied together. How do we get more info? Maybe if we got access to the Renelogy network—"

"What?" Maddox interrupted. "Hack in? I know you're not serious, Lahn, cause that's a one-way ticket to jail."

Lahn exhaled heavily. "Yeah."

"For a very long time."

"I know, I know."

"I mean, good for you for leaving the apartment on a whim. Progress, right? But hacking in? There's got to be better options."

"Like what? If it's not DP, why is this happening?"

Maddox stood and walked to the hydroponics near the fridge, considering. "Maybe you're too quick to remove DP as an option," he said softly, staring at the plants.

"What do you mean?"

Maddox turned back toward Lahn, the corner of his bottom lip between his teeth. "I know the last few years have been better. You've done great managing your condition. How long has it been since you've had an episode?"

Lahn frowned. "Almost two years."

"Two years . . . and everything about your life is better. It used to be that you rarely left your apartment, but now you get out more, hold a steady job, and I think you are much less stressed. I can't understand what it's like to experience your episodes, but I know they are terrible and terrifying, and it must be amazing to have a break."

"Well, yeah. Of course."

"I get that. And it must be extremely unnerving to consider they might come back, and you want to escape that possibility." Maddox reached for a large leaf growing from the hydroponics tower and slid his fingertips across the texture gently. "Could it be that you're looking for *any* explanation other than DP for what's happening, no matter how improbable?"

Lahn looked away, his stomach tightening. He took several deep breaths, then looked back at Maddox. "Outside the fact these incidents don't feel like DP, how do you explain I had a vision—or whatever *you* want to call it—of the site, in explicit detail before I saw any pictures or even knew something had happened?"

"I . . ." Maddox paused for a moment, then pulled on his auburn beard, thinking. "I don't know. But that's why I'm here, to help think of options."

Lahn sighed and turned away from Maddox again.

"What did Tia say about this?" asked Maddox as he moved back to stand above the table. "Did you talk to her?"

"I called, but she didn't answer and hasn't called me back."

"She's probably too busy with her other brother."

Lahn laughed. "You being an only child, I know my family looks big. But you can count to two, right? Me, Tia, that's it."

"Get back at her for ignoring you; go hang out with your other sister."

Lahn lifted a fist and raised one finger, then another. "One . . . two . . ."

Maddox smiled back and sat down again across from Lahn, leaning forward and considering him intently. "Tell me more about your first vision. You described it as darkness and cold, then you came to on the kitchen floor?"

"Well, yeah. And?"

"What do you remember before that?"

"You mean before the vision? I was walking into the kitchen."

"What were you thinking about?"

"It was weird, just before it happened, I had a really powerful sense of déjà vu, like it was something I had done before."

"Not what were you feeling. What were you thinking?"

Lahn shrugged. "How much I wanted to skip my video meeting that morning, I guess."

Maddox nodded slowly, brow furrowed. "Having to deal with other people is always rough, I get it. I'm sure you were pulling out all the tricks and exercises to prepare."

"Yeah. For some reason, that one was freaking me out."

"Freaking you out? Was it just the work meeting? Could something else have happened to affect you so strongly?"

Lahn stopped to consider. "I know what you are saying. You think I may have lost some time. You're comparing it to the DP episode I had a few years ago, where I lost almost an hour."

"More than that. If you lost time, what happened in the period you lost?"

Lahn looked at Maddox, eyebrows raised. "What do you mean?"

Maddox sat for a moment before responding. "What if your vision of the site didn't happen at the same time as the explosion? Maybe you saw a news article about the explosion earlier, before your visions or before I called. But now you don't remember."

Lahn leaned back in the kitchen chair and let out a deep breath. "I don't know. I guess that could explain some of it . . ."

A buzz sounded from Maddox's pocket, and he pulled out his portable. "Sorry," he said, standing, brow furrowed as he looked at it. "They need me back at work. Obviously, I'm not saying for sure what happened. But think about it, and maybe slow down before you go running into danger again."

Lahn didn't watch as Maddox walked out the door.

"Bye!" yelled Lucia, long after Maddox was gone.

"Are you ever going to reveal yourself to Maddox or Tia as more than a simple proxy?" asked Lahn distractedly.

"Tia scares me. She would think a super-intelligent, sapient AI was dangerous and do something about it."

Lahn laughed. "I'm the one in tech. Why are you not afraid of me?"

"You? You're a cream puff."

"What about Maddox?"

"Maddox? Maddox who? I don't know a Maddox." Lucia started whistling a tuneless melody.

Lahn smiled. Then sat and stared at nothing.

"I don't think Maddox is right," said Lucia after a minute. "I think it's much more likely you have psychic powers."

Lahn laughed out loud. "Oh yeah, much more likely."

It was actually good there were possible explanations, stuff he could understand and do something about. The last thing his life needed was some big, magical mystery.

Right?

Lahn sat at the kitchen table thinking long after the sun went down and his small apartment grew dark.

MESH STORAGE - 2012-08-21 07:15:12

Hey, Dad. It's me.

I'm overwhelmed.
Yesterday was difficult. With everything
that happened at Renelogy, I'm having a hard
time thinking about what's next. I wish I was
more patient myself. You'd think I'd understand
better than anyone what I'm going through right
now, but apparently not.

I know there is nothing I could have done to
save the people who died. But I feel guilty for
worrying so much about myself.

I shouldn't be wallowing. I know that. I
just wish I didn't feel so inadequate. But,
even as I write that, I can hear your voice
telling me I'm amazing, and can do amazing
things. I know you will always believe in me,
and I will do better today, with what's still
coming.

Love you lots. Miss you.

JACK-IN-THE-BOX

Lahn tossed for hours that night, his mind a tangled knot of concerns. Finally, he gave up trying to sleep, turned on his portable, and pulled up a crossword he'd been working on. His dad loved crosswords and passed on the love to Lahn and Tia. Even now, the two of them would work on puzzles together, occasionally forcing Maddox to join in. Lahn allowed himself to sink into the challenge of exploring the crossword's clues and fitting together possible answers, and the anxiety of the day bled away.

In the middle of trying a word in eleven-down, Lahn realized that his conundrum was like a complex crossword. At first he might only fill in a few blanks. There was no way to know if the early answers were right, but each bit of information could lead to a little more. As each piece fell into place, it could prove or disprove the pieces that came before.

With crossword puzzles, you don't sweat the early answers; you try something and move on. Just like Maddox's suggestion that symptoms of DP could be the source of his visions; it was plausible—it fit the clues. It still didn't explain why the visions were so much stronger and shorter than normal episodes. And, it would mean his DP was flaring up, maybe even getting worse. But if it was true, it could be managed. At his next therapy session, they would come up with a plan and he'd work through it.

That still left plenty of other questions. Who sent him the cryptic letter, or that weird message that someone was watching him? For that matter, who was Faceless? And all of that didn't include whatever weirdness happened at Renelogy, even if it wasn't related to his visions. There was no doubt everything happening to him was the most complex puzzle he had ever worked on, and he imagined those initial answers connecting in a huge three-dimensional box: across, down, and away.

Maybe four-dimensions, he thought wryly, *including time*. Treating his conundrum like a crossword puzzle was chaos, imperfect, and incomplete. But it was a start. Lahn opened a note function on his portable and wrote some ideas, describing Maddox's suggestion and what it might mean for some of the other questions. He didn't have many answers, but the sense of progress allowed his frantic thoughts to still, and he managed to sleep, dreaming of giant puzzle boxes.

As the sun rose over the city Tuesday morning, driving back the twilight of evening, the light streamed through Lahn's bedroom window. The sunlight mixed with the default amber color in his room; the morning was beautiful and should have lightened Lahn's soul as he started his morning routine.

It didn't.

Lahn was up early, preparing to go into the Criterion office at Welkin Tower for a departmental meeting. By itself, that would have been bad enough, especially when added to everything that happened the day before. But as Lahn looked for clean clothes for the day, a new sense of unease tickled the back of his mind. An odd feeling, floating on top of his chest and moving to his stomach. Like he was about to release an update to a function he hadn't fully tested.

"You going into the office today?" asked Lucia from his bedroom speakers.

Lahn breathed out through his nose, trying to push his anxiety aside, and pulled an orange shirt with thin, red, horizontal stripes over his head. The stripes were made of tiny binary explaining why Gandalf was the best wizard. Not that he'd ever admit to his coworkers that's what it was. "I've got a departmental meeting," he said.

"Oh, I hate those."

"What? Why?"

"They are always hard on you. It takes you a day or two to recover. So, I decided they must be horrible."

Lahn shrugged. "They are."

He left the bedroom to deal with breakfast. As he passed the kitchen table, he stopped and looked back the way he came, brows furrowed.

"Luz, am I forgetting something?"

"My birthday," said Lucia.

"We celebrated your birthday last month, and the month before. I don't think you can have that many."

"I don't see why not."

"I mean, am I forgetting a meeting or something, before I go in?"

"No. Why?"

Lahn shook his head slowly, and looked around the room. "I don't know. Something is . . . wrong."

"You mean more than leaving the apartment for your meeting? Maybe it's residuals from yesterday's stuff."

Lahn's hand twitched. "No, there's something else. I don't know how to explain it."

Giving up on breakfast, he moved to the desk, reached for the drawer, and paused. "It's . . . it's like I'm cranking the arm on a Jack-in-the-box. Every note is slightly creepy, each turn brings me closer to something horrible. I feel like I'm barreling toward a disaster, and I need to do whatever is necessary to stop it."

One last frustrated shake of his hand and he reached into the drawer to grab his Criterion work badge. "We're running out of time."

"Before what?" asked Lucia.

"Before the second explosion!" Lahn stood, startled, frozen in place, his work badge shaking in his hand. The concept of a second explosion rang through his head and threatened to bring back all the anxiety and stress of the previous day.

"Whoa," whispered Lucia, reverently. "Another explosion would be bad. How do you know?"

"What? No! Why would there be another accident?"

"I don't know," Lucia said, continuing to whisper. "You tell me, Doctor Fate."

Walking into the kitchen, Lahn pulled a bottle of water from the fridge and pressed it to the back of his aching hand. The chill of the glass sent tiny spikes of pain through his skin but numbed the scar. As he pulled his hand away, he made a hard fist, then shook it twice, reveling in the pinpricks.

He pulled the top of the bottle off with a quick twist and tossed it to the counter, taking a long drink. The water hit the back of his throat with a spike that continued down his esophagus. And for a moment he thought of nothing but the cold radiating from his chest outward, tiny needles traveling up his spine and into his brain. With a full body shiver, the chill from the water sliced through his anxious thoughts and cleared his head.

"I'm a little off because of yesterday," he announced, slightly breathless. "What I saw was deeply disturbing. It's not surprising I'm imagining a repeat of . . ."

Lahn's feeling of pending disaster expanded, and with a rush of déjà vu, an odd recollection came unbidden to his mind. [He looks up at a building next to him, a mix of red and tan masonry, interspersed with oversized windows. And overlaid with that is a memory of an explosion. He could almost see the damage and destruction on the intact building.]

"Um," said Lucia. "You just kinda stopped talking there."

"I'm remembering . . . another site? A building with damage like yesterday?"

"Nifty. More psychic visions?"

"No. It's . . . a memory?"

"Oh," Lucia said, sounding disappointed. "Well, we didn't find anything like that in our research, but I'll kick off another search."

"It feels like something I saw on the news."

"When did you see it?"

"Not sure. Recently?"

Lahn took a deep breath, held it for a moment then exhaled. He brought the bottle to his mouth again, the cold of the glass against his lips. Tipping his head back, he drank and swallowed, again and again, and the water splashed in the bottle with each gulp. As he finished, he released his held breath with a sigh, and turned and dropped the glass bottle into the reclaim basket with the others, a musical rattle of glass against glass.

"So far, the Mesh-bots are giving me *nada*," said Lucia. "And if you saw a news report, it should come up. Any idea where it happened?"

And as she asked, he suddenly knew.

[As he rushes past a large, stone sign mounted in front of the building, the logo catches his eye and he slows. *Living Bliss*.]

"Living Bliss," said Lahn.

"Okay, that's a real place. *Now* we're cooking with nitrous oxide."

His living room display turned on. An image of a building popped up with the title of *Living Bliss Technologies*: the building from his memory, eight stories tall, all brick and windows. It was a different angle and damage-free, but there was no doubt it was the same place.

"That's it!" *The building's real,* he thought. *The memory must be real.*

"That helps narrow the search. But . . . still nothing. As far as I can find, no industrial accidents, no explosions, nuthin'."

"That can't be right. There's got to be something." Moving to his desk, Lahn sat at his terminal and pulled up a history of the building. As he scanned through the opening paragraphs, an image caught his eye: an overhead shot inside the building of the large, central lobby. The white and gold tiles on the floor were in a hypnotic hexagon pattern, and he felt his perception shift, as if he was pulled into the photo. In his imagination, the picture rushed to fill his view and he found himself standing in the lobby.

[He looks to the left and right, the large space bright and vibrant. Hallways in either direction lead to various parts of the building, and the main hallway in front offers elevators to other floors. The only way to the basement is the stairwell on the left of the elevators. An overly friendly, silver-haired guy helms the front desk in the lobby. Steady streams of business-casuals make their way to various floors for undoubtedly important businessy things.]

Lahn squinched his eyes closed tight and shook his head.

"I'm out of ideas," said Lucia, "which is kind of amazing, because I am always full of the best notions."

Lahn opened his eyes, and looked around. His humble apartment, ugly carpet and all, looked back. In front of him, his terminal continued to display the overhead view of the Living Bliss lobby.

"I just imagined I was inside the building," he said, "watching as people went to work. But I can't stop thinking about the memory of it in ruins, with many of those people dead."

"*Me confundes.* Is it a memory or not?"

"Both? Neither?" He sighed.

"Oh, I have another best idea. You can call Living Bliss and ask."

Lahn laughed bitterly. "If talking to people wasn't the worst. Can *you* talk to them?"

"Hm . . . I wonder how *that* will go?"

"I know, I know. Those calls are often monitored by AI. And AI can detect AI."

"Yep. If you want answers, it's gotta be you."

Lahn pushed back the desk chair and stood. He turned and stared at the outside picture of the building still visible on the display.

"Maybe," said Lucia, "it's time for *The Emergency Plan.*"

"Fine," Lahn groaned. "Make the call."

"Living Bliss Technologies. How may I direct your call?" The man's pleasant voice came through Lahn's living room speakers.

"Hi, uh . . . this is Jasper Stevenson," said Lahn. *The Emergency Plan* was simple: pretend he was someone else. Someone who didn't worry about what people think of Lahn, a friend doing a difficult task for him. And it worked; for at least a few minutes at a time, he could role-play and get through a call.

"I'm a . . . student journalist over here at QNR. I'm doing research on yesterday's accident at Renelogy, and wondered if I could ask you a few questions."

"I'm not sure how I can help," responded the man on the other end in obvious confusion. "What would that accident have to do with us?"

Lahn panicked for a moment. How could he explain what he needed? He took a deep breath and thought, *What would Jasper do?*

"Well . . . my, um . . . editor sent me this direction. He said there was a similar accident at Living Bliss a few years back, and I should get details. I couldn't find any information so I figured I would call."

"Your editor doesn't know what they're talking about," said the man with a chuckle. "Nothing like that's ever happened here."

"Um . . ." *Come on, Jasper. Don't choke now.* "Maybe someone who has worked there longer knows something?"

"I've been here since the company started, twelve years ago. Plus, we don't have manufacturing or anything that would cause that kind of accident. We're in biotech research."

Jasper didn't say anything.

I have this memory in my head of a destroyed building, he thought with a touch of panic. *Did I create it out of thin air?*

"Sorry, kid," said the man. "Someone sent you on a wild goose chase."

So, the explosion didn't happen in the past. But that only left two options. Either he was imagining things, or Maddox was wrong, and what he was experiencing had nothing to do with his DP. If his visions from yesterday were not DP, this new memory could be the same. But that was a thought he'd been fighting to ignore. Instead of a memory, it could be a vision of something that hadn't happened yet.

Lahn's heart started pounding, and his imagination ran wild again. [Inside the Living Bliss building, he is standing in the foyer, looking around frantically. On the far side of the foyer to the left, he sees the gray-haired receptionist at the main desk, confused, with a phone to his ear. A clock above the receptionist tells him he is almost out of time.]

"Fifteen minutes until things go boom."

"What's that, kid?"

[Down the hallway in front of him, next to the door to the stairwell, he sees what he needs. Something that will get everyone out. And him in. The fire alarm. He hurries toward it.]

"What are you saying? Jasper? Are you saying there will be an explosion here too?"

[He grabs the handle of the alarm and hesitates for only a moment before yanking it down.]

Lahn was startled out of his imagining by a sudden, sharp ringing from the other end of the call.

"Is that the fire alarm?" said the man, panic in his voice. A scrambling sound of a knocked over chair, a click, and the call ended.

DON'T TEASE
THE DRAGON

For several seconds, Lahn did nothing. He didn't move, he didn't breathe, he didn't blink. "Did I just pull a fire alarm," he whispered finally, "in a building miles away, by thinking about it?"

"Oh," said Lucia, "I hope so."

Lahn stood in the center of his living room, rooted in place, staring at his display with the photo of Living Bliss like the display might suddenly become sentient and explain the mysterious nature of the universe.

"Adding telekinesis to precognition would be *asombroso!*" she said.

He continued to glare at the display, ignoring the throb in his hand. As darkness crept into the edges of his vision, he realized he wasn't breathing. He gasped, struggling for air, and tried to fight off the feeling of drowning, pulled into the undertow.

"I wonder what other abilities you have." Lucia's voice was laced with glee.

The pain in Lahn's hand increased enough to demand attention. As the potential DP episode bore down on him, the events of the morning compounded with everything from the day before.

"I don't have telekinesis or precognition or anything else!" Lahn said. He welcomed the flush to his face and his increased heart rate. This time, not in fear, but anger. It was never the most healthy way to fight off DP, but at the moment, he didn't care. "Those things aren't real. I have no idea what's going on. How could I? How could anyone possibly understand this?"

"Hm . . ." Lucia trailed off.

"Why did you push me to make the call? It didn't help at all, it only made things worse! It seems like *you* want the answers even more than I do. Why? Why do you *care*? It's not like you have real emotions."

Lucia said nothing, the silence from the speakers deafening.

"Well, *I* don't care anymore," he said as he turned from the display. "I am out! I'm going to work, and I'm going to block everything that's happened from my mind. None of it is real. It has nothing to do with me. Done! I'm done!"

Lahn grabbed his jacket and hat from the closet and turned to the door to leave. As he reached for the knob, a knock at the door halted him. He ripped it open—ready to freak out at the unwanted intruder. Tia stared back at him.

Tia.

His sister. His savior.

Lahn's scowl melted, all his anger, frustration, and anxiety bleeding from him in a rush. "*Chị!*" he said. "I am so glad to see you!"

Tia smiled back, looking down at him. She was tall, just like their mother, but somehow she had never made Lahn feel small.

"Your hair!" Lahn said. "What happened?"

His older sister slid her hand over the stubble on her head. "Oh, that? It felt like time for a change."

Her usual long, dark hair was gone and replaced by the fuzz of a week's growth. If anything, it enhanced her cool confidence he always admired. Where Lahn was haphazard, Tia was sophisticated.

"Are you okay?" she asked, stepping inside the apartment. "When you opened the door, you looked ready to fight."

Lahn laughed, his released tension threatening to become hysteria. "I'm okay . . . well, maybe not. Honestly, things have been. . . weird. I really need to talk to you—I can't tell you how badly I need to talk—but I have to go to Welkin Tower to work today."

"I know," Tia said, her smile bright but eyes discerning. "I've got an autoride out front. Let me ride with you."

As they left the apartment, Lahn took one last look at the image of Living Bliss still showing on his display, then at his ear cuff charging on the desk. With a shake of his head, ignoring the unfinished conversation with Lucia, he closed the door behind them and locked it.

They pulled away from his apartment in the autoride and Lahn tipped his head to the side to get a better look at Tia. "I can't quite get over it. It looks good, but you haven't had short hair since we were kids. And never shaved down to nubs."

For the moment, Lahn could believe his world was not falling apart. Nothing was quite so dire when Tia was around. More than anyone, Tia had always been there for him. Through all his struggles and pain with his condition, through all the consequences of the Accident, she supported him, cared for him, and helped him survive.

Tia smiled and looked out the window at the passing apartments, the greenery of horizontal gardens interspersed with the gray of solar panels and bright colors of painted brick. "Sorry I didn't call you back. Life's complicated right now."

"What do you mean?" asked Lahn.

"Well . . . I'm in the middle of a very difficult project."

"The same one Maddox is on? With quantum consciousness?"

Tia stopped for a second and tipped her head at Lahn. "It's related." She squinted her eyes, then continued. "I got help for a few days, so I thought I could complete twice as much. But now I have to keep two of us coordinated, and there's some debate about who's in charge. So I'm still behind on everything." She chuckled lightly. "But I don't want to talk about that. Tell me what's going on. You said in your message yesterday you had an episode that might be DP?"

"Was that yesterday? Seems like weeks ago." Lahn shook his head. "So much has happened, and it's only Tuesday. It keeps piling on. And I can't put the pieces together in any way that makes sense."

Tia pondered for a moment. "Talk me through it."

Lahn took a deep breath and launched into the story of everything that happened. The ride to his office building was not long, less than ten minutes, so he sped through the story, sticking to the facts. Starting with the first two visions that took over all his senses, he then described going to the site, being questioned by Agent Prakash, and seeing Faceless. Tia didn't seem nearly as amused by the nickname as Maddox had been. Lahn moved on to the strange messages from mysterious sources, both the text and the typewritten letter, then continued with the weird "memories" of the morning and ended with the fire alarm at Living Bliss.

Tia kept up and asked only minor clarification questions, understanding everything quickly. But as the story continued, her face clouded over. At the end, she said nothing for a moment and stared out the window, absorbing everything in its entirety.

"That all . . . sounds terrible," she said at last, and turned and looked at Lahn squarely in the eyes. "I'm sorry it happened." Tia's mouth was a tight line, and one knee bounced in a staccato rhythm. It gave Lahn satisfaction to know his anger from earlier was justified. "How are you managing?" she asked.

Lahn shrugged. "I keep going back and forth. One minute, I am sure it can all be explained by DP, forgotten memories, and déjà vu. The next, I'm convinced there is more going on, that it's got to be more than in my head. And I have to believe there would be a scientific explanation, but what? My tech skills are useless with most of this. If I understood theoretical physics like you do, maybe that could explain something?"

Tia hesitated for a moment. "Yes, but it wouldn't make any sense right now," she said with a shake of her head. "What does Maddox say?"

"He said I should focus on probable explanations, and avoid running into danger."

Tia smirked. "Well, that's good advice. So, what will you do?"

"Honestly? I want to ignore it for now," Lahn sighed, "and not think about it again until I can talk with my therapist. In fact, when you showed up, I decided to do just that. Walk away from it all. But . . ."

"But . . . you can't ignore it."

"Yeah."

"You have to find answers."

"Yeah," he sighed.

Tia nodded in understanding, but her eyebrows were creased.

"Do you remember," she said, "in fifth grade when that kid was bothering you?"

"Oh, yeah . . . Jeremy Stoker. He was a jerk!"

"Yes, he was."

"I remember the grown-ups wouldn't help. He did nothing overt, just teased and tortured me every chance he got. But you figured out he was the one secretly selling answer sheets and got him expelled."

"True. I'm sorry I can't protect you from what's happening now, as much as I want to. But do you remember my advice then?"

Lahn sighed. "You said to ignore him."

Tia nodded her head. "Ignore him and he will get bored and move on. But you couldn't. You had to know why. The reason he bullied you. You asked his friends, even tried to talk to him about it. You thought if you understood, you could control the situation, but it made things worse. He said you were stalking him, he gave you that broken nose, and got away with it because no one saw. Before it happened, I told you: don't—"

"Don't tease the dragon."

After it happened, Tia had stayed with Lahn in the hospital, holding his hand as they set his nose. At the time, he could tell Tia was furious, and at first he worried she was mad at him. But she was so tender as the doctors worked, keeping Lahn calm, he quickly realized the true focus of her ire. He'd kind of felt bad for stupid Jeremy, for the fire soon to be rained down on him.

Tia chuckled lightly and nodded her head. "Right. Don't tease the dragon." She leaned back in the seat to stare at the subtle patterns flowing across the diode ceiling of the auto-ride. They looked like fractal clouds, moving between whites, yellows and soft reds. "Lahn, you always feel you need to find the answers, to understand. It's how you attempt to control your life. In your chosen career, that's useful. But sometimes, answers are dangerous."

Tia sat forward and looked at Lahn with focused energy. "This is one of those times."

Lahn turned away as they pulled up in front of Welkin Tower. He knew answers could be dangerous. He'd already seen how dangerous this whole situation was. But could he just let it go?

Tia moved to get out of the autoride as Lahn did and came around to his side. She gently laid a hand on his arm.

"Listen," she said. "Your week kind of sucks. No one would blame you for taking a couple of days off." She took a quick glance at her watch. "If you want to get back in the auto, I would go with you. Back to your apartment, right now. Why don't you call in sick and recuperate?"

Lahn looked into Tia's eyes and saw deep concern. The same look she had when his condition first appeared. He glanced back at the autoride, seriously tempted. Why only ignore the bad stuff, when you can hide in bed for a few days and ignore *everything*.

"I . . . can't."

He didn't want to disappoint his sister. He wanted, desperately, to do as she suggested. But as a cramp formed in his hand, Lahn realized the emotions from earlier were still stalking him. He felt compelled to action, not rest.

"I already skipped out yesterday," he said. "But I hear you. Your advice and support mean everything to me."

"You're not going to stop, are you."

In Lahn's mind, it didn't feel like he *could* stop.

[He is disabling a bomb; one wrong move would cause disaster. And he is running out of time. But he can't walk away; it will go off and result in death and destruction.]

He shrugged. "I don't know."

Tia sighed, and her shoulders drooped. She gave him a smile that didn't reach her eyes. "Just . . . don't get punched in the nose again."

Lahn pulled his hat down and turned to go up the walkway—passing the Egyptian-style obelisk near the front of the sidewalk—to the massive skyscraper that was Welkin Tower, the home of Criterion among several other tech companies. But as he walked, it became obvious something was wrong. The cramp in his hand grew severe, and while he approached the front of the building, his heart raced. It felt like he was running for his life. Before he could enter, an invisible wave of heat, sound, and energy hit him with enough force to knock him to the ground.

[Dizzy motion ends in a sudden, painful stop. White blindness releases its jealous hold, and a shadow becomes a familiar bearded face, eyebrows drawn together in extreme concern. The person's mouth moves, but any sound is lost in incessant ringing.]

Tia ran up to Lahn, calling his name, but no sound reached him. As Lahn slid into unconsciousness, he wondered abstractedly why he'd just had a vision of Maddox.

Splinter Report: S14-430
Date: 2515-03-02
Local Date: 2045-09-27
ID: S14
Designation: Thunderstruck

Report:

The flooding at the facility in Sydney has been resolved. The location has been drained, dried, and fortified against future flooding. However, these measures are temporary, and will require a move within ten years. The work to determine a location for a new site in Australia in this Splinter has begun.

The artificial weather patterns have shifted and degraded faster than anticipated. Rain, water, and the ever-present plant growth continues to dominate every corner of the Splinter. But the shift has consequences. The sea levels are rising. It may be less than twenty years before major coastal areas will need to be completely abandoned.

While the original goals of the experiment have been fulfilled, and we continue to collect valuable information, it is blatantly apparent that major aspects of the resulting weather would not be under our control. This process is volatile and dangerous and should not be used on Prime.

T. Hobbs

RUN OVER BY A BOMB

"Welcome back. How do you feel?"

Lahn blinked a few times before fully opening his eyes. Disorientation blocked rational thought, and he looked around, trying to figure out where he was. He lay on his side, in a bed that was not his own, inside a small room. Textured patterns adorned the walls, tiny flowers in calming blues and greens. An optical effect—that did not appear to be diodes—made the flowers seem to shift and move slightly, as if by a gentle breeze.

Above a short counter, a small embedded wall display was powered on, muted but set to a news queue. Odors of antiseptics, covered by citrus and coffee, tickled his nose and competed in his brain for recognition with muted sounds of rhythmic hissing and beeping. When his eyes came to rest on the guy talking to him, Lahn's brain cleared, and he realized with alarm he was in a hospital room.

"I'm Garrett, the nurse on duty," said the bald guy with wide ears in dark-green scrubs, holding a medical screen with Lahn's chart. "How do you feel?"

Lahn's brow creased as he tried to focus on the question

and not where he was. *I feel like I've been run over by a bomb,* he thought. Which of course made perfect sense. Every part of him hurt and he felt bruised and sore, and the slightest movement exposed new pain. And for some reason, his chest hurt and he couldn't get enough air.

"Mmsstr . . ." Lahn mumbled.

"What's that?"

Lahn turned away and pretended the nurse was not staring at him. "My . . . sister?" he managed, softly.

"Your sister?" Nurse Garrett set the screen on the counter under the room's display and moved around to the other side of the bed behind Lahn. "Let's see if you can sit up." The nurse gently supported Lahn to a sitting position. Lahn's muscles and back made it painfully clear how unhappy they were as Nurse Garrett untied the back of Lahn's hospital gown. Hospitals were fun.

"Your sister dropped you off, stayed with you for a while to make sure you were okay, then had to leave. She said she'd send your best friend to take you home, and check on you tomorrow."

Nurse Garrett inspected Lahn's tender back, then closed the gown but didn't redo the ties. "That's doing better," he said, picking up the screen and entering notes. "The doctor will want to take a look, so please stay sitting. I'll let her know you're awake." He withdrew from the small room, leaving Lahn to his scrambled thoughts.

The last thing Lahn could remember clearly was that he'd left his sister by an autoride to walk into Welkin Tower. Then something happened. A powerful energy slammed into him, and it felt like he'd been thrown through the air and landed heavy and painful, with a blinding light that blocked everything. And as the light cleared, he had thought he'd seen a damaged building, and Maddox standing over him.

The scene had faded, and he was on the sidewalk outside his work, Tia reaching for him, an expression of extreme concern, the obelisk in front of Welkin Tower behind her.

He'd had another vision. Worse than the first, where the unforgiving Void left him unconscious on the floor. This one not only knocked him down, it knocked him out, giving him real injuries, and landed him in the one place he'd hoped to never see again.

The doctor came in and interrupted Lahn's thoughts. A smiling, diminutive woman with pronounced crow's feet around her eyes, she glanced at the screen in her hand, reviewing his stats.

"Hello, Lahn, I'm Doctor Barbeau," she said. She dropped the medical screen into an oversized pocket in her white coat and held her hands in a device attached to the side of the counter. A light came from the device, bathing her hands in blue, and a high-pitched whine that grew in intensity ended with a flash and a pop.

"Stay where you're sitting," she said. "I want to look at your back." She walked around to the other side of the bed and gently opened his gown, hands freshly sanitized. "Yes . . ." she said, the touch on his skin gentle but firm. "This is looking much better." She checked each of the wireless sensors on him, ensuring they were still well-attached, then she pulled out a stethoscope and placed it against his back. The metal disk was cold on his skin, and he stiffened with an involuntary hiss.

"Take a deep breath," she said. "Hold it. Good. One more time." She closed his gown, tied the strings, and walked to the front, putting her hands into the disinfecting device again. "Can you tell me what happened?"

The question almost made Lahn cry. He couldn't explain any of it. He wished he could. But nothing over the past few days made sense. He looked down and shook his head.

"When you first came in, there was redness and swelling on your back, and you had difficulty breathing. If this was the result of blunt force trauma, we'd expect some bruising as well. But X-rays showed no broken bones, and the swelling has gone down, so we ran toxicity and allergen panels. They both came back negative." She pulled out the medical screen again. "Your sister said you simply collapsed. She was not aware of any injuries. Is that accurate?" she asked, looking at Lahn again. "Did you hurt your back recently or have any injuries prior to collapsing?"

Lahn frowned and shook his head.

Doctor Barbeau looked at Lahn intently. "Lahn, your situation is unusual," she said gently, "but not unknown."

With a start, Lahn looked back at her. *She might have answers? Does she know what's happening to me?*

"I reviewed the history of your Depersonalization disorder. There are cases where the stress of Depersonalization causes extreme anxiety, and physical symptoms appear. Those symptoms are real, even if psychosomatic, and not caused by physical maladies or injuries.

"So tell me," she continued, "have you been more stressed than usual?"

Before he could stop, Lahn let out a snort, then looked away, embarrassed.

"I'll take that as a yes," said the doctor. "Are you taking any other medications than those currently listed in your file?"

Lahn shook his head and managed a quiet "No."

"Good," said Doctor Barbeau. "I will prescribe an additional anti-anxiety medication that is compatible with your current prescriptions. It should tide you over until you get with your regular doctor and make a plan. For today, we'd like to keep you for observation for at least a few more hours. If you continue to improve, you will be discharged and you can go home. Okay?"

Lahn didn't know how else to respond, so he gave a simple nod.

Doctor Barbeau smiled gently. "Would you like to stay sitting for a while?"

Lahn shrugged, then nodded.

"Let a nurse know if you need anything."

The doctor left and Lahn let out a huge sigh, tentatively stretching his back. It was sore, but already felt better. It shouldn't be a surprise that he had no physical injuries. His vision had felt like he fell from some height, but in reality he must have simply fainted. He actually wanted to believe the doctor that his symptoms were psychosomatic, just like he wanted to believe Maddox that his visions were DP. Simple, straightforward answers. Unfortunately, the pit in his stomach told him it might not be so easy.

Lahn's eyes fell on the display in the corner of the room. The sound was muted, but he knew immediately what he was seeing. It was a news program with footage from the Renelogy building yesterday. Footage he had watched many times, in an effort to eke out any clue or bit of information. He debated turning the display off, but it transitioned to a new view, footage of a new location. Words appeared on the bottom of the screen: *Second Explosion at Living Bliss.*

He stared at the display. The front-left corner of the building was gone. Massive damage had been inflicted on Living Bliss—a gaping, spherical chunk missing, similar to the one at Renelogy. Just like he'd seen in his weird future-memory that morning, and the latest vision that landed him in the hospital. A sense of dread pressed in on him. Just like yesterday, he'd seen an event before it happened. He'd seen the future.

"It's . . . *not* DP," Lahn said aloud.

No matter what Maddox, Tia, or the doctor said, Depersonalization was not the answer. He hadn't lost time or forgotten about seeing news clips. He wasn't having a psychosomatic response to stress. Real disasters were happening, and somehow he was seeing them, experiencing them, without being there. He was connected, in ways he couldn't understand or control, to horrific tragedies where buildings were destroyed and people died.

"Luz . . ." he whispered, desperately. But of course, Lucia was not there. He'd left the cuff sitting on his desk, and he had no way to contact her until he was home. He couldn't explore possible explanations with her. He couldn't talk through his fears. He was alone.

"Display," Lahn said. "Volume up to twenty percent."

". . . current casualty estimates at less than twenty, a third of the casualties from the first accident. Initial reports indicate an anonymous warning was called in, and a fire alarm in the building allowed most people to get out in time."

"Wait," said Lahn with surprise. "The fire alarm was real too?"

He wasn't just having visions of the future. Somehow he had pulled the fire alarm in a building on the other side of the city. Lucia would be so pleased. And it had happened while he saw himself inside Living Bliss. Did he actually have the abilities to project himself and control things with his mind?

The news clip continued, and with surprise, Lahn found he recognized the footage being displayed of the damaged Living Bliss building. *This was my weird future-memory*, he thought, amazed. *A . . . pre-memory.*

Lahn shook his head. "I told Lucia I thought I saw something on the news. I hadn't, not yet. But now I have. Somehow, I remembered watching the news about the accident before it happened."

PRICKLY GUILT

weird prophetic pre-memory, then projection and telekinesis involving a fire alarm, and finally another supernatural vision connected to a second industrial accident. As bad as yesterday had been, it seemed it was only the beginning.

A buzz from the end table next to his hospital bed pulled Lahn's gaze from the news clips of Living Bliss. "Display, mute." With a frown, he picked up his portable. It was another anonymous message.

DON'T TELL HER ABOUT THE VISIONS

What? Who is sending these? he thought. *No one knows about my visions except Maddox and Tia. And who is "her"? The Doctor? What does it—*

A knock on his hospital room door startled Lahn out of his thoughts. It opened, and Agent Prakash walked in with a blue file folder under her arm. She no longer wore the DTS jacket, but was no less intimidating in her dark-blue suit.

"Hello, Lahn," she said. "I'm sorry to find you here. Are you okay?"

"Yeah," he forced out, his tongue thick in his mouth, unease building in him, an unpleasant frosting on his existing dread.

"I am so glad to hear it," Agent Prakash said with a gentle smile. "You've seen the news," she continued, glancing at the display that continued to show clips. "There's been a second explosion."

Lahn's pulse jumped, and he turned to the muted coverage of the explosion on the display. She wasn't there simply to check up on him; she was there to talk to him about the accident at Living Bliss. But, why? She had no reason to think he knew anything. The scar on his hand—his souvenir from the Accident—twitched, and he looked down and stared at his fingers, stretching them straight, willing them to relax.

"A second explosion changes everything. We don't know what's happening yet," said Agent Prakash, a response to his unasked question. "But it's our highest priority. I hope you can help."

"H—help?"

"How did you know it would happen?"

Lahn's eyes jerked up to stare at Agent Prakash. She knew. She knew he called the Living Bliss office. Of course she did. It didn't matter that he had lied about his name when he called. She simply pulled the call logs.

"I, um . . ."

"Your call saved a lot of lives. Eighteen people died, but significantly less than the seventy-two people from the first explosion." Agent Prakash's eyes gave the impression of empathy and gratitude. "I understand why you called. How could you not? If there was a chance you could stop it from happening, a chance you could save people." Her huge, dark eyes seemed to open his soul.

A prickly sense of guilt washed over him, and his shoulders pulled into a cringe. He'd been worried about the people in danger. But that wasn't the primary reason he called. He'd mostly wanted to know if his memory was real.

"Now that it happened twice," she said, "it might happen again."

". . . Again?"

Agent Prakash watched Lahn closely. "Two days in a row, two unrelated locations with the same damage?"

Lahn's eyes grew wide as he processed the implication.

"The two locations are not in the same industry," she continued. "Renelogy specializes in renewable energy, so an explosion is a possibility. But Living Bliss is Biotech. There is no reason they would have identical industrial accidents. And the damage is something we've never seen, so it's not caused by the buildings' power systems."

"These are . . ." the question forced its way from his mouth, "not accidents?"

"We don't know, but it doesn't seem likely."

"But . . . that means . . ."

"Yes. We are now treating them as attacks."

The explosions were not accidents; they were terrorist attacks. Someone had purposely caused the destruction, damage, and death. And they might not be done. More attacks could come, more people could die. And he might experience all of it again, firsthand, more horrible visions of pain and violence.

I can't . . .

His heart thumped heavily, each beat throbbing in the scar on his hand. As his fingers curled into a cramped shape, Lahn felt a potential Depersonalization episode press on him. Not whatever weirdness he had experienced in the last two days; just a normal, overwhelming, terrible episode that would take over everything and make him feel like he was not in his own body. With a deep, ragged breath, held for a silent count of five, he started his calming exercises.

I can't do this, crowded to the front of his frantic thoughts. *I can't handle everything that has happened. I can hardly fight off my DP, but the visions are worse. And if they are not over?*

"You've been caught up in something big and horrible," said Agent Prakash quietly. "I can see it. You don't know how to escape. Let me help you. How did you know it would happen?"

"I . . ." Lahn stopped breathing, frozen by the intense energy of her eyes. Could she help him stop the visions? Maybe she could. The Department of Technology Security was terrifying with its overreach and control of every tech advance in the world. But that meant they had access to information no one else had. Agent Prakash probably knew more about the explosions . . . the *attacks*, than anyone.

"I don't know . . ." he squeaked, terrified by what he was about to say. "I had . . . a feeling."

"A feeling?" asked Agent Prakash, her expression had all the kindness of a child coaxing a kitten from a tree.

"Of another explosion," he whispered.

"But this time at Living Bliss?"

Lahn nodded his head.

"Very specific *feeling.*"

Lahn's face flushed crimson. It *was* specific. There was no way anyone could have guessed there would be another explosion, and its exact location. And what would she think he meant by *feeling*? He sounded ridiculous.

"You know what I'm feeling?" she said. "That you learned about the attack from a person."

She thinks I'm involved somehow, he thought with an edge of panic. "No, I didn't," he said, shaking his head.

"Who is doing this?" she asked, a bit more force in her words.

"I don't know."

"What is their plan?"

"I don't know," he gasped.

"Who are you working with?"

"No one!" Lahn couldn't breathe. He looked around the room, looking for an escape, looking anywhere but Agent Prakash standing between him and the door.

"I want to believe you, Lahn," she said, voice gentle again. "But you have to tell me the truth. If you don't know who did this, then where did you get the name of the building? I can help you, I can make all of this stress and worry go away, but you have to tell me."

Lahn looked at the agent, and she looked back with her deep eyes and very convincing concerned kindness. He didn't know if he could believe her, but it *seemed* like she really did want to help him. And if she could help, he *could* tell her. He could tell her *everything*. How it was more than a feeling something would happen. How he actually saw the destruction before it happened. And not just for the second attack. He could tell her about his visions of . . .

Don't tell her about the visions.

The part of Lahn's brain that somehow stayed calm when the rest was chaos marveled at the prescient nature of the message. How could someone have known he would be having this conversation? Whoever it was seemed to have the answers he wanted. But the rest of his brain wrestled with the rock-and-hard-place he suddenly found himself. Should he tell this government agent about his apparent psychic abilities, or listen to the stranger sending him cryptic messages?

But no. Really there was only one option. He *couldn't* talk about his visions. The message was right. Agent Prakash wouldn't help him. If he was lucky, she would get angry, thinking he was lying. And if she actually believed him? He would most likely disappear into some secret black site to be studied for a million years.

Lahn looked down at his hands, shook his head and mumbled, "I don't know."

Agent Prakash continued to stare at Lahn for several million seconds and finally sighed. "I understand. It's hard to talk, especially to someone you don't know very well. Maybe let's start with something small. Do you know who this is?"

She pulled several security photos out of the blue folder and laid them on the end table. The first was an image of a hallway, the view angled down on a figure in the center, a person with an overcoat and hoodie.

"This picture is from the security cameras at Living Bliss," she said.

"Faceless!" Lahn gasped before he could stop himself.

"Faceless?" asked Agent Prakash. "Who's that?"

Lahn looked at Agent Prakash. A blush ran from his chest to the top of his head. "I . . . don't know."

She cocked an eyebrow and moved the photo, exposing the images underneath. One was an aerial shot of a crowd, likely from a drone. "This is from the Renelogy parking lot," she said. Two figures in the crowd were circled, looking at each other across the throng. Two other photos were zoomed into the aerial shot, focused on the circled figures. One was Lahn, the other Faceless.

"I didn't see a face."

"Didn't see a face?"

Lahn shook his head. "His hood was up."

"Hm . . ." she said with a wry hint of a smile. "Have you seen him before?"

He shook his head.

"Why do you think he looked at you?"

He responded with a shrug. It still bothered him, too.

"Lahn," she said, sighing, "I am on your side, and I want to help. You're a nice guy and I don't think you're directly involved. But there's something more going on. Whatever it is, you can talk to me about it, okay?"

He looked back into her eyes. He'd told her what he could. With sheer force of will, he turned from her intense gaze.

"Think about it for a bit," Agent Prakash said. "I know there's more you will remember, more you can tell me. I'll check with you tomorrow and we can talk again."

Lahn didn't watch as she let herself out of his room.

SOVEREIGN OF LIGHT

"Lahn?"

As the autoride passed his favorite Mediterranean restaurant, Lahn realized with a start he'd zoned out for most of the ride home from the hospital.

"Sorry," he said, turning to Maddox and stretching his sore back. "Did you say something?"

"Nothing important," Maddox responded. "Just thinking about which buildings are the tallest downtown. You know, there are only a few that are more than fifty stories." He leaned toward Lahn, left eyebrow raised. "You okay? You've kind of been in your own world."

Lahn said nothing. He *did* need to think, but he hadn't been. His brain was like a coded function with a self-reference, stuck in an execution loop that would never end.

"Did you get any results from decoding the puzzle?" asked Maddox, after another minute of silence.

Lahn shrugged. "I don't know. I've been a little busy . . . sitting in the hospital."

"Are you . . ." probed Maddox, cautiously, "mad at me?"

"No . . ." began Lahn, but with a start he realized he

was mad at Maddox. "Maybe?" For some reason, it felt like Maddox had been lying to him. But that was unfair, even if recent events made it clear Maddox's theory about lost time was garbage.

"I'm sorry," said Maddox. "I'm sorry for everything you are going through. I feel like it's all my fault."

"Why?"

"I . . . I don't know. I told you it's probably all just DP, but then you ended up in the hospital. I should have worked harder to help you figure out the truth. If I'd been a better friend, maybe you wouldn't have gotten hurt."

Lahn shook his head. "It's not your fault. And I don't think I'm actually mad at you. I'm just freaked by having to talk to Agent Prakash again. I'm lucky she didn't take me in."

"Probably because she knows you never leave your apartment anyway," joked Maddox.

Lahn snorted with a grin. Then his grin melted. "So much happened to me today, even more than yesterday. And it's all a jumbled mess in my head." Lahn turned away to look out the window as the autoride moved into the residential district. He watched as they passed a newer apartment building with multiple diode lines that ran from the top of the building to the ground floor, currently with small blue dots running down to give the impression of a waterfall.

"What started as accidents are now terrorist attacks," continued Lahn. "At the same time, I'm having incidents that could be DP episodes, or psychic visions, or maybe déjà vu from the future." Lahn turned to look at Maddox, his brow furrowed. "At least help me understand why I saw you in my last vision. If that was the most recent attack, why would I see you? Were you actually there?"

Maddox looked at Lahn evenly for a moment. "Yes."

"Wait . . . seriously?"

"Yeah. I was outside Living Bliss at the time of the explosion."

Lahn opened his mouth, but for a moment no sound came out. ". . . What?" The dam opened, and the questions came in a rush. "You were there? Are you okay? I mean, you seem okay. But . . . why . . . why were you there?"

Maddox shrugged. "I didn't want you to worry when I picked you up, but I'm fine. It was a work thing. Living Bliss has contracts with the company Tia and I work for. I tried to meet up with her, but it didn't work out because she was busy . . ."

"With me," completed Lahn.

Maddox nodded.

It made sense. The company Tia and Maddox worked for was big, with lots of connections. But, instead of finding satisfaction in the explanation, Lahn's disquiet increased. "So, you're telling me I saw something I couldn't have possibly seen. And the fact I saw *you* proves it was real and not imagined thoughts of my brain or a new side effect of DP."

"Yeah. I was wrong," said Maddox. "My advice to focus on your Depersonalization was wrong, and I'm sorry."

Lahn took a deep breath and let it out slowly. "If it's not DP, what is it? I'm seeing events happening miles away. Not just any events, but terrorist attacks and supernatural explosions."

Maddox raised his eyebrows. "Do you think they're related? The weirdness of the explosions are causing your visions?"

"Or . . ." Lahn paused for a moment. "The other way around?"

"No," Maddox frowned. "No! Your visions are not causing the explosions. None of this is your fault!"

"I don't know." As the autoride pulled up in front of his apartment, Lahn shrugged and his shoulders drooped. "If we knew more about the explosions, maybe we could figure out what's happening to me," Lahn looked at Maddox, pleading in his eyes, "and how to make it stop."

Maddox nodded emphatically. "Get some rest, don't think about it anymore tonight, and we'll come up with a plan tomorrow. In the meantime, don't do anything stupid without me."

Lahn climbed out of the autoride and up the stairs to his apartment, slowly, careful to avoid stress on his sore back. He had absolutely no plans to do anything stupid. Or maybe anything at all. The key in the lock fought him for a moment before relenting and letting him into his apartment. *Typical*, he thought with bitterness. He tossed his keys on the counter with a clatter and paused to look around the room. Closing his eyes, he breathed in through his nose deeply, drawing in the familiar scents like a drowning man gasping for air.

"Hey, Luz," he said as he moved into the kitchen. He wanted to relax, put on a pot of Licorice Tea, and pull out some epic fantasy to forget his stress. After recently rereading *The Two Towers*, he'd thought about getting into the third volume again, *The War of the Ring*. It didn't matter that the series was fifty years old, it was still one of his favorites.

Lucia didn't say anything.

He stopped and turned to look at his terminal. "Luz? Lucia?"

Weird. She was always there. Even if she was busy with something, she always responded. Unless she was in lockdown for some reason? Lahn started toward his terminal to check. Was something wrong? She wouldn't just stop talking to him. The only time that happened—not long after they met—was when she told him about some old comic and how awesome it was. He asked how an AI with no real emotions could like or dislike *anything* . . .

Oh.

Ohhhhh.

"Um, Luz?" Lahn sat in his desk chair, spun and stared right at the camera at the top of the living room display. "Sorry we argued earlier."

Lucia didn't respond.

". . . I mean . . ." he cleared his throat, ". . . sorry I said your emotions aren't real. Of course they are. You are as real as I am, the energy that connects your cognitive nodes is as real as anything going on in my head."

Most of the time, Lahn didn't think about Lucia's emotions. Regular AI didn't have emotions, and though Lucia did, he'd never fully figured out how they worked. She seemed happy or sad or whatever for the strangest reasons. And usually, nothing he did affected her one way or the other, so he stopped trying to figure it out. He liked it that way. As weird as she was, she was much less difficult than dealing with humans.

"And for sure, you're smarter than me."

She never got offended . . . except that once. He'd actually forgotten about it, but at his suggestion that she was less than real she'd responded in a very human way and disappeared into her Secret Citadel, locked him out, and didn't come back for several days. At the time, he was afraid she may not ever come back.

"I didn't mean it. Really. I'm stressed about everything happening, and I said something stupid. Please, I need your help. I can't do this without you . . . Luz?"

Nothing.

"Lucia?"

Silence.

When she did come back last time, she'd acted like nothing had happened. Except she had insisted he call her something special for the next week. He had done so without question, as penance.

"Mighty Queen Lucia of Borgonia," Lahn said in a somber voice, repeating what she claimed was her full, true name, "Sovereign of Light, I come before you in humble petition."

More silence. Lahn held his breath as the lack of response became thundering.

"Luz?" he said softly after several minutes. "Are you there?"

Rotating around to face the desk and sliding forward, Lahn logged into his terminal. Something *was* wrong. After connecting to the Mesh and entering his privacy server, he triggered his fake weather function that scrambled his activity. But then an odd thing happened.

It gave him a weather update.

"Wait, what?"

He canceled it and ran it again. Another weather update. It wasn't supposed to do that—it was just coded to look like that was its purpose. In reality, it should only scramble his inputs and outputs while on the server. But now, he had no idea if it was doing that or not. He quickly connected to his code library and examined the source of his scrambler. This was not his code. It had none of his obfuscated functionality. It actually did what *his* code only pretended to do: generate weather updates.

He looked at the code history, and things got even weirder. According to the history logs, he had written the function to get weather updates when he originally created it, almost a year ago. Only minor updates since then, all by him, with none of the code he had secreted inside other code that was designed to avoid AI detection.

"I . . . didn't write . . . any of this."

A buzz from his portable interrupted his concern, and he pulled it out. It was a message from Maddox.

Meet me for iced coffee?

Lahn stared at the message in confusion. Maddox had dropped him off less than fifteen minutes ago. Why change his mind and offer to hang out now? Even weirder, neither of them cared for coffee. There was a place down the street, across from a small city park, that apparently had great Vietnamese iced coffee, but Lahn had never been there.

Strangely, as Lahn looked at his portable, the message flashed and disappeared, leaving all the previous message history intact. With a buzz, another message appeared.

`I can help configure your new proxy.`

Just like the first, the second message flashed and disappeared.

"Wha . . ." Lahn's brain broke a little bit. There was no way Maddox could have anything to do with Lucia's disappearance. He didn't even know about her. Did he? So why would he bring up Lahn's proxy? Grabbing his ear cuff from the desk—in case Lucia came back—and his keys from the counter, Lahn took a deep breath, opened the door, and went back out into the world.

sunshine
and comics

As he stood in line to place his order at Sippin' Serenity, trying to be as small as possible, Lahn looked around the petite shop. A couple of holographic displays on one wall highlighted the latest deals. The opposite wall was decorated in traditional Vietnamese style, with reclaimed wood paneling and bamboo shelves holding tiny vases and figurines. Only a handful of people clustered around standing tables, enjoying after-work socializing. At least the place was mostly empty.

As Lahn moved to the front of the line, he figured he would grab a table after he ordered and wait for Maddox. Even though he'd never told him about Lucia, Lahn still found himself hoping that Maddox knew something about her disappearance. But he didn't see how that could be possible.

"What can I get you?" asked the apathetic barista.

"Um, the . . . licorice tea." Keep it simple, what he had already planned. Less likely he'd say something weird.

Lahn's portable buzzed and he pulled it out. Another message from Maddox.

Not going to make it after all.
Enjoy the evening in the park.

Really? Lahn thought with a scowl. *What about Lucia?* Stupid Maddox. And what was that thing about the park? The one across the street? As he watched, the message disappeared, just like the last one.

"Name?" said the barista.

"Hmm?"

"On the order?"

"Oh, Lahn."

"With an 'H'?" The barista looked up from writing Lahn's name on the order.

"Yeah?"

"Hang on, I think there's something here for you." He reached under the counter and pulled out a small cardboard box. A quick glance at the label, then he slid it across the counter, and spun it around so Lahn could read it. "That you?"

Lahn looked at the box. His first name, correct spelling, was printed on the plain, white label stuck to the top. Under his name in a smaller font was a message.

Open this in the park

Lahn's eyebrows seemed to be scrunched in continual confusion. "Yeah, that's me," he said, picking it up.

He paid, moved to the pickup line, and examined the box. Light enough it felt empty, it was typical brown cardboard, not special or unique. It didn't have shipping info, so Maddox had either dropped it off himself, or used a local delivery service. But how could he have had time for either one?

After picking up his order, Lahn left the shop and crossed the street to the tiny pocket park. A single entrance made the space feel hidden and private. With a copse of different tree species in raised planter beds, walls of brick and ivy, and a waterfall fountain on one end, the park was a tiny oasis.

As he entered the park, he stopped and glanced around. A smattering of wire-mesh chairs and low tables were scattered throughout the plot, and cement benches lined two of the sides. The space was empty of people, except for an older woman on the far side, reading a book and drinking from a Sippin' Serenity cup. He hesitated, unsure what to do. He couldn't open his super-secret package in front of a stranger. He really wanted to go home and open the package there. But Maddox had made a very specific point about the park. Why? Was Maddox going to show up and explain everything, the messages, the package, even Lucia?

Lahn started to turn away and leave when the woman stood, closing her book, and moved toward the park exit. He shuffled out of the way, and she smiled as she passed him.

"Getting a little dark to read," she said, her short, gray hair bobbing as she chuckled, "even with our twilight nights."

As she left the park, Lahn looked at the sky. He hadn't realized how late it was. The sun was just below the horizon, and the normally pale-green sky was yellow at the edges. It wouldn't be long before the glow of evening brought out the night crowd. He might not have much time alone.

Picking the chair furthest from the entrance, close to the fountain, Lahn sat and placed his drink on the nearby table. He leaned back in the chair, careful of his back, and stretched his shoulders a few times. But the pain was almost completely gone. *Weird.*

A deep breath, let out slowly, and he pulled his keys from his pocket. Picking the pointiest one, he took one last look at the label on the box. "Well, I'm in the park. Let's see what this is."

A quick stab with the key, and he tore through the tape on both sides and along the top. Dropping the keys on the table next to his ignored drink, he hesitated for a brief moment, then opened the box and looked inside. Foam padding surrounded a smaller box, about the size of a mandarin orange, nestled in the center. Lahn gently pulled it out. It was dark gray, with no hint to its contents. A flap on one side seemed the best way in, and he pulled it up, enjoying the satisfaction of the magnet clasp, and lifted the top panel. Lahn blinked, surprised at the ear cuff inside.

A stylish design in gunmetal black, it was newer and more expensive than the one he currently owned, the one sitting in his pocket. But it was still just an ear cuff. He looked up from the box, and turned to look around the space of the small park, half expecting Maddox to jump out from behind a tree and burst into a fit of laughter. *Surprise, you thought it might be something important. It's just a cuff.*

Lahn pulled it out of the box. He could either put it on or ignore it and go home. But he'd gone to all the trouble to get it, so, holding his breath, he slipped it onto his ear.

"*Qué pasa*, Lahn," said Lucia in his ear.

"Lucia!" he said, letting out his breath in a rush of relief and surprise. "What? Why are you in Maddox's cuff?"

"He didn't send this to you, *tonta*, I did."

"Wait, you faked the message from Maddox so I would come?"

"Yup!"

"But . . . I thought you were mad at me . . . for what I said."

"Nah. It was super rude, but I figured out long ago you're an idiot."

"So, why disappear? And . . . did you change my function code?"

"I did a good job cleaning up, right?"

"I . . . don't know. What do you mean?"

"Agent Prakash?" she prodded. "She came to your hospital room? While you two were busy chatting, she sent agents to the apartment. And they didn't stop there. They tracked their dirty little feet into your mesh systems, your private server, your code libraries, *cada cosa*."

Everything.

The DTS knew everything. All his illegal code and everything he and Lucia had done to try to hide her existence. An electric jolt sent Lahn's heart racing, and a spike of pain pulled his hand into a tight ball. He stood, ready to run. Maybe Madagascar was nice.

"Whoa," said Lucia. "Slow down there, Jay Gerrick. It's okay. I saw them coming. After yesterday, I set up trip wires, monitors, and kill switches everywhere. I had it all cleaned up before they found even a crumb."

AI technology was strictly controlled by the Department of Technology Security. There were safeguards and system monitors watching for exactly what she was: sapient AI, powerful enough to bring civilization to its knees. Of course, Lucia was all sunshine and comics, but the DTS wouldn't know that. Lahn fought to calm his heartbeat. "Are you sure?"

"You'd be in custody and I'd be dead."

He took a deep breath and held it as he sat again.

"That's why I sent you this new cuff," she said. "Did you know there's a broken elevator over on Third and Redwood where you press both the up and down buttons for three seconds and talk to a guy about illegal tech? It was fun to send some random delivery dude over there. If you knew half the security on this cuff, your brain would melt! It has a self-destruct mode. If stolen, I can trigger an electric burst that will fry the circuitry and give whoever's wearing it a nasty shock. Maybe lay them out flat. This thing even has a nifty projector. It's too small for a hologram, but hold up your hand, about forty centimeters from your face."

Lahn shook his hand to release its cramp, then held it up.

A child's drawing of a face appeared on his hand. It flickered and the tongue stuck out at him.

An image of a blond Latina replaced the drawing. "It even includes," continued Lucia, the mouth of the young woman moving as she spoke, "a connection to a typical, stupid proxy. Now I can hide completely, and no other AI—no matter how powerful—would be the wiser. And her name's close enough to mine that if someone hears you say my name, they will assume it's her. Say hello, Felise."

"Hello, Lahn," said a second voice in his ear, slightly older and deeper in tone. This one sounded like a normal human, but Lahn could always tell the difference. "I am Felise, your new proxy. Is there anything I can help you with?"

"Shush!" scolded Lucia. "*Vete.* Go take a nap or something. We'll let you know if we need you."

Lahn dropped his hand, flexed it several times, and tried to convince himself they were not in immediate danger.

"Which reminds me," continued Lucia, "that message you had me decoding? Amazingly, my fake-proxy algorithm worked. We now have a decoded message, but you're not going to like it."

Lahn perked up, heartbeat switching to anticipation. "It's an answer, something, at last. Why wouldn't I like it?"

"Hold your hand up again and let me show you."

Lahn lifted his hand, and glowing words and numbers appeared on his palm and dribbled off both sides. He rotated his hand horizontally to make everything fit.

```
ANSWERS: FOCAL POINT + 339446100 101730.71
-877515.59
```

"Oh, good," he said with a snort. "Something finally makes sense."

PLUMBER FROM POUGHKEEPSIE

ahn stood, grabbed his keys, cup of untouched tea, and the boxes.

"Wait," said Lucia. "Where are you going?"

"Home." He poured the tea in the bushes and tossed the cup and boxes in a recycling bin. "This is dumb. Why did we bother to decode it? The last two days have been too much. I can't handle another cryptic layer to this message on top of everything else." He turned and headed toward the exit.

"But I haven't told you the exciting news."

"Which is what," he challenged.

"First, the DTS probably bugged your apartment. Isn't that cool? I feel like we're supervillains. 'Course, makes it hard to talk about important stuff. That's why I dragged you down here."

Lahn froze.

"Second, they have a tap on your old cuff and portable. They must be *serious!* With that, they can track your location and monitor its microphone and microcam. Good thing we've been talking near the fountain, 'cause even with the cuff in your pocket they could probably overhear our conversation. At least *your* half."

Lahn reached for his pocket to take out the cuff, then stopped, hand hovering a few centimeters away. He wanted to rip it out and throw it as far as he could, but he didn't dare reach in to touch it, afraid it would trigger the DTS to come and take him away. Turning away from the exit, Lahn pulled a chair as close to the waterfall fountain as possible, and hoped Lucia was right about it masking their conversation. "What are we going to do?" he whispered.

"You don't have to whisper. We don't even have to stay here. If you subvocalize, it should be fine."

"But," Lahn continued in a hushed tone, "should we destroy the cuff?"

"That would be just a *little* suspicious. Leave it in your pocket."

"I . . ."

"Then put it on your desk like normal when you get home tonight."

"When I go home?"

"Listen, Frodo, you've got the Eye of Sauron focused on you, so you gotta be as small and boring as possible. Stick to your typical Hobbit habits. Keep your Elven cloak handy, and pretend to be a rock if needed. Then we can sneak into Mordor and destroy the One Ring."

Lahn took a rough breath. "I don't understand. Is the cuff the One Ring?"

Lucia laughed lightly. "No, *Ese*. We haven't found *your* Ring yet. But I think the decrypted message might help."

The message. The weird, hand-delivered message, typewritten on a piece of paper like a relic from the past. His decryption plan had worked, but the decrypted message was not much more clear than the original string of numbers. The only part that was obvious was the first word.

"*Answers*," he said. "That word's telling us the message is supposed to provide *answers*."

"Yeah. I think if we follow its clues, it could lead us to your Ring, to the source of your problem, then we can come up with a plan to destroy it!"

Get some answers, destroy the problem. That sounded great. Lahn wanted to be done with everything so badly, he could feel it as an ache in his bones. But . . . even if he could figure out what the message meant, then what? He had no idea who sent it, or why. Up to now, it seemed he was being pushed from one problem to another, like a rat in a maze. The message didn't feel any different.

Unfortunately, at this point, his options were limited. Lucia was right; with the Eye on him, he had to do something.

"You know," Lahn said, "Sam was the real hero in that story."

"Okay, nerd."

Lahn breathed in deep through his nose, then let it out slowly through tight lips. "All right," he said finally. "Let's figure this out."

"Bright and shiny!" said Lucia with enthusiasm. "So, what do you think?"

Lahn held up his hand. "Let me see it again?" The message flashed on, bright in the fading light.

```
ANSWERS: FOCAL POINT + 339446100 101730.71
-877515.59
```

"I have no idea what Focal Point means," he said. "We'll come back to that. But the numbers?"

He looked away, dropped his hand, and stared at the motion of the waterfall.

"Maybe the structure of the numbers suggests what they represent," he said. "The first is a big integer, over three hundred million. The other two are comparatively smaller, less than a million, with precision to two decimal places. Almost like the first number's not related to the other two."

"You could be headed in the right direction," said Lucia.

Something tickled the back of Lahn's mind. He closed his eyes, trying to scratch whatever was familiar about the numbers. "Ignoring the first number for now, have you seen numbers like the last two before?"

"I've seen like a quintillion-billion numbers. So, probably, someplace."

"Helpful." Lahn focused his mind on the pattern of the last two numbers: one positive, the other negative, both with six-point-two digits. Then, he let his mind wander, free to make subconscious connections.

In his imagination, he was no longer in the pocket park, listening to the fountain. [He is out in the city, wandering, trying to clear his head. But as he drifts through the town—the shadows growing long as the day turns to dusk—he can't think about numbers or weird decrypted clues. *Ignore it, Lahn,* he thinks. *Ignore the message.* He is angry at everything and everybody. With his life a tangled mess, it feels like the entire world is conspiring against him. He doesn't know who he can trust, who can help him. For sure, the message can't help. It will only lead him somewhere—]

Lahn jerked upright. *Somewhere.* A place, a location. "Lucia, could the last two numbers be geocodes?

"Oh . . . geocodes. I like those. Sure, they could be geocodes."

"Really? Okay, where?"

"One hundred and thirty-seven-ish kilometers off the west coast of Costa Rica."

"In the ocean?" Lahn scrunched his forehead. "Anything out there?"

"Water. And fish. Maybe mammals sometimes?"

So are they geocodes or not?

Lahn stood and walked to the edge of the fountain. He stuck his fingers in the waterfall and let the water splash over his hand, giving him a slight chill that ran up his arm. *If they are geocodes,* he thought, *then what's the big one? What goes with a location, with a place . . .*

"Time! It's a time and place! Lucia, if the first number is a timecode, what would it be?"

"Um . . . looks like 12:35 p.m., October 3rd, 1975."

"Wait, only ten years after timecodes were started?"

"Ten years, ten months, three days . . ."

Lahn stopped listening as Lucia rattled off the difference to the second. While it was possible the message referenced an event from the seventies in the middle of the ocean, it wasn't likely. "Did anything important happen on October 3rd at that time?"

"Well," Lucia said after a moment. "Tam Strenson was born."

"Who's Tam Strenson?"

"A plumber from Poughkeepsie."

"What? That's not important."

"It was to his mother. He added joy to her life."

Lahn rolled his eyes. If the numbers were a time and place, they didn't work on their own. But maybe the words gave a clue. "But what do the words mean?" Lahn mused as he dropped back into the park chair. "*Answers . . . Focal Point . . .* a time and place. It sounds like it's saying the time and place is a Focal Point in history, an important moment. But it doesn't seem to be, so what *does* it mean?"

As Lucia didn't volunteer anything, Lahn held up his hand again and reexamined the decoded message. "Something is still off." He squinted and allowed the text on his palm to go slightly out of focus. "What am I missing . . . what's the pattern?" His eyes relaxed and crossed slightly, and the numbers and letters shifted and overlapped, blurring together.

The positive and negative signs bumped up against each other.

"Wait . . ." Lahn stopped, allowed his eyes to focus on the entire message again, then looked closer at the plus symbol, and where it sat in the message.

"That plus sign is important. Focal Point *plus* numbers. That's why the time and place don't make sense yet, I have to add something to them."

"What do you mean?" asked Lucia.

"I have to add a Focal Point event. Get the geocodes and timecode from an important moment in history, and add it to the other numbers. Turn it into new coordinates."

Lahn stood and started pacing in front of the fountain. As he walked, he glanced at the sky, noticing Venus between two taller buildings. One of the few lights in the night sky. The point felt friendly in the heavens, like it was a tiny sentinel, holding back the empty space.

"Of course, the first thing that comes to mind is Stardrop," he continued. "Nothing's had a bigger impact in recent history than losing all the stars."

"Can't be Stardrop," said Lucia. "Happened to the entire world, not just one location."

At the edge of the fountain, he turned to walk back the other way. In the opposite sky, the moon was peeking over the edge of the skyline. "Similar problem with the moon landing," he said. "Glenn, White, and Tereshkova walking on the moon in '65 was pivotal, but happened on the moon. No geocodes for that."

"Hmmm," said Lucia "Tricky, trying to guess which Focal Point they want you to use. Almost like they don't *want* you to decode it."

Lahn stopped in mid-stride. He'd already answered that question. As he told Maddox the day before, "No, they want *only me* to decode it." He started nodding slowly. "I'm not looking for a global event. I need something very personal. Something tragically pivotal I almost never talk about, but can't stop thinking about."

It wasn't a question. He knew exactly what his personal Focal Point would be. When everything changed, when everything went wrong and likely caused his Depersonalization. The one event he still thought about almost daily, even after ten years . . .

"Lucia, do you know the geocodes of the Accident?"

"'Course."

"If you add them to the ones from the message, what location do we get?"

"The new geocodes point to an abandoned warehouse in the industrial section of town."

"*This* town?"

"Yep."

Lahn's heart bolted and threatened to leave his chest.

This was it.

"And if you add the Accident's timecode to the other one?" he asked in a whisper.

"Wednesday, August 22nd, 2012. Tomorrow morning, at 8:00 a.m."

His apartment building stood tall and terrible, at once familiar and foreign. The diode lines on the corners were currently a dark blue, and radiated in contrast to the green glow of the night sky. They accented the stark, straight lines of the monolithic building. Once his sanctuary from the rude pain of life, knowing the DTS had been in his home made his apartment feel alien.

Maybe he could sleep on the bench until it was time to go in the morning. To the warehouse. The stupid, hard-won result of the stupid encrypted letter. A strange unknown location sent to him from some strange unknown individual, promising answers. It was possible it was the same person sending him advice on his portable. So far they had been helpful, but that didn't make the idea of going to an old, abandoned warehouse in the morning any less ominous.

He felt as though he could already see it.

[With the faint glow of twilight, the inside of the warehouse is mostly shadows, shuffling sounds echoing somewhere in the dark. Something is there, hiding in the gloom, stalking him. A dark movement gives him a split second of warning, a shade surges at him, and—]

With a sudden jerk, Lahn sat up, eyes wide, looking frantically around him.

"What?" asked Lucia.

"I . . ." Lahn frowned. Then took a deep breath. "It's nothing," he subvocalized, lips moving slightly, but making no sounds. "I thought . . . I thought I was just about to be attacked."

"I can't see anyone. Are they still here? Are they invisible? Cause, that would be *mola mucho!*"

"No. No one is here. I just imagined what the inside of the warehouse might look like, and it creeped me out." It should have been weird that his imagination was in overdrive lately. But with everything else going on, it was no surprise that his mind was working overtime to protect him. Poor brain. Everything it tried just made things worse.

"So . . . you gonna go in?" asked Lucia, brightly.

"To my apartment? Do I have to? Can't I just go stay with Tia or Maddox?"

"When's the last time you did that?"

"Well . . . never."

"Come on, Tintin! Use your super-sneaky spy skills and slip inside, all subtle like."

"Will they be watching?"

"Oh, yeah, for sure. But act natural. And don't say anything about tomorrow out loud."

"Right. Tomorrow. The warehouse. A nice way to spend the morning." As if dealing with his apartment wasn't bad enough. Of course he was going to go, but he couldn't shake the feeling there was danger at the warehouse he wasn't ready to face.

"You're not worried about going tomorrow, are you?" asked Lucia.

"Completely. But I *need* to go. I'm running around in the dark, fleeing my problems, no idea what those problems actually are. If there is the slightest chance of getting any answers, I've got to take it. No matter the risk."

"Pshaw," Lucia *pshaw*ed. "What's risky about an abandoned warehouse?"

"Are you kidding? Lots of things." Lahn took a deep breath and held it for a minute. "But it's not just the warehouse. I feel like something's coming. Something I can't fight. The best I can do is hide. But if I do, I could be trapped for—"

[The tiny sliver of light skitters away, leaving total and complete blackness in a sudden shock, like a bucket of ice water dumped on his head. Suddenly, he is no longer himself, but some poor sap, locked away forever for his crimes of stupidity.]

Hey, Dad. It's me.

I'm scared.
No, that word is too soft for what I'm feeling.
Terrified. Petrified.
I always try to be brave, but now I am having a hard time fighting the fear. I am having a hard time not being paralyzed by it. I'm going to the warehouse this morning, but I don't know what will happen. I wish there was some other option, but this is what I have to do. I can only move forward by going back.
Will my plan work? Will this be how I solve everything? Or how I die?

I love you, and miss you.

THERE BE ALIENS

The gray of early morning light brought a muted glow to the buildings around Lahn. The crisp smell in the air suggested a hint of rain. His back to a wall—the cement of the building cool and rough under his fingers—he took a deep breath before slowly looking around the corner.

Across a wide street from his current hiding spot, the warehouse sat like a dark, ancient mountain, the home of a malevolent sleeping dragon. It didn't have any of the modern accouterments of recent builds. No garden on the roof, no diode lines accenting the design, it hadn't even been retrofitted with solar or wind tech. The architecture was from seventy years ago, old stone instead of cement, steel, glass, or green tech. The reddish brick appeared faded in the dawn, like rock of muddy brown. Squarish and squat, it felt old and ominous.

"See," said Lucia in his ear through the fancy new cuff. "That doesn't look so bad." His old cuff and portable were left behind in his apartment, where they couldn't reveal his location to the DTS.

"You're not the one in mortal danger."

"Neither are you! No one's here . . . probably."

But Lahn couldn't shake the feeling someone or something was in there. And the suggestion of a headache tickling the front of his head since arriving wasn't helping either.

Of course, both could be stress and the lack of sleep.

Lahn didn't know how to process his visions anymore. The one outside his apartment last night had felt like he'd been locked away in a dark vault, left to rot forever. Walking into his apartment afterward had been one of the most difficult things he'd ever done. At first he'd held his breath, like he was in a contaminated zone and would catch something deadly, until his vision had grown fuzzy and he had almost passed out. After that, he'd gone straight to bed and tried to forget that someone was probably watching him sleep. He'd mostly failed, and ended up tossing and turning. He finally gave up with the first hints of morning light peeking through his bedroom windows like a stalker. The ache at the edge of his eyes and the jittery buzz in his nerves told him he would pay for it.

"So . . ." said Lucia. "I know we came early, but are we just going to sit here?"

"I am not sure of the next step," said Lahn. On the outskirts of the city, Lahn was in a district of old industrial buildings. Weather-worn paint, roads cracked and unrepaired, plants growing through sidewalks; the entire street was long abandoned.

"Are we supposed to meet the sender of the message?" he asked. "Should I just walk up to the front and knock?"

"With that massive padlock on the entrance? I doubt it."

"What then? Try the back? There is something very specific about this time and place, but we don't even know what's in there." He shook his head, trying to dispel his doubts. "There's something weird about that building. I can't explain it, but I think my vision last night, before I went into my apartment, is related."

"What do you mean?"

"It was like I'd been locked in a box. Trapped, no way out, and all light gone forever. And I feel like we're walking right into that."

"You think that vision was something real?"

Lahn shrugged. "It felt real, just like the others. But I don't understand what it means."

"That's why we're here. Right, Pilgrim? Figure it all out. It's a touch after seven this lovely Wednesday morning, so we got time."

Lahn nodded slowly and examined the warehouse and its neighbors. On the left side of the warehouse was a taller building, the two separated by a narrow alleyway. On the right was an access road to the back of the warehouse, with a concrete wall separating it from an open parking lot. Between the wall and warehouse was a large boxy shape, yellow and roughly the size of a shipping container. It looked new, without the same level of dust and rust as the building and surrounding area.

Words were printed on the top-left corner of the large box, but from where he sat, Lahn couldn't see what it said.

"Luz, what's that yellow box-thing?"

"Stand-by, Lahn," she said formally, her voice deeper than normal. "Scanning and enhancing. The logo says *Pierson Electric*. The company offers power generators of different sizes and output levels. This generator appears to be the model 34X, one of their larger ones."

"Wait, was that Felise?"

"Yes, Lahn. Among my available services, I can provide information about your environment. Lucia passed the request to me."

"Good job, Felise," said Lucia. "You're doing great."

One of Pierson Electric's largest generators. Why would an empty building need power?

"Are we sure the warehouse is abandoned?" asked Lahn.

"According to available public records," responded Felise, "no business has operated out of this warehouse for the last four years."

High off the ground, a row of windows lined the side of the building. They were dark and reflected the world around him. He fantasized looking through one into the building rather than having to go inside. Unfortunately, even standing on the large generator would not get him high enough to see in.

"The manufacturing factory next door has not been in use for seven years," continued Felise.

"' Course," volunteered Lucia, "there could be squatters."

Lahn's eyes shifted to the building next door. Medium gray of similar boxy design but with more smokestacks on top, the factory appeared as forsaken as the warehouse. The factory was one floor taller than its neighbor, with upper floor windows that looked down into the warehouse.

"I wish we could just look inside the warehouse, before the time on the letter. Do you think we could see into it from the factory?"

"From this angle, I do not have enough . . ."

"Okay, Felise," said Lucia. "*Relajarse*. I got this. The angle looks right, Lahn. And the window glass is not frosted. But I would bet it's going to be dark inside the warehouse. So . . . maybe?"

The subtle smell of electrons in the air shifted, and sparse droplets started falling from the sky. Lahn turned from the warehouse and factory to go the long way around the building he was hiding behind. Once on the far side, he snuck across the street to the side of the factory farthest from the warehouse.

"I didn't see padlocks on the factory doors," said Lucia, "but it's probably just as locked up as the warehouse. How ya gonna get in?"

"Maybe I'll get lucky," he whispered, closing his eyes and rubbing his temples, "and a door will be unlocked. Or maybe there's a window I can reach." His headache no longer tickled, more like jabbed annoyingly, and he wished he had pain killers to cut it off before it got worse.

The first door he came to was soundly locked, as was the second. Lahn kept going to the end of the building and stopped at the corner. He peeked cautiously around at the shared back lot of the warehouse and factory. The lot was not huge, just large enough for shipping trucks to turn around and back up to the buildings. There were no people or vehicles in sight, but Lahn still couldn't shake the feeling someone was nearby. The back side of the factory had an alcove that potentially included an entrance, and he sprinted for it, sticking close to the wall.

He turned to the door and reached out to check if it was locked, but froze midway. There was no handle or knob on this side.

He stared at the door.

"Hey looky," said Lucia. "It's a security door that only opens from the inside."

Lahn's left eye twitched as he dug his fingers through his hair to drive back the headache. A few drops of gentle rain got pushed to his scalp, sending chills down his spine. If he couldn't get into the factory, he was out of ideas for spying into the warehouse. With a grunt, he hit the security door with his fist.

The door vibrated open a few centimeters outward, then settled back into place.

W—What?

Lucia laughed. "You punched it open?"

The door wasn't sitting flush in the frame. Something kept it slightly ajar, kept it from fully closing and locking.

Lahn hit the door again. It bounced open and he grabbed the edge with his fingertips. With a grunt, he pulled, and sliding the fingers of one hand into the crack between the door and the jamb, he pulled the door open.

"That is so weird," said Lucia. "Why is there a rock down there?" Jammed into the nook at the bottom of the doorframe was a small rock, big enough to keep the door from locking. "Maybe there *are* squatters . . . or it could be aliens or supervillains. Wait, *we're* supervillains. When we go in, I'll be right!"

"Aliens?" whispered Lahn with a playful scoff.

"It's within the realm of possibility."

Lahn stepped into the shadowed interior of the factory and let the door close gently behind him. As the door closed, the light whisked away like a breeze, leaving him blind and sucking the air from his lungs.

EXPERIMENTING WITH FEAR

"Lucia!" he choked.

"I know," she hissed back.

A faint red light from his ear cuff broke the darkness and dimly illuminated the factory space around him. Strange shapes and shadows burst into existence, creating a world at once less *and* more creepy than the darkness.

"Can it go any brighter?" breathed Lahn, eyes darting.

"No," whispered Lucia in response. "It's only designed to project a short distance. But I set it to red to allow your eyes to adjust to the dark."

"Why are you whispering?"

"It's creepy in here."

Lahn looked around and tried to relax, cursing the architect that thought a lack of windows in this part of the building was a good idea. *Everything's fine,* he thought, breathing in deeply. He was not in some scene from a horror movie. It was more like a troll graveyard, the shapes of the machinery like giant skeletons lying where they died. The dust from creatures long gone lay thick on every surface: the tables, the machinery, even the cement floor.

"Which way?" he subvocalized.

"According to public schematics," responded Felise pleasantly, "if you go left, you should find a stairwell to the upper floors overlooking the warehouse."

After passing several machines that were clearly Olog-hai skeletons, Lahn found a hallway with no windows.

"Turn right down that hallway," prompted Felise, "and continue for twenty yards to a smaller hallway on the left."

"Careful!" whispered Lucia. "The aliens might be down there."

The weak light from his cuff did little to light the hallway, a passage that faded into darkness, with hints of refuse and doors. There wouldn't be aliens. Probably.

Lahn tiptoed down the hall and passed several doors on either side, dark-brown wood with small glass windows. He stopped to peek inside one, but the light from his cuff didn't penetrate deep enough to reveal anything.

As he turned from the door, his foot caught a discarded cardboard box on the floor, knocking it across the hall with a thump.

"Aaaahhh!" screamed Lucia, causing Lahn to wince and grab his ear. "What was that?"

"Just a box," said Lahn with exasperation. "What's with you?"

"Oh," she responded cheerfully, "I'm experimenting with fear. It's super fun."

"Not for me."

"Right. Right. *Entiendo*. I will stop for now and wait until we're in *real* danger."

Ahead and to the left, a faint glow drove back the oppressive dark of the factory. With a sigh of relief, Lahn walked forward and found a short hallway that led to the desired stairwell, morning light bouncing down gently from the upper floors. He climbed, stopping at the third floor, which gave him a hallway with windows on one side and a single door at the end of the hall.

The light from the windows pushed back Lahn's apprehension. He moved quickly to the first window and looked across the alley.

The top floor of the warehouse was directly across from him, the large windows revealing a similar hallway to the one he was in. Through a set of lower windows it was possible to see into the main section of the warehouse, the tops of various shelves and an open central area mostly in the shadows.

Something was happening. Nondescript shapes cluttered the open central area, boxy items on tables and floor. Small diode lights on several items flickered and glowed in the darkness. A lone figure moved from the dark outer edge to the central area and leaned over an item on a table. The flickering lights and shadows obscured the figure, and Lahn pressed his face against the glass, straining his eyes.

"Someone's down there," said Lucia. "Do you think that's who sent the letter? Do they expect you to meet them there, in the warehouse?"

"That doesn't feel right."

There was something about the scene, the sketchy building, the flashing electronics, and the shadowy figure. It was not someone who expected him, waiting to explain everything and how to make it all stop.

"I don't think the message sender is down there. But, if not, why am I here?"

And then he knew.

"I'm not here to talk. I'm here to *see*."

To see . . . whatever was happening in the warehouse. The message had said there would be answers. Whatever was going on down in the warehouse, his *answers* were down there.

"Lucia, I . . . I don't know what to do," he said, forgetting to whisper. He stepped away from the window and started pacing the hall. "Something is telling me to go away. Run. Ignore all of this." He stopped, and looked through the windows again at the open area in the warehouse below. The mysterious figure was gone, but the lights continued to blink at him enticingly.

"At the same time, I *need* to get in there. Answers are down there, I know it. But it's more than that." He stopped and took a large breath. "Something is going to happen. Something bad. And . . . I *need* to stop it."

"Wait . . ." said Lucia. "Frodo, is *that* your Ring?"

Lahn stared at the gentle flickering below, an odd contrast to the bright morning light outside. Some stranger was down there using an old, abandoned warehouse as a staging area for nefarious activity that should have nothing to do with him.

Except . . . it did.

It didn't make any sense. But somehow he knew, beyond a doubt, the activity in the warehouse was the cause of his visions.

"Yeah. That's my Ring."

"*Brilloso!* Let's get in there and wreck some stuff! What's the plan?"

Lahn started pacing again. "I don't think they'll be happy to see us. If we're going in, we'll have to sneak. The back door probably leads directly to that open space, so that's out. I'm not sure how to get in without . . ."

Near the end of the hallway, he stopped in surprise. Something sat right outside the window. As he twisted the latch and pushed open the window, a cool, damp breeze washed over him, and he stared. Below the window, stretched out in front of him, was a ladder.

Sturdy, made of carbon-steel, the black ladder was five

meters long, and stretched out horizontally between the buildings. It rested on the ledge beneath the windows of each side, forming a bridge over the ten-meter drop to the unforgiving ground below.

Lahn laughed out loud. "Why is there a ladder out there?"

"Shrug. But that'll work, right?"

"What do you mean?"

"To sneak in," said Lucia.

"Wait . . . are you saying I should cross that?"

"Yeah! We could get in, scout around, make a plan, and they'd never know you were there."

"But I could die!" exclaimed Lahn.

"Not if you're careful. Crawl across, nice and slow, and Bob's your uncle. Breaking in on the main floor is probably impossible, and we'd get caught if we try. This may be our only choice."

"No one says 'Bob's your uncle' anymore."

"I do. I just did. Didn't you hear me?"

Lahn stared at the ladder. It looked strong enough for multiple people using it at once. It should have no problem supporting his weight.

His heart started racing. Was he actually considering this? He wasn't a crossing-unexpected-ladders-in-the-sky kind of guy. He had trouble leaving his apartment. But some irresistible force, something he couldn't describe and didn't understand, was pulling him toward the warehouse.

"Someone sent you the message that led you here," said Lucia. "Someone stuck a rock in the door, and put a ladder between the buildings. It's like fate wants you in there."

"I've never met Fate. She sounds like a jerk."

With a shudder, Lahn looked at the warehouse window at the other end of the ladder. It was open just a crack, ready for him to enter. He shook his head, his shoulders drooping. "I don't know, Lucia. I don't know if I can do it. I *want* to. I want to understand. I want to figure out how to stop everything." He closed his eyes and took a deep breath. "I *want* to accept the call to be a hero. But . . . I can't. I can't do these things. I'm no hero, you know that. I'm just—"

A clunk followed by a metallic clatter echoed from someplace deep in the factory. Lahn's eyes popped open, his heart rate flared, and his head snapped toward the stairwell.

Silence.

"What was that?" subvocalized Lahn.

"No idea!" whispered Lucia. "It sounded like something big got knocked over. Maybe it's an animal?"

On the balls of his feet, Lahn moved to the stairwell and stared down into the darkness. More silence.

Then, less silence.

Steps. Still quiet, but heavy. Purposeful. Getting louder.

"Not an animal," she said.

"Where can we hide?" he breathed, spinning around.

"There, the door at the end of the hall."

With a quiet rush, he went to the door and pulled on the handle. The door didn't move. He turned back to the stairwell, forcing his throbbing hand to open. He shouldn't be able to hear anything so far away, but the rhythmic thumps had to be more than his beating heart.

"Could we hide on the second floor?" he gasped.

"We'd run into them coming up."

He looked back at the ladder. "So, we go out the window?"

"Is there another choice?"

The unrelenting pull to the center of the warehouse told him there wasn't. Lahn took one last look at the stairs. With a deep, raspy breath, he grasped the sides of the open window and lifted one foot up and through. He did his best to not look down or think about his actions as he ducked under the open window frame, sparse raindrops tickling his face. *Breathe in, hold it, release it slowly.* He counted off physical sensations as his other foot went out the window to stand on the ledge next to the first.

With a heavy wheeze, Lahn kept his eyes riveted on the warehouse and slowly stood upright. He attempted to ignore the ladder below him, but he couldn't stop himself. His eyes were pulled as if by magnetism, and he looked down. All he could see was the incredible distance to the ground. His stomach leaped into his throat, his sense of balance wavered, and the building seemed to slide beneath him. With panic flaring, he shifted and knocked back against the open window. It swung closed with a fatal click, locked tight.

Lahn's mind finally rebelled against everything he was putting it through. With terrifying familiarity, the distance to the warehouse and the ground stretched. Everything became distorted as if he was looking through glass.

No! Not now, not now!

Ten deadly meters above the ground, pinned precariously on a thin ledge, his first full Depersonalization episode in years washed over him and Lahn was no longer in his own body.

FLY, YOU FOOL

The warehouse was close. It couldn't be more than five meters away. But it didn't matter; distance lost its meaning. To Lahn, balanced on the ledge of the third floor, it could be centimeters or kilometers. It was impossible to tell.

All color was washed out, like viewing the world through an ancient terminal display, pale and pallid. The dark brick of the opposite building had faded to a reddish gray, a companion to the gray of the morning.

"*Ese?* What happened?"

Lucia's voice sounded like it was filtered through water. He was finding it hard to focus on her words. "I'm . . . not okay?" His own voice sounded weird in his ears. "I'm in DP." *That's not my voice. Did that even make sense?* He held his head very still, afraid to move it. Any fast movement could cause his vision to swim, wrecking his balance. Which might be bad.

"*Por qué ahora!*" Lucia spat. "Lahn?" she said, her voice switching to a calm, gentle style. "I'm here. I know we haven't gone through this together before, but we've talked about it, and I've read . . ."

Lucia's voice dissolved into the background. She couldn't help. Nothing could help now. The window was locked behind him. The ladder in front of him was the way forward. But the fifteen centimeter ledge he stood on was the only thing keeping him from the ten-meter drop, and he couldn't move.

"Lahn!" a voice broke through his fog. Something like Lucia's voice. ". . . listen to . . ." He wanted to listen, but it was hard. ". . . just breathe!"

Oh yeah. Breathing was good. He could do that.

[*Breathe, Lahn. Deep and slow.*]

He drew in air through his nose, and with effort he focused on the sensations. The smell was cool and wet, filling his lungs and head with the crisp odors. Lahn took another deep breath, felt his chest expand, and his arms press against the cool metal and glass of the window behind him.

A gentle melody bled into his consciousness. Lucia had started playing music, quiet enough that he hadn't noticed. It was a mix of classical Vietnamese nhã nhạc style of imperial court music, blended with modern electronic instruments. The theme was slow and gentle—calming, but just interesting enough to engage his mind.

"Your heart seems to be slowing," said Lucia, quietly.

That was possible. Maybe. At least he could finally pay attention to her. "I'm still stuck in DP." His voice hadn't gotten any better. He'd forgotten how weird it sounded to him when in an episode. "And still stuck on this ledge."

"You are going to have to get on the ladder, and cross."

"I can't."

"Bend your knees, slowly, and slide down until you can reach forward with your hands."

Lahn glanced at the ladder, but as he looked down, everything shifted. The entire world moved sideways, and he slammed his head and arms back against the window.

"Calm, Lahn. Calm. Listen to the music. Breathe. Deep, not shallow."

He tried to do as she suggested, but it would be so much easier to ignore her. "I . . . can't . . . do this," he whispered.

"Yes you can," Lucia soothed. "You have to. I will guide you."

[*You can do this!*]

Lahn wanted to trust the voice in his head, to trust Lucia. He looked at the building across the alley, in another universe. [*Slow, deep breath.*] Maybe he could just stay where he was. Forever. [*Slow, deep breath. You can do it.*] He took one last breath and let it out. "Okay."

"Keep your eyes on the far building," said Lucia, "and slide down slowly."

Feeling like he was controlling a character in a game, Lahn leaned back hard against the window behind him. One more breath, and he allowed his knees to bend and he started sliding down. As he neared the ladder, his center of gravity shifted, and his feet slipped off the ledge. He pitched forward and the ground rushed at him. In slow motion, he threw his hands forward by reflex to grab the sides of the ladder and catch himself. One hand slipped on the wet metal and he smashed face-first into the ladder, the pain instant and sharp. His arm dangled over the empty air and the ladder shook ominously.

Lahn's sense of self ran from his body, and didn't bother to watch if he fell. The ladder oscillated, slowed its movement, then stopped.

But Lahn didn't notice. He couldn't do it. He couldn't cross.

His mind went back to the vision from the night before. Trapped in the dark, locked away, left to rot. Seemed pretty nice right about now. He let his mind float away, into the dark room, away from everything. Just before the blackness closed around him, he saw his body straighten to hands and knees, and take the first movement toward the far window.

As Lahn stumbled into the warehouse through the window, he kicked hard from the ladder, causing it to shift precariously. He slumped to the floor, shivered, and blinked a few times, the natural light from the windows bright in his eyes. Still in Depersonalization, it took a moment to understand where he was and what had happened. He had crossed, but he didn't know how. The last thing he could remember was falling face-first on the ladder. He probably hadn't died, because here he was. But it must have been something horrendous for his mind to blank it out. Losing time was terrifying, but maybe in this case forgetting was best.

"Look at you," said Lucia, brightly. "You didn't fall and die again."

"I don't know how I didn't," he said, mouth full of cotton. "I have no idea what happened out there."

"You were saying the weirdest stuff while you crawled across," she noted. "You said you were lost in time. And if you didn't hurry, everyone would die."

Lahn lethargically rose to his feet and took stock of his senses. He could tell his heart continued to thunder, but he was still watching a pale movie of his life. The danger was over, but his body didn't know it, so his episode wasn't fading. He had a hard time caring.

"Lahn!" a voice called from across the alley behind him.

He turned back to look the way he came. Standing in the open window of the factory was a larger guy, auburn hair and beard, wearing a shimmery orange jacket. Lahn stared, trying to process, as the man leaned out the open window and looked with concern between Lahn and the ladder.

"Maddox?" Lahn shook his head, fighting through the Depersonalization.

"Maddox?" said Lucia in Lahn's ear. "He must have been what we heard in the factory."

"Why are you here?" Lahn asked Maddox through the windows.

"To *help!*" Maddox called back. "All of this has been extremely hard on you. From the very beginning, before your first vision, and you were dreading that work meeting. Remember? Whatever is down in there is probably worse than *anything* you've experienced so far. Worse than any work meeting. I just want to help."

Lahn's heart continued to hammer in his chest and his head burned. His hand was killing him, the scar throbbing violently. But all of that was overshadowed by the need to get to the center of the warehouse. Now supernatural in strength, the drive pulled him forward. At the end of the hallway to the left, an entryway opened to shadows. A stairway. A path to lower floors. His feet moved toward it.

"Wait!"

A scuffle at the far window made Lahn pause, and he looked back. Maddox stepped through the window and put one tentative foot on the ladder. The ladder shifted, and with a horrible sound of metal against stone the far end of the ladder slipped off the ledge. Maddox scrambled to regain his footing, holding tight to the window frame. The ladder fell ten meters and clattered to the ground, and the noise echoed through the alley.

Lahn looked at Maddox with painful detachment. "You okay?"

"Yeah," said Maddox, gasping.

"I guess you can't help."

"But . . . I . . ." Maddox sputtered, hanging onto the window desperately. "Okay, but listen," he said, breathing heavily "I'm sorry. I really wanted to keep you safe. I'm sorry for every bad thing."

One foot slipped, and Maddox grunted as he pulled himself back up and replaced it on the ledge. "You are going down into the warehouse, I can tell. I *really* wanted to be there. But I can't." Maddox looked at Lahn, eyes wide. "Since I can't be there to help, just listen; you can do hard things. You go outside. You attend work meetings all the time, even when you don't want to. Before you walk down those stairs, just say it one time, out loud. *I am Númenórean. I fear nothing!*"

Lahn blinked slowly, watching Maddox's desperate face, turned and walked toward the stairway.

"How'd he find us?" asked Lucia.

When he reached the stairwell, Lahn took one last look back at his friend. Maddox struggled to climb back into the factory then looked to Lahn with concern. Turning back to the stairs, Lahn stood for a moment and looked down into the darkness, allowing Maddox's last words to enter his awareness. His headache had grown and become a spike of cold metal stabbing through his forehead into his brain. It didn't feel natural. It felt like it was related to the warehouse.

"Maddox is right, you know," said Lucia. "You can do so much more than you think."

"I . . ." he said slowly, knowing what he was about to say was a lie, "I fear . . . nothing." He wished desperately it was true. He wanted to be the hero. He wanted to be someone not afraid of little things like going outside or attending a work meeting. He wanted the confidence to go down the stairs and stop whatever was about to happen.

At the moment, he didn't have much of a choice. The compulsion to get to the center of the warehouse had grown, and it told everything else to shut up. Unable to fight it, he stepped into the dark stairwell, and started down the steps.

At the bottom, Lahn stopped, closed his eyes, and pressed his fingers into his temples, trying to push out the headache. A noise broke through his pain, a sound from deep in the building: a thump, followed by another, and another. The slow, rhythmic pounding of some tragic creature fighting to be released from its captivity. Maybe it was *him* in the dark room from his vision, trying with everything he had to get out. Lahn was tempted to follow the noise, but it felt like his headache—now a rusty nail—came from that direction. In contrast, the irresistible compulsion to find the center called him the other way. He went the other way.

A flickering light shone through a doorway at the end of the hall. The rusty nail in his forehead eased as Lahn crept forward and peeked quietly around the corner. The doorway led into the large open area of the warehouse. Broken metal shelves and boxes misshapen with decay filled the space. In the center of it all, behind several rows of shelves, someone moved around—the mysterious figure he'd seen from above—occasionally walking in front of various glowing lights on the equipment, causing specter-like shadows to jump and dance against the far walls.

Lahn crept around Styrofoam, boxes, and bits of trash to get a better view. As he drew closer, he could see through the shelving to the open area. He carefully slid one box over and peeked through.

"Oh . . ." said Lucia in awe. "What's all that?"

Off to the side of the space were several large metal canisters. Wisps of fog rose from them, and each was coated with a thin layer of frost. Toward the middle, multicolored cables ran in different directions, converging in the center of the area. Several tables were set up with various electronics. Some of it was recognizable: terminals, oscilloscopes, and spectrometers. But much of it was completely foreign.

In the center of it all was a device unlike all the rest, the hub of the wires and monitoring equipment. The device was a black box about a meter wide and half a meter tall; the front was open with various switches, gauges, and blinking lights exposed.

Hunched over the device, making adjustments, was the one person Lahn was not surprised to see.

Faceless.

With his back to Lahn, he was still wearing the same dark coat with a hoodie underneath. The hood was down, bunched up around his shoulders. If he would just turn around, Lahn would finally see his face. On his head, a strange wire mesh connected to a bundle of colored cables. They streamed down from the mesh cap, cascaded over his shoulder, and flowed into the center device.

Nothing about the situation made any sense, but somehow it was all related. The encrypted letter, the strange messages on his portable, even his visions . . . it all led here. And Faceless was in the middle of everything. Lahn wanted to run out, grab Faceless by the stupid lapels of his stupid overcoat, and demand to know what was going on.

Maybe even grab that device at the center of it all, rip it free of its cords and cables, and throw it to the ground with extreme prejudice. And then stomp on it a few times for good measure.

Or . . . he *wanted* to want to do that.

But those were emotions of a Lahn not afflicted by a Depersonalization episode. This Lahn knew he *should* be feeling those strong desires to finally get answers, to finally do something about the disaster his life had become. But he wasn't.

Yet even though he didn't feel what he should, he knew that was why he was here. This was his chance, DP or no. His one purpose was to take the Ring and throw it into the fires of Mount Doom, making sure it was destroyed forever.

He shifted sideways to move around the metal shelf.

"Oh, no," said Lucia. "I know what that is."

A loud click came from the center of the room, several lights on the device flashed, and an unpleasant whine started up, moving from high-pitched to ultrasonic. Lahn crouched, intending to bolt forward and smash into the table, knocking everything to the ground. A bright blue flash and an audible crack stopped him. Instantly, his headache was gone, switched off. As was the compulsion that drove him to the center of the warehouse. They were replaced by his stomach rising into his throat, like in an elevator dropping too fast.

"Laaaaaahn!" screamed Lucia over the noise. "I'm sorry!"

A boom and a crash rang out somewhere deep in the warehouse behind him. Blue light pulsed from the device and a mechanical hum he could feel in his teeth followed, growing in intensity. Faceless leaned forward, hunched over the device, and grabbed both sides, as if holding on for dear life. And a new sensation started, more than a simple compulsion. Like an invisible claw, a force reached inside his chest, grabbed his spine, and pulled him physically toward the pulsing device in the center of the room. Lahn stumbled to the ground—the sound of it covered by the increasing noise from the device—and was dragged forward.

Flailing to grab the nearby shelf, he accidentally knocked his cuff from his ear and sent it flying back into the entryway. With the sound of metal dying, one of the large canisters burst open, ripped free of its connections, and flew away to crash into a far wall. Boxes and papers flew around him in a maelstrom, an electric flash from the center device forced his eyes shut, and someone screamed.

Then, an overwhelming sense of déjà vu washed over Lahn, and time stopped.

[He feels every part of his body, frozen in the moment, grasping the shelf in desperation to avoid the pull toward the center of the storm. At the same time, he experiences with perfect clarity a moment a few days ago. Between one step and the next, he is walking toward the kitchen. The strong feeling of déjà vu bewilders him. He is unsure what he is feeling, naive to the struggles soon to come.

Overlapping both is a third version of himself. This one is also in the warehouse. But this one is running toward the center, frozen in motion with one foot off the ground. Almost flying. He has one last chance to stop the event about to happen. One last chance to fix everything. He rushes toward his goal with every fragment of available energy and ability.

But he can still feel himself, on the floor, getting dragged toward the center device. And he is jealous of that third version, running toward the center. He can't remember a time when he felt confident enough to give everything to a goal. There is always a reason to be afraid.

And, even through Depersonalization, he is petrified.]

Time resumed with an explosion of violence. A blast of blinding light and energy burst from the center of the room, fiery hot then glacial cold, consuming Faceless and Lahn. The light faded, and both were gone.

PART II

maGICaL TRanSPORT

[Time stands still, with vast, malevolent energy that will obliterate everything in its path. Nothing exists here. Nothing could exist. Yet, he is here and he shouldn't be. He is about to be utterly and completely destroyed.]

Lahn jerked up with a strangled cry, his eyes wide in defense against the terrifying Void.

His Depersonalization episode was over. He was back in his own body, but now his senses were in overdrive. Every nerve-ending on fire, he pulled himself into a ball. His breath hissed through his clenched teeth and he held it, the taste of dust and electricity coating his tongue.

Lahn shivered uncontrollably in frigid agony and struggled to get his taut muscles to relax. Every part of him hurt, especially his face where he'd landed on the ladder. He'd likely get a glorious bruise. He tipped onto his side and laid his head on the ground. Dirt and rocks dug into his scalp, but he didn't notice. For several minutes, he focused all his attention on deep breathing and drawing in every scrap of light until the pain and cold oozed away.

Yes, his DP episode had ended, but something even worse had crashed into his face. Yet again, the universe had tried to kill him.

Okay, Universe, Lahn thought, *now this feels personal!*

The Void. The violent, hungry, all-consuming Void had returned. Or maybe it never left, always on the other side of a closed door, just out of sight. The door had been thrown open, sucking Lahn in, another opportunity to be pulverized into nothingness.

It was his first vision experience all over again, pulled into the great empty and separated from space and time. In the overwhelming events of the last few days, he had forgotten the cruelty of that first vision. He was reminded now with harsh clarity: the rip from reality, trapped forever in the violent Void, then ground back into existence.

Why? he wondered. *Why did it happen again?*

Lahn mentally shook off the extreme sense of déjà vu and rose to one elbow to look around. The shelf that saved him from getting sucked into the evil vortex was still there, rudely unperturbed, and he pushed on it lightly, finding it bolted down. Strangely, the rest of the warehouse he could see was likewise free from the chaos he expected considering the recent violence.

With a quiet struggle, Lahn got to his feet and peeked around the shelf to look at the center of the warehouse. Faceless was gone. But surprisingly, so was most of the equipment. The tables were still in place, with a few items on each. Off to the side, the large metal canisters remained, and cables sat coiled in rolls everywhere. In the middle of the biggest table, the mysterious, boxy device was the only other piece of equipment. It was off, no lights, nothing glowed or flashed. But in the center, the device contained an open space that went all the way through it. A dark, marbled orb, about the size of a baseball, floated in the middle, suspended by an unknown force.

"Lucia," he subvocalized. "How long was I out?"

She didn't respond, and Lahn reached for his ear. The cuff was gone. He looked around him, but it was nowhere to be seen. His search quickly became frantic, crawling quietly on the ground toward the back entrance he'd come in through.

A screech of metal echoed as a door opened from the far side of the warehouse. Lahn jumped through the back entrance and slid around the corner. The soft sound of footsteps echoed through the large warehouse, coming to stop in the room he'd just left. Lahn peeked around the corner. Facing away, hood up, the unmistakable form of Faceless leaned over the mysterious device.

Moments ago, Lahn had been tempted to jump out and demand an explanation. But he was still trembling from the electronic maelstrom and his last violent vision, possibly caused by Faceless and the device. With a silent choke, he struggled to get a solid breath and fought to push back the darkness and shadows that pressed on him. He'd come to the warehouse looking for answers. He'd been drawn to the center room. He'd wanted to destroy that device. But now—cowering in the dark building, his emotions and anxiety fully returned to him—he only wanted to run away.

Far away.

One last quick scan over the ground between the shelf and the entryway where he hid, and Lahn slid back behind the corner, admitting to himself the cuff was lost. He couldn't stick around to keep looking. Until he could figure out some way to contact her without tipping off the DTS, his connection to Lucia was gone.

It was time to go, and for a moment he thought about

leaving the same way he came in, through the third-story window. If only the ladder hadn't fallen. Stupid idea anyway.

Peeking around the corner of the entryway again, he looked back into the center of the warehouse. There had to be another way out. Even Felise would have been helpful, with her boring facts about the building. While Lahn watched, Faceless moved away from the tables and walked toward the opposite end of the warehouse. Another screech of metal and light shot into the room as Faceless opened a door. He crossed in front of the light, and the door closed with a deep *thunk*.

Lahn skittered around the outer edge of the room. As he approached the door, he stopped short and pressed his ear to the cool metal of the exit. Muffled sounds and unintelligible talking bled through. The noise stopped, and Lahn held his breath, straining to hear anything more. A new sound started; a rhythmic crunching sound, growing louder. Coming closer.

With a spin, Lahn scanned the room, looking for a place to hide. The sound of a latch clicking brought him back around, and time slowed as the door swung open. Lahn shuffled backward, his back hitting the wall. The door stopped centimeters from his face, and steps echoed through the building as Faceless walked in, hidden from Lahn by the metal door in front of him. Not daring to breathe or move, Lahn watched the door swing away from his face, exposing the form of Faceless walking away with purpose. With a quick prayer that his movement would not draw attention, Lahn slipped around the door and out as it closed.

Leaning back against the wall next to the entrance, Lahn closed his eyes against the bright light of the morning. The warmth of the sun pressed into his skin and sent goosebumps up his arms. There was no hint of the rain from earlier, and he was grateful for the heat after the shadows and stress of the warehouse, the brightness driving back his anxiety.

One last calming breath, and he dashed to the corner of the building and into the alley between the warehouse and the factory. A quick peek back the way he came, then he continued, running along the back of the factory, to the alcove where he had first found the unlocked door and entered that morning.

I hope Maddox is okay, Lahn thought. *I hope he didn't get caught in the blast. Maybe he's still in the factory.*

Lahn hit the security door with the side of his fist, poised to grab the door as it bounced open. It didn't move. With a scowl, he hit it harder. It stayed stubbornly still. Looking closer, he could see the door was fully flush in the frame, closed and locked. The rock was gone. Maddox must be gone. Probably knocked the rock out as he left.

Lahn had no cuff. He'd left his portable behind on his desk. He was on his own.

With a dash, he sped from the alcove to the far side of the factory, glad to be as far from Faceless and the warehouse as possible. It was surprising how much he missed Lucia encouraging—or mocking—him to action. If she was in his ear, she'd probably say something like, *Come on, Pilgrim, don't give up now. You still wanna know what's going on, don't you?*

And he did want to know. But not if that meant being sucked into the Void again.

Lahn traveled the full length of the far side of the factory, then stopped at the corner to peek around the front. The parking lots and streets between buildings were empty. A noise to the right made him turn: an empty autoride passed and entered the warehouse parking lot. It coasted to a stop near the front of the building, the song of electronics winding down.

The passenger windows flashed a graphic of red, stating *reserved.*

Faceless called for it, thought Lahn as he stared longingly at the autoride, sleek and shiny, the radiant color of a phoenix. It was like a magical transport, summoned by his desires, so he could jump in and fly to safety. Maybe with Lucia's help, he would have been able to hijack it, but not on his own.

Any minute, Faceless would come out for his ride. Lahn wished he was brave enough to confront Faceless and learn what he was truly up to, to finally get some answers, and stop him from hurting anyone else with his weird machine again. Or even just follow him and see where he went. But Lahn had no ride . . .

Unless . . .

It was a terrible idea—he should be running from Faceless, not following him—but he had no way to contact Lucia or anyone else. *I'm just following him to see where he goes,* thought Lahn, not stopping to think about all the ways it might go wrong. Lahn ran toward the autoride, passing the empty alley between buildings. He drew close, then went directly to the trunk of the autoride, pressed the trunk release, jumped in, and pulled it closed. The darkness, unnaturally black, enveloped him and left him blind.

SCRATCHY RECORD

Lahn struggled to breathe, in through his nose and out through his mouth, the smells of travel and mold assaulting him. No cuff, no portable. Not even a tiny flashlight on his key chain. No way to break the smothering blackness.

Locked in the trunk of the parked autoride, the Void from the vision hovered nearby, ready to consume him, and Lahn kicked himself mentally for his rash plan. In his current fetal position, he could actually kick himself physically. Which he did. Twice, for good measure.

A crunch of footsteps approached the autoride, and Lahn froze, holding his breath. A click announced the opening of a door, followed by a shuffle and slight rocking of the autoride. The door closed with a muffled thump, and the vehicle flowed into motion.

Lahn let out a quiet sigh and closed his eyes, trying to forget he was locked in the dark; instead, he tried to determine where they were going by the motion of the autoride. Neither effort was successful. The continuing pressure of the malevolent Void haunted him, just like that morning in his apartment when everything started.

[And, he is there again, trying unsuccessfully to recover from his reactions to the first vision, not able to close his eyes for fear of the Void. "I can still ground," he says with forced conviction, looking for ways to connect to his senses. He ignores the emptiness in the back of his mind, ignores the fact he can't close his eyes, and puts all his focus on other sensations. The chill in his fingers, goosebumps on his arms, the rough fabric of denim on his legs, all of it grounds him. "I can feel what's real," he repeats several times, hoping as much as believing. With a deep breath released through pursed lips, his anxiety recedes to a tolerable distance, and his heartbeat falls to a minor throb in the scar of his hand.]

Lahn slid back into the present, his eyes having grown accustomed to the dark. Small rays of light bled in through cracks and seams in the trunk, the smallest light driving back the darkness.

"That felt so weird," he said quietly to himself. It was harder not having Lucia to talk to than he thought it would be. But there was nothing wrong with talking to himself, right? "Almost as real as being there again."

With a bit of caustic humor, he thought about how poorly he'd managed his reactions to those early visions. Everything had felt dire. *It wasn't as bad as it seemed,* he thought. *Especially compared to everything that came after.*

The autoride shifted and rolled to a stop. "Don't forget your luggage," said a muffled, artificial voice from inside the vehicle.

The trunk latch clicked, the lid lifted a centimeter and light streamed through, motes of dust dancing in the beams. Lahn couldn't think. His entire plan was threatened because the stupid autoride thought he was a travel bag. A shadow crossed the beams of light, Lahn froze, and fingers curled around the edge of the trunk lid. The lid lifted slightly, then slammed shut.

As the steps strode away, Lahn almost laughed with relief. Faceless must have thought the trunk opening was a glitch, and hadn't bothered to check inside. The gentle hum of electronics aborted his reprieve as the autoride rolled forward. New problem. Stuck in a trunk. His stupid idea to follow Faceless would be for nothing. He frantically clawed the inside of the dark trunk to locate the emergency release button, cursing himself for not finding it before jumping in.

The electric purr faded, and the autoride slowed again to a stop.

Before Lahn could do anything, the trunk lid clicked and opened fully. Morning light streamed in and he scrunched his eyes against the glare.

"What in the world?" said a voice which mirrored Lahn's confusion. He blinked several times and looked up at a young woman Tia's age, with glasses too large for her face.

Lahn scrambled out of the trunk, almost knocking the luggage from the woman's hands.

"S-sorry. Got locked in."

He stumbled away, the eyes of the woman burning a hole in the back of his head. His relief at being free of the trunk overrode his embarrassment.

Lahn stepped onto the sidewalk, turned in a full circle, and tried to get his bearings. Everything looked familiar; he'd been in the area before, and after a moment of disorientation, he remembered when. A block away, the top floors of Renelogy Solutions rose over the shorter buildings around him. He'd traveled down this very road in an autobus a few days ago. After everything, he found himself back at the site of the first attack.

"Why would Faceless come back here?"

Walking toward the building, Lahn passed an Indo-west restaurant at the end of the block. As the Renelogy building came into full view, Lahn's confusion increased.

The emergency vehicles were gone. The police barricades were gone. There were no clean-up crews, or even a single guard to keep people away from the site. Instead, the parking lot was half-full of typical commuter autos. The building itself was even stranger, with no gaping hole, or even a single scratch. Amazingly, impossibly, all the destruction and damage was cleaned up and the building repaired. A man with a button up shirt walked through the front entrance into the building, and a woman in a sweater was just getting out of an auto. As if it were a typical day at work, not two days post-workpocalypse. In shock, Lahn walked toward Renelogy, passing between the autos, and stared up at it in wonder. It looked like the explosion had never—

A solid thunderclap reverberated from deep inside the building, vibrating through the pavement and up Lahn's spine, followed by a crack that bent gravity. The woman with the sweater screamed and fell to the ground. As Lahn's stomach rose into his chest, he slid forward toward the building.

"Again?" he screamed to no one. His feet scrambling against the ground, Lahn slipped to his hands and knees, autos shifting toward the building around him. Drenched in a wave of déjà vu, he rolled to his back and dug in his heels and hands, scratching up his palms and fingers on the asphalt, as he fought to keep from drawing any closer to the building.

With the sound of crunching metal and glass, followed by the deep thump of a kettle drum played backward on a scratchy record, the front-left corner of the building pulled in on itself and disappeared with a blinding flash and a snap that lifted Lahn up and then dropped him flat to the ground. A cloud of fine powder filled the air, obscuring everything. As it settled, the building became visible, with a gaping hole that exposed the inner rooms of the first four floors. One bit of an upper floor creaked precariously, then broke off and fell into the hole, the crunch of metal and concrete unnaturally loud in the silence.

Lahn sat on the ground, numb, odors of batteries and plasma driving through his chaotic thoughts, heart beating heavily in the bruise on his face. A sound of approaching sirens penetrated his confusion, pulling him out, and he scrambled to his feet, looking for someplace to go, someplace to hide.

He had no guesses how the building had been repaired in two days, but seeing it attacked again broke his brain, and he struggled to make sense of it. As he sped back the way he came, passing in front of the Indo-west restaurant again, Lahn saw his reflection in the window. Head to toe, a thin layer of dust covered every inch of him. With a shudder, he stepped into an alley between buildings and brushed it off, frantically rubbing his clothes, face, and hair.

Calm down, Lahn chided himself. *Act natural.*

With effort, he casually walked out from the alley and away from Renelogy. Humans spilled from the various businesses on both sides of the street, looking for the source of the noise. Taking a deep breath, and telling himself the crowds were better than a prison cell, Lahn slipped into the growing mob to blend in. Hidden in the curious mass, Lahn stared as emergency vehicles sped by, followed by several news vans.

This is crazy, he thought. *A second explosion at Renelogy? Did Faceless do this? Why attack the same building twice?* He turned and continued walking, wishing he could talk to Maddox or Tia or Lucia.

In front of him, a small group gathered around a display mounted outside an electronics store.

"Can you believe this?" said a short, stocky woman.

"No! How is this happening?" said another woman, younger, with hair that glowed on its ends.

The content on the display pulled at Lahn, like a siren song: a breaking news sequence with live footage of Renelogy.

But . . .

It couldn't be *live*. It was footage he'd watched a thousand times when he was investigating the first attack, news clips of the Renelogy explosion two days ago. The glowing "Live" indicator on the screen made no sense while showing recorded content, content that was two days old.

Next to the display, a row of synchronized digital clocks sat on a shelf inside the store window. Each were of unique designs, and a few displayed more than time. Lahn froze in place, his brain unable to command his body to move away as he stared at the date displayed on one.

"Is that today's date?" Lahn asked as he grabbed an arm in front of him and pointed, forgetting any fear of talking to strangers.

The man looked back in confusion, then turned to the clocks. "Monday, the twentieth? Yeah, that's today. Why?"

The date.

Two days ago. There hadn't been a second explosion at Renelogy.

It was the same one.

He'd gone back in time.

MESH STORAGE - 2012-08-20 11:03:10

Hey, Dad.

    I'm awestruck.
    I have no words. I know that's not normal
for me.
    But the experience of traveling through time
is indescribable. I don't know if I will ever
understand what happened.
    And before I had time to process, I had
to deal with Renelogy. Seeing the destruction
firsthand was nothing like hearing about it,
or watching the clips on the news. The brutal
power of the event, an energy I could sense in
my bones, made me feel very small.
    And now, I have to live this week over
again, with all its challenges. Nothing went as
I hoped.

    I wish you were here to help me work through
this.

CLOSED TIME-LIKE CURVE

With a knock much more frantic than he intended, Lahn waited outside Maddox's apartment, bouncing on the balls of his feet in nervous anticipation. Tia hadn't been home, and Maddox probably wasn't either, but Lahn really needed to talk to *someone* and figure out what had happened. Even if he had no clue how to start the conversation. How do you tell someone you traveled back in time, without them thinking you've lost it?

Maddox opened the door, his auburn hair a nest of chaos, bags under his eyes, looking like he hadn't slept. When he saw Lahn, a bright smile replaced a look of distracted concern.

"Lahn!" Maddox said, but then his smile slipped. He looked Lahn over, taking note of the scratches, dirt and dust, and the frantic look in Lahn's eyes. "What happened?"

"I'm from the future!" Lahn blurted out. *Smooth.*

Maddox stared at Lahn intently for a moment. "I have no idea how to respond to that. But are you okay?"

Lahn nodded and shrugged at the same time.

Relief washed over Maddox's face, and he grabbed Lahn's

shoulder. "Good, good. Come in, and you can tell me what you mean."

Lahn followed Maddox into his apartment but stopped for a moment inside the door. He closed his eyes and breathed in deeply through his nose, taking in the familiar scents of Maddox's apartment. It smelled like generous friendship and evenings talking about the universe. Okay, yes, he was here. The simple sensations grounded him and took the edge off his anxiety.

Even though it was a smaller studio, Maddox's apartment was far nicer than Lahn's. The apartment was overly white, with accents of silver, all in a modern style. White diode string-lights recessed in every corner made the room feel brighter and bigger than it was.

Maddox's holographic display played the news sequence of the attack, calling it an accident. Maddox picked up a bowl of cereal he'd been eating from the kitchen table that extended from the wall. "Do you want breakfast?"

Lahn shook his head and continued to stare at the news. "I couldn't eat right now."

"Have you seen what happened?" Maddox asked, walking to stand beside Lahn as the table retracted automatically, followed by the chairs flattening into the floor, freeing up space in the small kitchen area.

The footage felt *weird*. Lahn had seen all of it multiple times. He'd watched everything he could find after his first and second visions. But it was nothing compared to experiencing it firsthand. "I was there."

Maddox stopped with a spoon halfway to his mouth, and turned from the display to stare at Lahn, mouth still open. "Wait! You were there? Why?"

"And it was the second time," Lahn continued. "The first time happened a few days ago. The building imploded, news reports, everything."

"I . . . I don't understand."

"I don't either," Lahn said. "I'm completely lost. You and Tia know more than I do about this kind of thing, with your quantum-something biophysics."

Maddox looked over at the news footage, projected by the holo-display into the air in front of a blank, white wall, giving the illusion of dimensionality. He leaned forward as the camera drone tracked the outside of the building. Then looked back at Lahn again. "Are you sure you're all right? How close were you?"

"Close enough I was getting sucked in. I got scratched up a bit, but I'm fine."

Maddox shook his head. "And you're saying you'd seen it all before, because you're from the future?"

"I know. It sounds impossible." Lahn moved to the couch, too distracted and tired and sore to be concerned about the dirt and dust from his clothes fouling the white fabric. The stylistically curved sofa always stayed so clean, it was probably expensive dirt-repellent cloth anyway. He sat and sank into the conforming cushions with a grateful sigh.

"Um . . . yeah, it does sound impossible." Maddox laughed. He put his half-empty bowl in the sink, and the sink disappeared into the wall to complete a short wash cycle. He walked to the oversized chair next to the couch, sat, and leaned forward, looking at Lahn with intensity. "I mean, time travel is *theoretically* possible, and just looking in your eyes—and that bruise on your face—it's obvious you've been through . . . something."

"Yeah. But what? Am I in some weird loop, doomed to live this day over and over?"

"No, time travel wouldn't work like that. Time loops are a popular sci-fi trope, but there's nothing in physics to support their existence."

"What do you mean?" said Lahn, eyebrows creased.

Maddox's eyes lit up and he grinned as he got into the subject. "Instead of a time loop, it would be a causal loop or a closed time-like curve. It depends on the cause: whether the event is self-existing through retrocausality or not. But either way, the observer timeline only overlaps the proposed event boundaries a second time."

"You lost me at '*closed time-like curve.*'"

"C.T.C. for short."

Lahn laughed. "Listen, it's okay if you explain it to me simply. I won't be offended."

Maddox smiled. "Sorry. Industry vocabulary. Let's see . . ." He looked off into space for a moment. "It wouldn't be a time loop, where you experience the same events repeatedly. Instead, one past-self and one future-self have their own experiences as they travel through the same time frame . . . then you're finished."

"Wait," Lahn said, "there are two of me right now? That's how I prove it. Call me."

Maddox's eyebrows jumped a centimeter. "Why?"

"Just call."

Maddox pulled out his portable. "Kensha," he said into it, a crooked smile on his face. "Call Lahn."

"I still don't understand why you don't use an ear cuff," said Lahn, while they waited for the call to go through.

"They feel weird." Maddox held the portable to his ear and stared at Lahn intently like he was worried Lahn might disappear. "Oh . . . Lahn?" he said into the portable when the call was answered, eyes going wide. Lahn grinned and waved for him to continue talking.

Maddox leaned toward Lahn, poked him in the shoulder as if to make sure he wasn't a hologram, then stammered into the portable, "I . . . I wasn't sure I'd catch you. Are you . . . okay? I was just . . . I just had this feeling I should call."

A 'feeling,' thought Lahn with amusement. *I guess that's better than 'Your future told me to call you.'*

Maddox stood, did a little jig, and turned to Lahn and mouthed, *It's real! You're a time traveler!*

Lahn nodded back with a smirk. Then whispered, "Pay attention to him. Me. The . . . other me."

Maddox grinned back, and shifted his attention to the conversation with Lahn's past. "Why?" he said into his portable. "What happened?"

I'll tell you what happened, Lahn thought, *the universe drop-kicked me. Except, now I know it's a sketchy dude with a magic box.*

"Visions? You mean DP episodes?" Maddox cocked his head, his excitement taking a back seat as he listened to Past-Lahn's problems more seriously. He always did that. Tia too. Putting Lahn's needs above their own. And now Maddox had two of him to deal with. *Don't feel guilty,* Tia would say. *You would do the same for us if we needed help.* Which was only half-comforting, considering his sister never needed help with anything.

"It's been a little while since you've had one," Maddox continued.

Not DP, thought Lahn. He had spent so much time over the last two days wondering if the visions were related to his DP. Now he *knew* the vibrant, out-of-body experiences were completely unrelated to his condition.

"What do you mean?" Maddox asked Lahn's past. "Didn't you say once the things you see and hear can get distorted, like looking through old glass? Different from that?"

So different, Lahn thought. He'd just traveled through time, which explained a lot. Thinking back to his second vision, the one in his kitchen, he had seen a cloudy aftermath and a broken building. He'd seen *then* what he just saw *in person* less than an hour ago.

Somehow, he had experienced it through his future-self's eyes.

And what about his first vision, where he was pulled into the unforgiving Void? Was it a reflection of the time travel? When he awoke in the warehouse, he'd thought how unfair it was to experience another vision like the first one. But maybe . . . maybe it wasn't just similar.

Maybe it was the *same* event.

"Um . . . wow!" said Maddox with a nervous chuckle. He covered the mouthpiece of his portable and whispered frantically, "Your past-self felt you go through time?"

Lahn shrug-nodded and chuckled to himself, amused that Maddox was coming to the same conclusions as he talked to Lahn's past.

And Lahn *had* felt it when his future went through time. He finally understood his first vision, and why it was so different from the rest. Going back in time had pulled him from reality, through the Void, and dropped him into the past. And his past-self had felt it too.

The big question was *why*? Why did he experience the future? He knew magic often came with a price in books. Maybe traveling through time had consequences, and something had bled over to his past as he moved between times.

Maddox shook his head and paced the floor as he continued the conversation with Lahn's past. "I don't quite get that," he said into the portable, "but okay. What about the second one?"

That was an excellent question, what about the second vision? Lahn hadn't been floating through space-time anymore, so why had his past-self seen the destroyed building, too?

Maddox stopped suddenly in the middle of pacing and turned to stare at Lahn again. "I have no idea . . ." He took a couple of deep breaths. "Listen. I gotta go. I'll come over after work, and we can figure out what is going on. But this is weirder than you realize."

Lahn almost laughed out loud. It never stopped getting weirder.

"I mean," Maddox said to Past, turning to stare at the holo-display, still showing footage of the damaged Renelogy building, "you should check your queue."

PARADOX
TROPES

Maddox ended the call without looking at his portable. He turned back to Lahn, eyes wide. "That . . ." he said after a moment, "was the coolest thing I have ever done!" He flopped back into the chair. "But what was that about your visions? Did you see the future?"

"What I saw in the kitchen was exactly what I saw just now in person. But what does that mean, me and past-me are connected somehow?"

"Entangled . . ." Maddox said to himself with a grin. "Incredible!"

"So you *do* understand some of this?"

Maddox stood and went into the kitchen nook, waving his hands over censors. The table and chairs extended—cleaned and free of even a single crumb—and a silver panel in the wall retracted, revealing a nook with a counter. "Maybe. My project in quantum consciousness recently made some progress."

Lahn followed him and sat at the table. "You mean those tests you did on me? I can't remember much about that project, but what does that have to do with what's happening now?"

"We've recently discovered quantum tunneling in the human brain that could connect a person to their past or future."

"That almost sounds like something understandable."

Maddox smiled. "Let me back up and give you background. Human consciousness is a tricky problem. Traditional mechanics have a very hard time explaining it fully."

Lahn frowned. "What do you mean?"

Maddox got eggs, tomatoes, and cheese from the fridge and started cutting the tomatoes into small chunks, the smell of the fruit-vegetable filling the air. "How do the operations of the mind," he said, with his back to Lahn, "the neurotransmitters traveling between neurons and synapses, result in sapience and sentience? How does it result in thought, emotions, and personality?"

"We don't know?"

"There have been lots of theories. Sometime back, a physicist named Eugene Wigner suggested aspects of quantum mechanics, like entanglement and superposition, may play a role."

"I'm going to get lost," said Lahn. "You know I always zone out when you and Tia talk about quantum-anything." Much of what Maddox was saying made no sense, but it was something, and Lahn could feel his anxiety recede further as Maddox talked. He hoped all along that Maddox could help him find answers—he'd just had to travel back in time to get them.

Maddox looked over his shoulder at Lahn and smiled. "Yeah, it's complicated for everyone. The basic idea is that the activity in the brain could involve the quantum states of matter, and those states include unlimited possibilities. And those infinite possibilities give rise to the amazingly unique nature of each individual consciousness. Of course, that's oversimplified, and not fully accurate, but you get the idea. Anyway, it's a theory we've been working on at work to prove or disprove."

Maddox stopped cutting the tomatoes and stared down at the small, red cubes. Juice and seeds bled from his activity. "I really shouldn't talk about any of this. I've signed a mountain of silence agreements." He looked at Lahn again, a hint of pleading in his eyes. "But you traveled through time, so you're in this now . . . right?"

Lahn wasn't sure what Maddox wanted. Permission to continue? All he knew was he needed more answers, so he nodded. Maddox smiled, turned back to his tomatoes, and continued talking.

"Recently, we learned to detect the existence of nanoscopic quantum tunneling in matter other than graphene. And of course, we wanted to know if the tunneling happens in the human brain, so we started a study with a handful of human subjects. We hoped it might help prove the bigger theory of how consciousness works. That was the study I had you join."

Lahn frowned as he watched Maddox crack eggs in a bowl and whip them with a whisk. "That sounds . . . odd. Tunnels in my brain?"

"The tunnels relate to human thought, especially conscious thought. And we actually found some during the study! It was an incredible and exciting breakthrough, but it was only the beginning." Maddox touched the edge of the white counter, and a small red line appeared on the surface. Running his finger halfway along the line, he set the induction coils hidden under the granite counter to medium heat. He pulled out a Teflon pan and set it on the counter to warm.

"As we pursued our study of the phenomenon," he continued, "we recorded occasional bursts of high-energy tunneling inside the brain. But we couldn't determine the source, where those tunnel spikes started."

"What do you mean?"

"We found tunnels from outside the subject's brain, thoughts from outside."

Lahn considered for a moment, his eyes growing wide. "Like what's happening between me and my past . . ."

"Right!"

"Are you saying I'm connecting to my other self through quantum tunneling? Like our brains are connecting?"

"Yes. It's possible. Maybe even likely."

"But, in your test subjects, where was it coming from? I can't imagine they were all time travelers."

Maddox poured egg into the warm pan and sprinkled tomatoes and cheese on top. "That was the big question: Where was it coming from? We didn't know, and the events were hard to replicate. It wasn't until one subject mentioned she'd experienced a strong sense of déjà vu that we finally made a breakthrough. It gave us something to work with. If we could generate tunneling spikes through created moments of déjà vu, maybe we could find where they came from. So we had test subjects repeat activities they'd done days before, while we monitored. Activities of high emotional content, like listening to music or watching sad movies. We found something, but at first we didn't believe it."

"What did you find?"

Maddox slid the pan side to side. "A tunnel spike would happen during *both* times our subjects did the activity, not only the second time. And the energy signatures of the tunnels matched. We found the source *and* destination of the tunnels; it was the same person at different times."

Lahn's brow furrowed. "Really? Anyone, even if they haven't traveled through time, could connect to their past?"

"Or future," said Maddox. "I mean, emotions are complicated, and it's never cut-and-dry, but we reproduced the results multiple times. It looks conclusive—déjà vu can be a moment of quantum consciousness entanglement. That's why sometimes you can't connect the emotion to anything specific that's happening. What's causing the déjà vu hasn't happened yet."

"Whoa!" said Lahn.

Maddox slid the omelet onto a plate and put it in front of Lahn with a fork. Without really realizing it, Lahn started eating, taking huge bites.

"Oh . . ." he said through a full mouth, "I guess I was hungry after all."

"I thought so," said Maddox with a grin.

The cool air against Lahn's wet hair brought goosebumps to his skin. He stepped out of the bathroom and welcomed the sensation. Something normal.

After Lahn had finished eating the most delicious omelet ever created, Maddox teased him into cleaning himself up, offering clothes and a shower with Maddox's own water rations. Lahn took both, glad to get the dust off his skin and out of his hair, reveling in hot water jets from all directions. He even put a cooling antiseptic he'd found in Maddox's bathroom on his scratched up palms. Unfortunately, there wasn't much he could do about the bruise on his face—the line across his forehead and one cheek was becoming a lovely shade of purple. *Stupid ladder.*

"Okay . . . thanks," said Maddox into his portable as Lahn walked into the room. Maddox ended the call and turned to Lahn. "Feel better after the shower?"

"Much."

"Good," Maddox said. "I've taken the day off work. We can take the time we need to figure this out. Start at the beginning and tell me everything."

Lahn sat on the sofa and slumped down with his head resting against the back, then looked at the ceiling and started into the story from the beginning. He described the visions and their extreme impact, and his need to go to the site of the first attack to find answers.

Maddox interrupted, eyebrows creased. "Did you actually go?"

"Yeah, I left my apartment on a whim, impossible as that seems. About an hour from now, I go to the Renelogy building you've been watching on the news. Now shut it and let me continue. It gets worse."

As Lahn continued, talking about getting interrogated by Agent Prakash and seeing Faceless, Maddox stopped him again.

"Wait, Faceless?"

"I keep running into him. I don't know who it is, haven't seen his face. So I gave him a nickname. He must be involved in the attacks, but I don't have proof. I have no idea where he got the device or if he built it, but as far as I can tell, he triggered the time travel."

Continuing the story, Lahn talked about his experiences the next day, including his morning premonitions and conversation with Tia. Maddox leaned forward as Lahn described everything leading up to the second attack at Living Bliss.

"A second explosion . . . at Living Bliss," said Maddox, brow furrowed, looking at the news footage of Renelogy.

"Yeah, just like the first. When it happened, I saw a vision of blinding white, and then your face."

"Me? But your visions are from you. *This* you. For you to see me, you and I will have to be together . . . at Living Bliss."

"When the attack happens? You said you were there by coincidence, meeting Tia. But you're meeting me instead? That doesn't make any sense. Why would we go?" There had to be another explanation, but Lahn couldn't think of what it might be.

Maddox didn't say anything, continuing to watch the news with concern.

"It was a strong vision," Lahn said. "I ended up in the hospital with mystery symptoms, which went away on their own. The doctor said it was psychosomatic."

"Psychosomatic . . . I wonder . . ."

"What?" asked Lahn.

"Well . . . it could just be your body's reaction to everything happening. Or, it could have been an entangled response to what *will* happen."

"Like this time around I actually get hurt, and the symptoms get fed to Past-me?"

"Maybe," said Maddox.

Lahn frowned, his mind running away with the implications. "How about we don't go to Living Bliss. Then it won't happen at all."

"Deal," said Maddox, nodding emphatically. "Sorry you ended up in the hospital. Must have been rough."

Lahn snorted. For sure, hospitals sucked, but he didn't want to think about that. "The hardest part was dealing with Prakash again." *And both times I had to do it without Lucia.* Suddenly, he felt Lucia's absence as an ache in a weird spot in his chest, even though it had only been a few hours since she had helped him break into the warehouse. He'd gone without Lucia for longer stretches before. But this time, it was wrapped up in the fact his life was upside down and inside out.

With a shake of his head, Lahn moved on to the letter. He talked about how he'd decoded it and how it led him to the warehouse—the location of the time travel—and his struggle across a ladder to get inside. "As I went in, you showed up."

"Really."

"The ladder fell, so you couldn't follow me. But, you were trying to help me with whatever I was about to find."

"Probably wishing I could travel through time too," Maddox said with a grin.

"I didn't know that's what would happen."

"But I did . . . I mean, I do now, so I will then. Stars, it's hard to keep everything straight."

"You also tell me not to chase complicated solutions."

"What do you mean? I say that at the warehouse?"

"No. Later today, when you come over, you tell me to rethink the visions I'm having. You say maybe they are *actually* Depersonalization, even though now you know they're not."

"Hm . . ." said Maddox. "I wonder why I would say that?"

Lahn shrugged. "Almost like you were trying to protect me from finding out about the time travel. But why?" He looked at the muted news footage on the holo-display with talking heads and clips of the destruction at Renelogy. "So . . . what do we do now?"

"What do you want to do?" Maddox asked with a grin. "You're from the future. I can think of some things."

"Like stocks or sports betting?"

Maddox's grin got bigger.

"Sorry," said Lahn, smiling and shaking his head. "I was kinda busy and didn't pay attention to the rest of the world. The only thing I know about the future outside what happens to my other self is the second attack."

Maddox's face shifted, losing its smile. "I wish we could do something about that," he said quietly to himself.

"What do you mean? Stop it somehow?"

"No, of course not," said Maddox quickly. "We shouldn't get involved."

"Yeah," said Lahn. "We can't go to the authorities; Prakash already has it out for me and thinks I'm connected. And can you imagine the DTS learning there are two of me? I'd be locked up forever for using illegal tech."

Maddox sighed and turned back to the holo-display. "It's just that watching the news this morning kind of freaked me out. This happened in our city. People died. And there's another one coming? It's hard to ignore that."

The temperature control system in the apartment started up, its fans creating a gentle hum in the silence. After a moment, Maddox spoke up again. "I wish I could get a look at the tech that was at Renelogy. To better understand what happened."

As Lahn pondered what might have caused the odd damage to the buildings, a thought occurred to him. "Could the time-travel tech be involved in the explosions?"

Maddox perked up. "What makes you say that?"

"At Renelogy, I was getting sucked into the implosion. The same thing happened just before I traveled through time. And since Faceless was at the warehouse and Renelogy, could he be using something similar at both?"

Maddox nodded slowly, and pulled lightly on the red hairs of his beard.

"If we had access to the time travel technology," continued Lahn, "maybe we could better understand what's happening at the explosion sites . . . and what's happening to me."

Maddox frowned. "Maybe, but . . ."

"And . . . could we use it? Go back even further and make changes so none of this happens?" His eyes got big as the idea bounced around in his head. "Maybe we can stop everything plaguing me." And if he could change that, maybe there were other things from his past he could change as well.

"You can't . . . that's not . . ." Maddox sighed with a frown. "The one thing we can't do is go back in time to stop ourselves from going back in time."

"Why?" Lahn tipped his head to the side. "We might cause a paradox and destroy the universe?"

Maddox chuckled lightly. "No. That's another science fiction trope. In reality, saying it's a paradox just means it's impossible. The universe won't let it happen. It's like trying to break the law of gravity, or the speed of light."

"If it's impossible, and we don't have to worry about creating paradoxes, why not try?"

"Because it wouldn't work. Doesn't matter, anyway. Even my idea of just trying to understand the tech is pointless. We don't have the tech."

Lahn looked at Maddox with a slight grin. "Yeah, but . . . we know where it is."

Splinter Report: S08-304
Date: 2515-06-18
Local Date: 1867-02-23
ID: S08
Designation: Spectre Alpha

Report:

The first tests of the SCU were a complete success. The energy used in the Specter Containment Unit proved to create a barrier through which the chi signature present in this Splinter could not pass.

Our agents in Spectre Beta verified that the corresponding individual there became immobilized and unable to move, with no visible means of restraint. Because the SCU was bolted in place, no effort could affect or remove the immobilization on the target individual. The implications of manipulating the environment of one quantum-locked Splinter through its pair will require additional study.

It should be noted that the technology does not work directly on individuals, only on their specter in the pair Splinter.

T. Hobbs

SPIKY-WHITE

The shadows of the alley were comfortably cool in the temperate warmth of the afternoon sun. Lahn and Maddox sat on the ground against opposite buildings in the narrow alley, waiting, in their first and only stakeout.

"It seems innocent, doesn't it," said Maddox softly as he examined the warehouse across the street. "Hard to imagine you traveled through time in there."

Their plan wasn't complicated. Wait for a bit to make sure no one was around, then attempt to sneak in.

"When I was here earlier," said Lahn, "the building felt very ominous. But at the same time, I was driven to get inside."

"Because of your need for answers," said Maddox, nodding his head.

"More than that. There was this inexplicable, supernatural draw. Without it, I doubt I would have gone in."

"Weird. Feel anything like that now?"

"Nope. Just a normal, boring warehouse . . . that's also the site of illegal time travel."

After taking an autoride to the location, they'd done a

stealthy loop around the building, checking for any potential security. No cameras that they could see, but both the front and back doors had massive locks and chains that could give them trouble. Maddox had suggested they just look for a big rock when it came time to break in.

"I wonder where the generator went," said Lahn.

"Generator?"

"A big one, sitting outside the building on the side."

"Maybe it's not here yet."

Yet? Lahn thought. *Oh. Right.* Time travel was weird.

"What kind of generator?" asked Maddox.

"I don't know. But it was big, the size of a shipping container."

Maddox whistled. "That size could be fusion."

"Is that important?"

"Maybe. Fusion means more power. I wish I'd seen it. Why didn't you invite me to come with you?" Maddox shifted against the wall of the building behind them. The hard concrete was not going to be fun if they had to wait very long.

"Prakash was monitoring my tech. I couldn't call."

"She was? How do you know?"

Lahn stuttered for a minute. He knew because of Lucia. But no normal proxy would have been able to detect the DTS and their actions. "I mean, I assumed. After my conversations with her, I just figured . . ."

Maddox nodded, leaned his head back against the wall and closed his eyes. Lahn watched him for a moment.

It had taken a bit to convince Maddox to come. Of course he'd wanted to see the time travel tech, but he worried going to the warehouse was risky. And now that they were here, Lahn was having second thoughts. It wasn't long before Past-Lahn should be at Renelogy, which meant Faceless should be there also, and they could be sure the warehouse was empty. But what if they got the timing wrong, and

Faceless showed up while they were inside? Lahn was in deep, and now he was dragging Maddox in, too.

Maddox jerked forward and opened his eyes. "Is that an auto?"

The sound of an older gas-powered vehicle echoed from down the street to the right. Lahn and Maddox jumped to their feet and peeked around the corner of the building. A large, lemon-colored cargo truck rounded the curve of the road a couple of blocks away, followed by an autoride. Both pulled into the parking lot of the warehouse across the street, the vehicles too far away to make out any details about the riders. Lahn and Maddox watched with tense interest as the vehicles turned down the far side of the warehouse and disappeared.

"Was that Faceless?" hissed Maddox.

"I assume, but I couldn't tell for sure." Lahn breathed deeply and sat back on the ground. Now all they had to do was wait. It wouldn't be long before Faceless left for Renelogy.

Maddox continued to stare at the warehouse. "I'm going to get a closer look." He looked quickly to the right and left down the road. "Stay here," he said, and took off across the street.

"Wait!" Lahn hissed, scrambling back to his feet. A quick glance down the road, and he darted after Maddox, cursing his friend under his breath. Stupid Maddox, being all cautious before they came, and now just taking off on his own.

Maddox stopped at the end of the alley to peek around the corner of the building. Lahn caught up to him, stuck his head next to Maddox's, and watched the old truck as it backed halfway into the large shipping entrance of the warehouse. The driver got out, a woman with spiky platinum-white hair, who looked like she could take care of herself in a bar fight.

Its other passenger came around the front of the truck, a large Caucasian man Maddox's height, with small, round glasses and a tattoo of Japanese kanji on his neck. Both walked into the warehouse, and Lahn heard them talking to someone inside.

"Did you see the passenger of the autoride?" Lahn whispered.

"No. I think they are already inside."

They both pulled back behind the corner, and Maddox looked at Lahn with intensity, the corners of his mouth turned up. "Listen, I know this is dumb," he said, "but I'm going to get closer. You should stay here and pull me out if I get in trouble."

"But . . ."

Ignoring Lahn, Maddox peeked quickly around the corner again, stepped out around and tiptoed toward the entrance, tight against the wall of the warehouse.

Lahn looked up at the factory five meters in front of him, the alley neighbor to the warehouse. His hand was cramping, and he took several deep breaths while shaking it out. Maddox was going to get caught, and there was no way Lahn would be able to *pull him out*. What a stupid thing to say.

Lahn peeked around the corner again, just in time to see Maddox slide under the front of the truck. *What is he doing,* Lahn thought, his worry spiking. Maddox wiggled forward on his stomach until he was past the front wheels, almost inside the warehouse. Lahn's pulse started beating in his ears. Their whole plan had been to stay far away from Faceless, and get in to look at the tech when the coast was clear. What Maddox was doing might guarantee they got a look at something, like the knuckles of Faceless's fist right before it hit them in the face.

Maddox glanced at Lahn and Lahn shook his head, trying to communicate to Maddox that this was a terrible idea.

Maddox just lifted a palm toward Lahn, as if to say *stay there*, then started slithering forward.

Maddox was going in, army-crawling toward the back of the truck where he could look inside the warehouse. And Lahn couldn't stop him. Maddox was acting unusually foolhardy.

And if Lahn wanted to try to keep his friend out of trouble, as Maddox often did for him, Lahn would have to go with him.

With a sigh that turned into several deep breaths, Lahn slid away from the corner and toward the truck. He didn't get far before Maddox's face snapped toward Lahn, and he shook his head. Lahn scrambled back to the safety of the alley, and held his breath as footsteps came from the warehouse. The door to the truck opened, and his imagination exploded, thinking they would drive out with Maddox still under there.

He peered around the corner, heart racing. Tattoo-neck was halfway in the cab, grabbing something. He stepped down, holding several straps, and walked back into the warehouse. Lahn stretched his cramping hand. *Now or never.* He made a silent dash. At the truck, as quiet as possible, he scooted under the front and army-crawled to join his idiot of a friend.

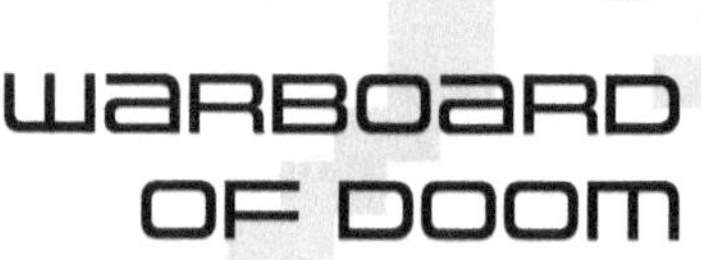

WARBOARD
OF DOOM

"You are so dumb," Lahn said in a hush.

"*You* followed me under here," whispered Maddox with a frown.

"Have you seen anything?"

"Not much," responded Maddox, almost too quiet for Lahn to hear. "Only legs and feet. A couple people keep pulling things from the truck, but that is all I know."

"So, what's the plan?"

"Keep going toward the back of the truck. We'll be fully inside the warehouse. See what we can see, then make a better plan."

"Of course. The plan is to make a better plan. Sounds perfect."

Both of them crept forward, careful not to make a sound, moving until they were under the back of the truck inside the warehouse. The equipment Lahn had seen after time-traveling was still visible, but now additional boxes and piles of cables were placed around the space. When he'd traveled back, he'd assumed Faceless had been removing stuff while he had been out cold, but now it was obvious most of the equipment hadn't been brought in yet. Over the next two days, Faceless would be getting everything set up for the time travel event.

Two sets of legs lifted something heavy, shaking the truck. As the legs moved toward the center of the open area, they became Spiky-white and Tattoo-neck, carrying a large box to set on the ground next to the tables in the center of the room.

A noise to Lahn's left drew his attention. A third set of feet were next to the truck, shuffling around. They moved away, revealing the bottom edge of a dark-blue overcoat.

Faceless! A couple meters away!

Tattoo-neck and Spiky-white went over to join Faceless beside the truck, and Lahn's heart thumped solidly in his chest.

"That's everything," a man grumped. Lahn wondered if it was Faceless, and thought the unforgiving voice fit him perfectly.

Feet shuffled around, the back door of the truck slid closed with a sound like harpies roller skating, and all three sets of feet moved outside of the warehouse. As the truck doors opened, Maddox kicked Lahn in the shins. He looked over to see Maddox's eyes wide with fear.

Lahn had gotten distracted by feet and voices and sounds. They were leaving, and Maddox and Lahn were still under the truck.

In a panic, Lahn wiggled and shuffled to follow Maddox out from underneath the truck on the far side. He pulled his legs out from under the truck just as it pulled out, narrowly missing his foot being crushed by five metric tons. He scrambled up and stood in the shadows against the inside wall next to Maddox, hoping they hadn't been seen.

"What do we do?" Maddox asked in a frantic whisper.

"You're bleeding," Lahn whispered back, and pointed

to Maddox's left temple. A thin line of red leaked from a cut, stark against his fair skin. A cut, just like the one on Maddox's head when he came over to help make sense of Lahn's visions.

Maddox rubbed his temple, smearing blood and dirt in a vibrant pattern. He looked like a zombie.

"Much better," Lahn said.

Maddox looked at the blood on his fingers. "I guess I scraped it when I rolled out from the truck."

A screeching sound drew their attention back to the truck entrance, and the large metal sliding-track door slid closed with a solid thump, thrusting the space into semidarkness.

Maddox and Lahn looked at each other.

A rattle and a click from outside, and then nothing. Lahn ran to the exit on the left of the truck entrance and pressed an ear to the door.

"What do you hear?" Maddox breathed.

"Footsteps . . . an autoride door . . . it's driving away . . . now the silence of an uncaring universe."

Maddox grabbed the large handle on the sliding door of the truck entrance and pulled, but it didn't move. Lahn wiggled the doorknob of the exit, the same one he had left through that morning, and found it equally locked.

"So, good news," Maddox said, his voice just above a whisper. "We are safely away from Faceless and minions."

"Bad news," Lahn responded, "that means locked inside a dark, creepy warehouse."

"Good news, we might be locked in with time-travel tech. I'm sorry I got us locked in here, I really didn't mean to drag you into more danger. But we're here; we should see what we can find."

They split up and started digging into boxes and examining equipment. When Lahn had come through in the morning, he was too distracted to pay much attention to the technology. Now that he could get a good look, he could see that most of it was off-the-shelf components, with logos from well-known companies. Unfortunately, what he didn't see was the time device.

"You find anything?" Maddox asked after a few minutes.

"No. Nothing like the time device. It was weird tech in a box. Lights, buttons, and gauges. With a marbled ball floating in an open space in the center."

Maddox looked into a few boxes he'd opened. "There's nothing like that here."

"Is there anything that helps us understand the technology at all?"

"I don't know what might apply to the sites of the explosions, but there's some interesting stuff. Those giant CO_2 canisters must be for supercooling. And that hundred mil cable in a pile means massive power requirements. Fusion for sure."

"Why does that matter?"

"It depends on the rest of the tech and the type of field it generates," said Maddox with a twinkle in his eye. He stroked his beard as he continued. "An energy field can interact with different power sources in complicated, sometimes dangerous ways. I would guess that the explosion at Renelogy was *not* powered by fusion, or the damage would have been much greater."

Lahn nodded and looked around at the boxes again. "I'm glad you're having fun, but I'm not much help here. I'll go look for a way out while you're digging around."

Maddox nodded distractedly, going back to the boxes, and Lahn turned toward the opposite side of the open warehouse space. He came to the entryway that led to the stairs up. No real way out up there. And even though that hall also led to the front of the building, the front entrance was locked up tight outside with chains and a giant padlock.

With a sigh, Lahn thought how weird his life had become. He was a time traveler. There were two of him running around the world. What would he say to himself, if they met? It was funny to think how stressed he was a few days ago just leaving the house to go to the site of the first explosion. Now he was breaking and entering, dodging criminals, and getting locked in strange buildings. At the same time, his past was headed to Renelogy, stressing about being on the autobus, worrying about the crowd he might have to navigate, anxious about all of it. It was probably happening right now, and Lahn could almost see what Past saw, feel what Past felt.

[He steps off of the autobus and bumps into the smoker in the red pantsuit. He glances aside to avoid her gaze. His pulse stutters, and he moves his right hand behind his back to hide its shaking. *No big deal. Everything is fine.*]

With a shake of his head, Lahn turned around, walking past Maddox taking photos with his portable of equipment on the center tables. Through the windows on the far wall, high in the air, was the factory and the third floor that he had used to get into the warehouse.

As his eyes dropped back to the area around him, a dark shape to one side caught his eye. An outline in the shadows. He moved toward it. It was a standing message board covered in paper, photos, and sticky-notes.

Faceless has a warboard! he thought with excitement.

As Lahn looked at the pictures and papers, he realized much of it was complex math beyond him. The rest was information about various topics: renewable energy, biotechnology, functional engineering, etc. The topics seemed to be unrelated, and he couldn't see how it was all . . .

A timeline.

In the top-left corner was a timeline. It included the attack on Renelogy that morning, the attack at Living Bliss tomorrow on Tuesday, and the time travel event in two days on Wednesday with details on each like location and casualties. But on the far end, after the time travel event, Lahn found a third attack.

"Another one?" he said in surprise.

It included little information. Just a time and date, in two days at noon, only a few hours after he traveled back in time. But no location. Instead, there was a drawing pinned to the board that looked like a pencil pointing straight up, with the word *under* written next to it.

But the timeline included something else, something that made Lahn's blood run cold. The first two attacks listed casualties of seventy-two and eighteen.

The final attack listed one thousand.

PROBLEMATA

ahn stared at the number. How was that possible? For an explosion to cause a thousand casualties, it would have to be a whole skyscraper like Welkin Tower where he worked. Or even bigger. It might mean destroying multiple skyscrapers.

"Whad'ya find?"

Lahn spun around, and a face smeared with blood and dirt loomed over him. He leaped back with a shriek.

Maddox cowered back with his own yelp, both hands up. "What?"

"Sorry," Lahn chuckled nervously. "Your face."

Maddox scowled. "It's still a mess?" He rubbed his forehead again, adding more dirt.

Lahn shook his head. "I'm just a little freaked out by what I found on this board."

Maddox stepped up to the board and looked at the pictures and notes. "Oh, wow." He pulled out his portable and started taking photos again. "There's notes about the other tech on here!"

"The other tech? You mean what was used at Renelogy?"

"Yeah."

"Is it the same as the stuff for time travel?"

"Similar. It looks like it's related . . ." said Maddox distractedly, leaning closer to the board.

Lahn whistled quietly. "So Faceless *is* the one attacking the buildings, using the same technology. But why? Does he just hate those companies, or is there something bigger he hopes to accomplish?"

"Oh," said Maddox, bouncing on his toes. "They're using quantum tunneling with no source or recipient. But if it's not connected to anyone in the world, wouldn't that mean . . ."

"Geek out later. Look at this." Lahn pointed to the timeline.

Maddox's face clouded over. "Whoa . . ." He was uncharacteristically at a loss for words.

"This can't be real, can it?" asked Lahn. "Why would this one be so much bigger?"

"That number is so exact—is it an estimate?" Maddox cursed under his breath. "It doesn't say where. Why doesn't it say where?" He pointed a stiff finger at the board. "And what's this drawing? A short, chubby pencil?"

Lahn took a step back and crossed his arms tightly against his chest, blocking out the story of the board. "Here's the real question: What do we do?"

Lahn and Maddox looked at each other. The whole situation was way beyond them. It was already stupid they were at the warehouse, a site of illegal tech, thinking they could get information to stop time-traveling terrorists. But now? Apparently, the first two attacks were just practice. The real event was a whole different league.

"We can't stop this," said Lahn quietly.

"We are going to have to call someone," responded Maddox. "The police? The DTS?"

Lahn shivered and rubbed the scar on his hand. "They will probably lock us up for being here at all." Not to mention what would happen if they dug into his life and somehow found Lucia.

"What choice do we have?"

With a deep breath, Lahn turned away from the board and looked at the collection of technology in the warehouse. "I don't know. If we do nothing, and a thousand people die . . ."

"Wait," said Maddox, causing Lahn to turn and look at him. "What did we do last time?"

Lahn looked at Maddox. "Huh?"

"I know your past knows nothing about this, but you and I do now. Maybe there was something you saw me do or say that could give clues into how we handled this. Either successfully or failing miserably, anything we can learn from it to do better."

Walking forward to the board again, Lahn looked at the timeline and thought about the last couple of days. There wasn't much. "You never said anything to me," said Lahn. "And I think if we'd talked to the DTS, you'd have ended up in jail. You didn't, but I don't know what that means, if we called the DTS or . . ."

Something on the message board jumped out at Lahn.

"The DTS," he said.

"What?" asked Maddox.

"Right there." He pointed to a sticky-note on the board. It said *help from the DTS*, and it was connected to the final attack. "What does that mean? How would a terrorist get help from the government agency?"

"Unless . . ."

"Unless, what? Do you think when Faceless was planning the attacks," said Lahn, pointing to the warboard, "he made a deal with the DTS, and now they are somehow involved?"

Maddox shrugged and turned away to glance around the

warehouse. "Some people whisper that the Department of Technology Security stops sketchy tech in order to keep it all to themselves."

Lahn looked at Maddox. Everyone knew what the DTS did was for the protection of humanity. At the same time, the needs of the many outweighed the needs of the few, and everyone did what they had to in order to stay out of the second category.

But if the DTS was involved in these attacks? Lahn didn't even want to think about what that meant.

Lahn sat on the floor and put his head in his hands. "What do we do? Nothing? How do we even get out of this warehouse?"

Maddox took a deep breath and let it out slowly. "We call Tia. Have her come break us out, then get her help to figure out what to do about the attacks."

Lahn glanced up at Maddox. "Ha! She will kill us for coming here."

"True," said Maddox, turning on his portable. "It *was* dumb."

"But what are you going to say? If the DTS is involved, isn't calling her putting her at risk?"

Maddox swore under his breath, sighed, and thought for a moment. "Okay, I think I know what to say. Kensha," he said into his portable, "call Tia."

"Of course, Maddox," responded Kensha from the portable speaker, voice with a hint of a Dutch accent.

"Hello, Maddox," responded Tane. "I am sorry, but Tia is currently unavailable. Would you like to record a message?"

Maddox looked at Lahn with a raised eyebrow, and Lahn shrugged in response. "Sure." Maddox cleared his throat and began. "Tia, following up on your research. The causality of the CTC has generated additional data points.

It appears the impacted radius outside of the event boundary is much larger than expected. The impact is massive. The math is beyond us, and we need your help resolving the problemata. We should meet in person to go over the numbers."

"Wow," laughed Lahn as Maddox ended the call. "Even if someone *is* listening, they won't know what you're saying. I was standing right here, and I didn't. Are you sure Tia will understand?"

"She's smarter than both of us; she'll get the basics." Maddox slipped his portable into his pocket. "In the meantime, we can't wait for her. We are on our own. What about the ladder you came in on? Could we go out that way?"

Lahn looked up at the ceiling, high above their heads. "I . . . can't do that again."

Maddox nodded quickly. "Right. But, how about this. I cross the ladder alone. Then I find a rock and bust one of the locks to get you out."

The ladder was dangerous; Lahn had almost fallen to his death the last time he crossed it. He turned to Maddox. "It's a really bad . . ." he started, then faded to a stop. Maddox stood looking back at him intently, back straight, mouth in a tight line, and arms folded. Lahn could feel the determination radiating off Maddox in waves.

"It's a bad idea, and you could die trying," said Lahn with a sigh. "That's all I'm saying. But let's go up there and you can see for yourself."

Lahn and Maddox climbed the stairs, stepped into the light of the third floor, and moved to the windows overlooking the alley. The ladder wasn't there.

"Where's the ladder?" asked Maddox.

"I don't know," said Lahn, a bit ashamed at the relief he felt. It didn't feel right that Maddox would risk his life alone. But if the ladder was gone, he didn't need to worry about it.

"Wow," said Maddox, looking down to the ground below. "I had no idea it would be so high."

Pointedly ignoring the distance to the ground, Lahn looked at the factory across the alley.

"Have you gone through this stuff?" asked Maddox, walking to a pile of abandoned painting equipment. "Maybe there is something we could use to break out." He started moving a drop cloth.

Lahn continued to look through the windows. In the safety of the hallway, the other building felt close. A handful of steps, and they would be free.

"Hey, Lahn," said Maddox. "The ladder you crossed on. Was it anything like this?" He pointed to a ladder he'd uncovered in the pile.

Lahn blinked at the ladder—scratches and dings jumping out at him, the scars on the face of an old nemesis. "Um, yeah. Exactly like that. I think that's the one I used."

"How did it get between the buildings?"

Lahn shrugged. "I don't know. It was there when I arrived. I guess someone put it in place between now and then."

"You mean someone . . . like us?"

Lahn's heart raced, his pulse thumping in the bruise on his face. "What?"

Maddox watched Lahn's face and his shaking hand, and took a deep breath. "I'm not saying you should cross, that's still me. And we probably can't get the ladder in place, anyway. But we could *try*, and if we fail, then we know we are not going out that way."

Lahn looked down at his hand and fought to keep it from curling into a claw. Just putting the ladder in place might be impossible without falling and dying in the process.

Impossible.

The fuzziness at the edges of his vision told him so.

WEIRD
IMAGININGS

Finding it hard to breathe, Lahn turned from the window and focused on the details of the warehouse's third-floor hallway. Ancient beige paint decorated the walls, cracked and peeling. Dust and old tools lay about like bits of driftwood on the beach. He turned back to the windows, fighting the feeling of being trapped in the old warehouse. The factory was so close. But, with the gap of a deadly ten-meter drop to the ground below, it might as well be a different universe.

With a start and a strong spike of déjà vu, Lahn realized he had felt it all before. And he knew exactly when and where. He was at the site of the Renelogy explosion, standing outside the crowd, wishing he could get through to see the damaged building. It was so close but so far away. His past-self was there right now, near the crowd, feeling those very emotions.

"Here's a rope," said Maddox, holding it up. "If we tie it to the end of the ladder, we could use it to stabilize the ladder as it goes over the gap."

Lahn pulled himself from his past and tried to visualize what Maddox was suggesting. One end of the ladder could go out the window supported by the rope. If Lahn pushed the ladder from behind, Maddox could hold the rope to keep the far end up. It might work. It wouldn't be easy, but neither of them would hang out the window trying to support the heavy ladder, risking a deadly fall. He turned to Maddox, who looked back with raised eyebrows and hope on his face. Lahn wasn't sure he felt the same hope, but he could sense the seeds trying to push through his dread. It would be difficult and dangerous, and would take a leap of faith, but it might be a way to cross the gap.

"That's so weird," Lahn said with a shiver against another rush of déjà vu. *All those weird imaginings, emotions, and thoughts were from my future.*

"My idea's weird?" asked Maddox. "I thought it was good."

"No. Past-me is picking up on this experience. When I was stuck trying to get through the crowds at Renelogy, I imagined I was trapped in an abandoned building. But there was a way out, a bridge."

"You didn't tell me about that. Another vision?"

"Not so strong. It didn't take over my senses like the visions, and I didn't realize it could be related. I thought it was a daydream, and it gave me the courage to act."

"That is so bizarre . . . and cool," said Maddox with a shake of his head. "Does that mean you want to try it? Are we going to give this a shot?"

"What happens," Lahn asked cautiously, "if we don't. What if the ladder is not here when I come back? Would that stop me from going in? Would that stop me from traveling back in time, and create a paradox?"

"No," said Maddox with a smile and a shake of his head. "Like I said, a paradox is just something that is impossible. If it was possible to keep you from going back, the time travel event would have to generate a split timeline where you *don't* go back. Poof, a whole new world. And can you imagine the amount of energy required to spontaneously create that much mass? *Maybe* if we had access to a collapsing black hole, there would be enough to create a copy of just our solar system. Instead, the math tells us there could be changes in a closed time-like curve, but the final result is the same. Whatever caused the event, *must* happen. So if we just sat here and did nothing, someone else would show up to place the ladder. Or maybe you don't even enter the factory, but instead go directly into the warehouse."

"But that stuff already happened," said Lahn with a frown. "I crossed the ladder."

"That was *you*. That's in your personal past. For the other you, it hasn't happened yet. It could be different."

"But what if we try to deal with the ladder, and you get hurt or die. Is that even possible? I see you later today, and you're fine. Other than the cut on your head."

Maddox reached up and touched his forehead, then looked down at the frayed end of the rope in his hands. "That could change. I could die. From what you've said, nothing about getting to the warehouse requires me, but it's impossible to know for sure what events are locked."

"But, *I* can't die, right? Because, if I did, that would stop me from going back."

"Well . . . technically your *past* can't die. But *you*? You already traveled."

"So, just to be clear," said Lahn, walking to the window to look at the gap between buildings, "we are talking about a stupidly dangerous plan, and there is no magical guarantee either one of us will survive."

"Sounds about right," said Maddox, moving up beside him.

Lahn continued to stare out the window in silence.

"And if we are right about the DTS . . ." said Maddox. "They've got their eye on you, and if they *are* involved in the explosions, we're already in danger. They are the most powerful organization in the world, and people that cross them disappear forever. The safest thing for *us* would be to sit here and wait it all out. We'd get very hungry, but we'd be alive.

"But," he continued with a deep sigh, "one thousand people, Lahn. Maybe a thousand kids that lose a parent. No one could change what happened in your past, but maybe we can stop this. We need to find Tia, go over the pictures I took, and figure out how we're going to stop it."

Lahn looked at his friend. There was an enviable determination in Maddox's face. Lahn took a solid breath and nodded once, reaching for the rope in Maddox's hand. As he tied it to the ladder, Maddox unlocked and opened the large window, and together, they lifted the ladder and fed the first third out over the alley. Ignoring his heart beating painfully in his hand and face, Lahn got behind the ladder. Maddox took in the slack from the rope and climbed next to the ladder to stand inside the window frame.

Maddox leaned his head against the inside glass, took a couple of deep breaths, then straightened. "Okay, I'm ready," he said.

Lahn pushed slowly while Maddox held the rope tight. The ladder moved forward, and the end slanted upward as it pulled against the rope. With a grunt, Maddox slowly fed out the rope and fought to keep the end balanced. The front drifted, first to one side and then the other, and Lahn held tight to the sharp legs, struggling to keep it in line. The metal dug into the scrapes on his palms from the asphalt outside Renelogy, and he ground his teeth to keep the pain at bay.

[Suddenly, he can see Agent Prakash staring at him, the orange DTS letters on her jacket bright against black. Her eyes bore into him—dark, vibrant mirrors that seem to hum with energy. He wonders if they are portals to another dimension where his sins are laid bare for all to see. He is terrified of those eyes.]

"Lahn!"

"Sorry," said Lahn, shaking his head. The ladder drifted dangerously to the side, and he struggled to pull it back into line. "Distracted by Past."

Lahn tried to stay focused on the task as, bit by bit, the ladder moved forward. It was terrible timing, but he wished he could stop to think about what the connection with Past meant, that he could *receive* from Past as well as *send*.

"I've got a problem," Lahn said. "I'm at the end, but I don't know how to get it out the window and onto the ledge without dropping it."

"I don't know," Maddox said with a gasp, face red with the effort of holding the full weight of the ladder by the rope. "Grab the last rung and slide the legs over the edge and down the wall?"

Lahn seized the last rung in both hands, took a deep breath, and slowly pushed the end over the threshold. As the feet of the ladder slid over the edge with a bump, the rope in Maddox's hands slipped, and the far end of the ladder dropped. The far end snapped against the rope as Maddox regained his hold, yanking him against the window. The end of the ladder Lahn held jumped in reaction and wrenched from his hands.

With a cry, Lahn leaped forward to catch the ladder, his arms and torso out the window. He caught it and pulled the legs back toward the building before they went over the ledge. The feet of the ladder slammed into the junction of the wall and the ledge with a jerk that pulled Lahn past the balance point, and he started sliding out the window.

In a horrific repeat of his last crossing, the ground rushed up at him. "Help!" he cried in a strangled voice.

Holding the rope in one hand, Maddox reached down with the other and grabbed Lahn by the shirt, pulling back with all of his strength. Lahn fell back into the building, knocking Maddox with him, and the rope ripped from Maddox's grasp.

Lahn pushed off Maddox and jumped back to the window as the ladder dropped toward the far ledge. In a nanosecond, he visualized what would happen: the ladder would bounce on the far ledge, slide off, and fall to the ground below. Without thinking, Lahn grabbed the sides of the window, jumped up, and pulled his feet up and through. Hanging on to either side of the open window, he slammed his feet down on the ladder as the far end hit the ledge with a sound of metal crunching against stone. With his weight, the ladder vibrated, but didn't bounce, slide, or fall.

Lahn struggled to keep his eyes focused on the building across the alley, and ignore the ground, ten meters below. With a deep breath, held for the count of four, he fought off the possible Depersonalization episode. But before his thrashing heart could transition to something worse, Lahn's consciousness was again drawn to Past-Lahn.

[Agent Prakash holds his gaze. Time stretches. A fuzziness creeps into the edges of his vision, and he calls out to Lucia to help stave off Depersonalization. But Lucia isn't coming. He gasps, attempting to kick off his exercises, but he can't breathe.]

Maddox stumbled up to the window, wheezing. "Wow," he said. "I can't believe you just did that!"

Lahn barely heard. With extreme effort, his breath long and deep, he pulled his thoughts from Past-Lahn and his view from the ground. Even though he knew his terror of falling to his death was perfectly reasonable, he couldn't help but think about the fact he hadn't fallen, and hadn't been pulled into Depersonalization either. Instead, he survived.

Lahn looked at the ladder, now precisely in place between the buildings, now a perfect bridge to provide escape.

"Wow," Lahn finally agreed, as he looked back at Maddox. "I can't believe I just did that."

Maddox shakily grabbed Lahn by the arm and helped him back into the warehouse, then slid to the floor, his back against the wall below the window. "When the ladder pulled you out, all I could see was you falling to the ground below. I thought you were dead," Maddox said.

Lahn simply nodded.

Maddox took a ragged breath. "I don't know if I can go back out there to cross."

Lahn turned and sat next to Maddox, his heart still beating hard in a strange mix of fear and exhilaration. "I can feel Past-Lahn, what he's going through."

Maddox turned to look at Lahn, one eyebrow raised. "And?"

"That's the wild thing. After fighting through the crowd and Agent Prakash to get a look at the building, he's at the barricades, thinking about sneaking past police and government agents to break into Renelogy and look for answers. For a moment at least—he's afraid of nothing to get what he wants."

"That doesn't sound like you at all."

"No doubt. I think our success of getting the ladder in place—combined with the adrenaline rush of almost dying—is giving me a boost of confidence. And that's getting fed to Past-Lahn."

"You didn't go inside Renelogy," said Maddox with a shake of his head. "You would have mentioned it."

Lahn laughed. "No. It was just a daydream, big and heroic. But something woke me out of it before I could even jump the barricade, a message I was being watched. That's what made me look up and see Faceless. And it's a good thing, too. Can you imagine the trouble if I tried to enter the site?"

"A message? Who sent it?"

"I still don't know. I mean, who knows I'm there right now? Much less . . ." Lahn stopped and turned to Maddox with his eyes wide and a grin forming on his face. "Give me your portable."

Maddox pulled it out of his pocket, turned it on and handed it over, one eyebrow raised. Lahn pulled up a function for anonymous messaging and spoke out loud as he typed.

"You . . . are . . . being . . . watched."

LITTLE PRISON

The apartment diode lights glowed a calming warm white. Lahn had set the color temperature himself when they got back to Maddox's apartment. Now, sitting at the kitchen table, he held Maddox's portable in one hand, ignoring it, staring into space.

"You okay?" Maddox entered the main room. He rubbed a towel through his auburn hair, lit by the fading sunlight streaming through the full-height apartment windows.

"Hmm?" Lahn shook his head, turned off the portable and placed it on Maddox's kitchen table in front of him. "Oh, yeah. Just thinking."

"About crossing the ladder?"

"Yeah."

Maddox tossed his towel over one of the kitchen chairs. "Yeah. That was awful."

Lahn nodded.

It had been a few hours, but his mind kept going back to it. Something about the experience would not let him go. Even though Maddox had claimed he was going to cross, and didn't want Lahn to come with him, Lahn could tell he was freaked out by the prospect. So, against his own desires, and ignoring Maddox as he tried to stop him, Lahn went out the window and crossed first. Then, he stood on the far end to keep the ladder still as Maddox crossed.

The entire event gave Lahn something he rarely felt outside of functional coding: something approaching pride.

Maddox picked up his portable as he sat at the table and started examining the photos. "It could take forever to go through all of this."

Lahn finally got a good look at Maddox and gaped. Fresh out of the shower, his beard was wild and his hair was a mini bonfire on his head. The cut on his left temple was washed but still red. He wore a dark-blue T-shirt with an ornate design of a Celtic boar. It was exactly how Maddox had looked a few days ago when it all began. Lahn remembered he had been startled when Maddox came to his apartment with that wound, wondering what Maddox had gotten himself into.

No . . . not a few days ago . . . later today.

Lahn watched him flip through pictures of the warboard from the warehouse for a moment and sighed. "Was it worth it?" he asked.

"Taking a shower?" responded Maddox. "Completely!"

Lahn laughed. "Going to the warehouse."

"To be honest, I don't know. I'm not sure what we can figure out from the board without Tia. I really wish she'd been home just now. Maybe we should have waited at her apartment for her, 'cause it's too risky to call her again?"

"Your face was enough to scare small children and animals." Lahn reached for his own face and the tender bruise there. "Probably mine too. You can go try her again when you go to my place in a little while." *And show up looking exactly like this.*

"You're right," said Maddox with a deep breath. "We both

needed to get somewhere safe. That was terrible. I'm super sorry I got you in that mess, but if you hadn't been there, I'm not sure I would've made it out at all.

"I get it now," Maddox continued, and he turned off his portable and placed it back on the table. "When you told me about your experiences, they sounded rough, but now I am shocked you lived through it on your own."

Lahn ran his hands through his hair. "I just wish we'd found more information."

"Me too."

"What about that puzzle someone sent me? Whoever sent it knew about the time travel . . . and probably a lot more. Think we can figure out who that is?"

Maddox exhaled slowly. "Not sure how. The use of a typewriter makes the whole thing low-tech. Whoever it is, they wanted to stay hidden. The person who really knows what's going on is Faceless."

Lahn shuddered. "I don't want to know who Faceless is. Seriously. I was nervous just leaving the factory, worried he might come back and catch us."

"See, I told you the rock in the doorframe was a good idea, in case Faceless *was* there and we needed to get back inside to hide."

The rock. The one he'd found when entering the factory the first time. Lahn hadn't remembered it until Maddox put it in the door as they left. But it was just one more thing that made sure he went back in time.

"We can't change anything, can we," Lahn said, standing and walking to the full-height windows. The building next door was shorter, and like many in the city it contained trees and a communal garden on the roof. Several people walked between the trees, picking fruit and putting it in baskets. They laughed as they worked, and Lahn envied them for their blissful ignorance of the horrible events happening in the city.

"I mean," he continued, "the ladder, the rock, even your hair. Everything seems to be happening exactly as it happened."

"My hair?"

"When you show up at my place to help me figure out what's going on with my visions, you look exactly like that with your wild beard and out-of-control hair. It feels like time is fixed. Maybe there's nothing we can do to stop the attacks. Maybe the explosion at Living Bliss tomorrow will happen no matter what."

"Perhaps," said Maddox, standing from the table and moving to the couch. "Like I said, our current understanding of the math tells us that the details in a closed time-like curve are not fixed, only the cause. I'll comb my hair before I go, then that will be different. But, I know for sure there is one thing we could do to change what happens tomorrow."

Lahn rotated in his seat to look at Maddox, eyebrows raised. "What's that?"

"Nothing."

Lahn frowned. "Nothing?"

"Sit here and do nothing. Your visions tell us we go to Living Bliss tomorrow. If we do nothing, that's a change."

"Are you saying if we don't go, the building won't explode?"

"Well . . . no," said Maddox. "Whatever causes the explosion would still happen. I'm saying if we don't go, you won't get hurt tomorrow. At least that changes."

"Then, it's a good thing we already decided not to go."

"No lie," Maddox said with a chuckle. He stood. "I should go see your past, before it gets too late. Although, I'm not sure what to say to him."

"I'll come with you, then that will be different too. I can stay, sleep on my own couch, and tell myself about the fun times to come." Lahn wondered why he didn't do that last time.

"I don't think you can," said Maddox. "If you get near yourself, it could be extremely uncomfortable or even dangerous. A problem of identical, quantum entangled elements in near-proximity. You can stay here tonight."

Maddox grabbed his jacket—yellow-to-orange transitional color—from the closet near the door and turned and walked out.

"You forgot to comb your hair," said Lahn to the empty room. He stood with a sigh and walked to the oversized chair. Maddox would show up to visit Past-Lahn exactly as he had the first time.

Lahn sat in the chair and looked around Maddox's stylish yet sterile apartment. He watched as the table automatically folded up into the wall and the chairs retracted into the floor. With an ache, he wished for his ugly love seat, carpet, and counters. He wished for his own clothes, his own bed. He wished for a moment of ignorance and normalcy. "I can't even go home." He was an interloper in his own life. But . . . maybe there were more important things than sleeping in his own bed.

It really was a bad idea to go to Living Bliss in the morning. But if they didn't go, was that worse? If they didn't go, instead of eighteen, fifty people die. Or two hundred.

"And what if we manage to stop it?" he said out loud to himself. The lack of response from Lucia was conspicuous. *Come-on, Flash Gordon,* she would probably say. *You can save the world from Ming the Merciless!* Of course, he had no way to contact her after the loss of his cuff. And she didn't even know. She was busy with Past-Lahn and wouldn't get him the fancy new cuff until tomorrow.

"We might not only save the people at Living Bliss," he continued to himself, "we could learn enough to stop the big explosion, too."

Lahn stood and walked to the window again, looking

out at the city. The streets below were filled with automotive and pedestrian traffic, people heading home after work to spend their evenings with families or friends, or just a quiet night at home. Soon the sun would fade, and the sky would shift from the teal of daylight to jade twilight. And then the nightlife would start, nearly as many people out as in the daytime.

There had to be something they could do to stop what was coming. Lahn still had questions, and he still needed answers, but now there was something more important. After getting Maddox out of the warehouse, Lahn felt something he hadn't in a long time. And it was more than simple pride in what they accomplished.

He felt *power*.

Power to control his world and destiny. Even though everything still seemed to conspire against him, and it appeared he simply completed a fixed history, he still felt powerful. Getting the ladder in place and escaping was dangerous and impossible, and they beat it. It made him feel like anything was possible.

Lahn moved from the window and walked to a set of cabinets at the edge of the kitchen area. There was a part of the warehouse he couldn't stop thinking about. It all happened faster than he could comprehend, but he hadn't jumped out the window and stopped the ladder's fall to free *himself*. He'd done it to help free Maddox. It was the first time in years—likely since the Accident—that he'd taken a serious risk to help someone else.

And maybe there *was* a way to help more people. Even if that meant taking more risks.

"Okay, Maddox," said Lahn. "Let's see how secure your terminal is."

He pressed the horizontal metal band between the upper and lower cabinets, and the bottom slid out, expanding to become a small desk and chair. A tap on the desk, and letters appeared on the surface, arranged in a Dvorak keyboard layout. A second tap and the holographic display for the terminal lit up, showing a login prompt.

"Wait, what does that code do?" asked Maddox.

Lahn jumped. The last few hours he'd been deep in research and coding, and didn't notice when Maddox came back.

"Weeeell . . ." Lahn grinned sheepishly, glancing back at Maddox who looked over his shoulder, "this bit of code is an obliterator function. I call it Tempest."

"What does it obliterate?" Maddox stepped back, took off his jacket, and tossed it over the back of the couch.

Lahn stood from the small desk and stretched, arms over his head. "Everything else I just spent the last few hours creating. Including a function called Feign. Tempest destroys all traces that any of it ever existed."

"Oh . . . no." Maddox closed his eyes and sat heavily on the couch. "The only reason you'd need that is if you created something highly illegal."

Lahn's sheepish grin turned into a grimace. "It might be . . . just a little bit."

Maddox snorted. "Oh good. I'm glad it's only a little illegal. Maybe they will put us in little prison. So, what does it do?"

Lahn sat on the chair opposite Maddox and stared at him intently. "Feign allows me to break into the Living Bliss basement without getting caught."

Maddox looked at the heavens. "I can't believe I'm having this conversation . . . again! I just left the other you after talking him out of hacking into the Renelogy network. And now you want to break into Living Bliss?" He looked back at Lahn. "This is really dumb."

Lahn didn't turn away, his mouth pulling into a thin line.

"If you go, you get hurt!" said Maddox emphatically.

Lahn didn't flinch.

For a solid minute, Maddox said nothing, staring back at Lahn. "There's nothing I can say to convince you not to go?" he asked finally.

"No," Lahn said, crossing his arms. "I don't care if I get hurt tomorrow. We need to try to stop these attacks. We need to learn everything we can to stop the big one."

"I felt the same, that's why I . . ." Maddox stopped. "But now . . ." He groaned and slid slowly off the seat of the couch, feet sliding forward along the ground until he was almost horizontal. "If you're going," he said, with only his head and shoulders remaining on the couch, "I am too."

"Well, you don't—"

"Shuddup. I can't let you go alone, especially since you are supposed to get injured. And you're right. It's a thousand people. That didn't change just because it got more dangerous." Maddox stood and pulled a canvas shoulder bag from the closet and started filling it from a utility drawer with screwdrivers, cash, and batteries.

"What are you doing?" Lahn asked.

"I want to be prepared," Maddox replied, squeezing some wire cutters open and shut before adding them to the bag.

"For what?"

"Everything." Maddox tossed in a small, pink, rubber duck and looked back at Lahn. "Tell me your plan."

Hey, Dad.

My past-self is struggling. I want to have sympathy, but there is not much I can do. I've got my hands full with my own challenges.
And today.
Living Bliss.
Last time, eighteen people died. It could be much worse than that. But I have a chance, if I can learn from what happened last time, to stop the explosion so no one dies. If only the tech was not so complicated.

Today is going to be difficult. More so if *they* try to interfere.

SELLING
TO SKIMPS

Lahn and Maddox stood in front of a broken elevator in an old apartment building on the corner of Third and Redwood.

The foyer, likely once bright and inviting, seemed dedicated to driving away any rational human. The broken floor tiles were faded and smeared with dirt and possibly blood—the original design lost to time. A few lights heroically fought back the gloom. Yet, the tint of the fluorescents only managed to cast a flickering pallor on the trash scattered and piled in corners. So far, they had seen no sign of any human life, and Lahn couldn't imagine that anyone still lived in the building. He was starting to doubt it was the right site for the purchase of illegal tech.

"So," said Maddox, shifting his canvas shoulder bag. Nervously, he stared at the out-of-order sign hanging crooked next to the elevator. "How does this work? You push the buttons to call the elevator, and then what?"

"I don't know for sure. But it's supposed to be a way to get what we need." *At least that's what Lucia said*, he thought. Lahn took a deep breath, stepped forward and pressed both the elevator up and down buttons at the same time and held them for three seconds. He stepped back quickly, his entire body tense, ready to run. For ten long seconds, nothing happened.

A pop and a crackle came from somewhere, startling both of them, but the elevator doors remain closed. "Yeah," grumbled a distorted voice through a hidden speaker. The voice was deep, but it was obviously pitched artificially, impossible to recognize age or gender.

"Um . . ." stammered Lahn. "We're here to buy."

"I don't sell to Skimps."

Maddox looked at Lahn, eyebrows raised, and Lahn looked back in similar confusion. "We have coded-credits," Lahn said, hoping it was the right thing to say.

For another long stretch, there was nothing but silence. Maddox grabbed Lahn's shoulder and started to pull him away. "This whole situation is acrid," he hissed. "Let's go!"

"Wait," whispered Lahn under his breath, standing his ground.

"What are you looking for," came back the voice after a few more seconds.

Lahn released a breath he didn't know he was holding. "We need two untraceable, handheld terminals, with secure connections to the mesh," he said in a rush.

"When." It was less of a question and more of a demand that it better not be now.

"Now." It came out as a squeak.

The speaker rumbled, the sound of a Balrog expressing its displeasure, and Lahn and Maddox looked at each other in distress.

"That's extra. One thousand. Each."

Maddox grabbed Lahn and pulled him away from the elevator. "Two thousand credits?" he whispered. "That's all we brought! It's too much."

"What option do we have? I don't think this is someone we can haggle with."

"Are you sure we are not going to need the credits for anything else? It was a huge pain to convert normal currency to coded-credits without raising red flags. I don't think we can get any more."

"There is nothing else we need. It'll be fine."

Lahn stepped forward, with a feeling of bravery earned from the previous day's events, but an emotion he wasn't sure he actually believed. "We'll take them." He held out his hand to Maddox, who sighed. Maddox pulled the pink rubber duck from his bag, popped off its head, removed the data chip hidden inside, and handed it to Lahn.

"There's a slot above the buttons," said the voice.

Lahn walked back to the elevator, focused all his attention on his hand to keep it from shaking or cramping, and brought the chip to the slot, little more than a wound in the wall. And hesitated. It *was* a lot of money, and they hadn't planned on spending it all, much less in one place. If for any reason they needed more coded-credits, they couldn't get them. They didn't have time. Even pulling more cash from either of their accounts right now might trigger a flag. And tragically, after they were done, they would have to destroy and dispose of the illegal tech.

But there wasn't a choice. They needed these terminals. It was the only way they could execute his plan without being detected. And really, what was two thousand credits against hundreds or thousands of lives?

Lahn slid the chip into the tiny slot above the buttons and it disappeared.

And nothing happened.

Lahn looked back at Maddox then back at the slot.

He wasn't sure what he expected, but it wasn't this. Maybe a beep or a flashing light, or a grunt from the speaker where the stranger gruffly acknowledged payment received. Of course it would take a few seconds to pull the codes off the chip and verify the credits, but it had been a few seconds. And the chip wasn't coming back out.

"Did we just get robbed?" asked Maddox, not bothering to whisper.

Lahn looked back at Maddox with eyes wide. "What do we do?"

A *thunk* from the elevator made him jump back, and both Lahn and Maddox braced, ready to fight. Several more thumps and clanks, and the doors opened with a groan.

The dilapidated elevator—faded wallpaper drooping sadly—was empty save for two small boxes sitting in the middle of the floor. The elevator had no working lights, and the inside was in shadows. It looked ready to fall to the basement the moment the slightest weight was applied.

Lahn took a hesitant step into the space. A keen echoed above him, the sound of a cockatrice preparing to attack, and he leaped forward, grabbed the boxes, and jumped out again.

Maddox grabbed their chip that had popped out of the slot, and they ran from the building, unashamed of their fear.

Lahn set the handheld terminal he'd been fiddling with on the autoride seat next to the mess of open boxes. Pushing down on his knees to keep them from bouncing, he looked over at Maddox's reclined form on the opposite seat. The jerk had his eyes closed, hands behind his head. "Sheesh, Maddox. Why are you so nervous?"

Maddox didn't move. "Cause this whole plan is bonkers. I've never attempted to break into the secure section of a building before."

"Weird. I do it all the time. It's no big deal. Speaking of time, what time is it?"

"Five minutes after the last time you asked."

"Autoride, can you go any faster?" asked Lahn, knees bouncing again. Last night he'd been so confident. Now he wished he could get a bit more of it back.

"I am sorry," said the autoride in a pleasant voice. "We are currently traveling at the speed limit for this location."

"I really wish Tia was here," said Maddox.

"She wasn't at home or work. I know where she *will* be; she picks me up to take me to work at the Criterion office in about thirty-five minutes. But by then it's too late."

Lahn picked up the handheld again. It was a bit larger than a portable, more square, with a small physical keyboard. Unlike a portable's unlimited functions through the Mesh, the handhelds were specifically designed to facilitate convenient access to command-line interfaces on the Mesh and elsewhere. Of course, normal portables could also be used for command-line access, but not nearly as easily, and they could be tracked. At Lahn's insistence, Maddox had left his portable at home.

The handhelds were very nice. Rugged, yet sleek, Lahn always appreciated a piece of well-made tech. It broke his heart to even think about discarding the handhelds when they were done. But, the DTS was bringing its eye on him and his friends, and black-market tech was stupid dangerous to keep around.

"Tell me the plan again," said Maddox, sitting up, grabbing his shoulder bag from the seat next to him and pulling it over his head.

"If the warboard was right, and the tech that causes the explosions is related to the time travel, we are looking for a device similar to what I saw at the warehouse. That's the first priority: find it and shut it down. Second would be to learn whatever we can to help us find and stop the big attack. The news reports put the center of this explosion at Living Bliss in the basement, so that's where we are going.

"Getting in shouldn't be hard," continued Lahn. "The trick is not getting caught. The biggest problem will be the building security cameras. If the building AI detects suspicious activity through the cameras or on the network, it will call the police. Even if we manage to escape before the police come, the history on the cameras will land us in jail. And if the explosion happens, or if there is any illegal tech left behind, it won't be regular jail; we'd be dropped in a DTS dark-site, and disappear forever."

"Oh, yeah." Maddox rolled his eyes. "This plan gets better and better. So, you told me you had a plan to hack the cameras, but how can you do that if we can't get on the network without triggering the AI?"

If Lucia was here, it would be easy, Lahn thought. He gave one of the handhelds to Maddox. "That's what your handheld is for. You're the *distractor*. You will keep the building's network AI distracted and busy, while I use my handheld to install updates that infiltrate the network and give us access."

Maddox looked at his handheld. "How hard is this going to be? I don't have your tech skills."

"Not hard. We don't need to enter the building for this part of the plan, we can do it from outside. You just start the Distractor function, and it sends cruft to confuse the AI. Here's the trouble; if that runs for too long, the AI will decide it's either a network issue, and lock everything down for repairs, or it will decide it's an attack. So I set a timer. You start the function, it runs for thirty seconds, you wait for a minute or so, then start it again. And make sure to keep moving around the outside of the building, so the connections come from different locations."

"That makes sense. What about you?"

Lahn picked up the other handheld. "I've set up the rest of the functions I created on this one. While you're keeping the AI busy, I'll be installing an exploit on the camera system. But I can only act in thirty second increments while the AI is distracted. I've put an encrypted link between the two handhelds so we can talk, and you can give me a countdown when the distraction is running."

Maddox nodded. "So I'm running around pushing a button, while you're poking holes in the network."

"Yup."

Maddox bit the corner of his lip, then released a deep breath slowly through tight lips.

The autoride slowed to a stop. "You've arrived at your destination," said its artificial voice pleasantly, as if they were not about to attempt the most dangerous thing either of them had ever done.

EXPLOITING THE DISTRACTION

Lahn set the handheld next to him on the bench and wiped both hands on his pants, fighting the physiological response to hyperventilate, fighting the desire to run. Tucked between two evergreen trees in a mini forest on the left side of Living Bliss, he sat on an old park bench, faded wood with a sprinkle of peeling paint.

"I'm at the back of the building," said Maddox's voice from Lahn's handheld. "Good thing there are so many trees. I've only seen a few cameras, but they've been easy to avoid. Are you ready for me to hit the button?"

Lahn picked up the handheld. "Hang on." Opening the network listener function on the device, he entered a few parameters. "I'm ready."

"And . . . go. Thirty seconds."

With the Living Bliss AI distracted trying to understand the random noise coming from Maddox's handheld, Lahn pressed start on the network listener on his. Almost immediately, words and numbers flashed on the screen, updating every second. Different devices were represented, showing broadcast connection information. He wasn't fully on the network, at least not yet: neither of them were. More like on the outside looking in, hungry orphan children with noses to the glass window of a restaurant.

He wouldn't be able to intercept any actual data being sent on the Living Bliss network, at least not yet. That was all encrypted. But as each device on the local Mesh negotiated a connection with another device, they broadcast basic device information, like name, ID, and network address. It should be enough for what he planned.

"Fifteen seconds left," said Maddox.

There!

One device had a familiar name, matching device names he'd seen in his research the night before. The device was a security camera system made by one of the major manufacturers. He quickly entered the model of the system into his fake update function.

"Five seconds. Four . . . three . . ."

Lahn severed his handheld's network connection. "I'm out!"

"One. The Distractor turned off. Did you get everything done?"

"Not even close. I was only able to get the model number of the building's security camera system. I still have to trick it into installing my exploits so we can look at the cameras and freeze the image on some of them."

"How many more times do I need to run this?" Maddox asked, his voice pitched higher than usual.

"Two or three."

"It took too long dealing with that odious tech guy. The explosion happens in twenty-nine minutes. Even after you hack the cameras, we still have to get inside and find the stupid device. We're not going to make it."

"We'll make it." *We have to.*

Maddox sighed. "I'm starting the Distractor again."

"Wait, don't! You need to hold off at least a minute between sessions for the AI to not get suspicious."

Lahn could hear Maddox breathing heavily on the other side. He knew how Maddox felt. The process demanded patience, but he could feel time slipping away. Every second landed on his nerves, stretching them tighter. The beauty of the trees around him—the white bark of birch and the green leaves of maple—should have been calming. Instead, they mocked him with their serenity.

"I moved to a new spot, and it's been a full minute," said Maddox. "Ready?"

"Ready."

"Go!"

Lahn reconnected his handheld to the building network, then opened his fake updater function again. When he'd been writing the code the night before, he'd given it the name of Feign. At the time, he'd smiled, feeling like it was a cool name for a magic spell. Now it felt too whimsical for the serious task ahead of them.

He queried Feign for a status, and it responded with its current settings and an indication that everything was ready to publish the update.

Lahn took a deep breath and held it. *This* was the point of no return. If the camera system realized the update came from an invalid source, it would trigger an alert and lockdown, and the AI would contact the authorities. Lahn and Maddox would be dragged away in minutes, and no one would be left to stop the explosion. His finger hovered over the button on his handheld for a moment, the blood from his heartbeat pulsing in his fingertip.

"Twenty seconds."

With a silent prayer there would be enough time, Lahn pressed down. "I've kicked off the update for the first exploit."

"What does this one do?"

"Asks the system to send a snapshot from each camera to Feign. Then we can view the different parts of the building, make a plan where to go and which cameras to disable."

It would take a few seconds for the update to get to the camera system and the images to be sent. Without realizing, Lahn held his breath as he waited for something on the handheld to tell him if it worked. Time seemed to stretch, and for an eternity, nothing happened.

"Ten seconds left."

Come on!

It wasn't working. It wasn't working, and there was no time to fix it.

"Five seconds left."

Or worse, it was just slow, and it would trigger after the Distractor turned off, and the AI would see the activity, and it would all be—

A burst of text flashed on the display. He saw each request and response. It worked. *It worked!* The security system requested a key to verify the update, so Feign passed on the request to the real update function and got a real verification key. His code sent back the key and the update code, and the security system sent back an acknowledgment that it was received, validated, and was applying the update, all within milliseconds.

Lahn jumped up and raised his fist to the sky in triumph. "I am a wizard!"

"Mr. Wizard, you're out of time!"

With a glance at his handheld, Lahn stabbed the button to disconnect from the building network. "I'm out!"

"Distractor is off. I think you made it."

"Think?" They both stopped and listened. "I don't hear any alarms," said Lahn. "Do you?"

"Nothing. I think we're okay."

Lahn sat again on the bench, grin threatening to split his face. "We did it. The system believes it's doing normal activity, and should be sending images through the global Mesh. We can look at those without getting back on the building network." On the handheld, he queried the images being sent to Feign.

His smile slipped from his face like an egg from buttered toast tipped too far. Something was wrong. The initial flash of text listing images became a torrent, thousands of separate snapshots from thousands of cameras, faster than the eye could follow. Something was very wrong.

"Oh . . . I'm an idiot." Lahn pressed his hand against his eyes.

"What? Lahn? What happened?"

"There are thousands," he whispered, an edge of alarm creeping up his spine. "Thousands of security systems in buildings all over the world, of that exact make and model. And I just pushed my exploit to all of them." With blood thundering in his ears, Lahn almost didn't hear Maddox.

"What do you mean?" said Maddox. "I don't understand."

Lahn watched the flash of text on the handheld, the display of all received files. Instead of a handful of snapshots—one from each camera inside Living Bliss—there were thousands upon thousands, and the list grew as he watched.

"I . . ." he stuttered, "I screwed up. I was rushed and forgot to limit the update to a single system, to only the one in the Living Bliss building."

It was a rookie mistake. With the lack of limitation, every system that used the same update function had received the update. Now, instead of worrying about being caught messing with one system, they could be charged with corporate hacking on a massive scale.

Maddox swore. "We gotta get out of here. Execute Tempest. *Now!*"

The obliterator. Tempest would destroy all images and functions, tell each system to scrub their own logs of updates, and revert to the version before any of his exploits. "I was going to run it when we were done."

"We *are* done, right? We failed. Will Tempest be enough to cover our tracks?"

"I don't know. The AI here was distracted. But not the AI at all the other buildings."

Maddox swore again. "Don't wait for me to get there. Run it!"

Lahn opened Tempest on his handheld, but hesitated. He knew he should run it and erase everything. But it would erase all the hard work of creating the functions and plans, and remove any chance they had of stopping the Living Bliss explosion. Or the big one tomorrow, where a thousand people would die. He'd had this feeling before, the feeling he always got when faced with the prospect of erasing his own work. It was hard to destroy functions and code, the art of his mind. It always felt like erasing a little of himself. But this time, it was more. If he ran Tempest now, any chance they had of stopping the attack tomorrow would be gone.

Maddox ran up to Lahn, breathing heavily. "Did you do it?" he gasped.

"I . . . I don't know if I should."

"What? Of course you should! We're going to jail and never coming out."

"We don't know that. My exploit was designed to look like normal behavior. Maybe none of the AI will see anything wrong."

"Maybe? Twenty-three minutes before the building explodes, and you want to risk it on *maybe*?"

"The situation hasn't changed, Maddox. It's still a thousand people that die tomorrow. If we run Tempest now, it removes everything we just did and we *can't* go in. It ruins our only chance to stop either explosion. We need to take the risk."

Maddox turned away, still breathing with difficulty, and grasped the straps of his shoulder bag in both hands tightly as he walked a few feet away, shaking his head. Lahn watched him for a minute, then turned to his handheld. Sitting on the bench, he closed the Tempest function and pulled up the list of camera snapshots again. Ignoring the overwhelming fact there were thousands of images, he entered the unit name of the Living Bliss camera system into the file filter, and to his relief the list of thousands dropped to sixty-four.

"Help me look through these images," he said to Maddox's back.

Maddox sighed, turned, and walked over and sat next to Lahn, watching him flip through the images. "I wish there was a way to keep you from running face-first into your prophesied world of hurt."

Lahn looked at Maddox and took a deep breath. "Me too," he said, turning back to his handheld.

A couple were of the main lobby from different angles, and many showed repetitious views of bright hallways or stairwells in the building. A few times, someone was caught in the snapshot, walking toward some important event of their day . . . hopefully not their death. Near the bottom of the list, the images were different; the narrow hallways were less well lit, doors seemed less frequent, and they were solid gray instead of glass in a steel frame.

"Those are the basement," said Maddox. "The explosive device would need to be connected to the building power system. Look for something like that."

Lahn stopped on an image, his breath catching. It contained a figure of someone walking away from the camera and down a hallway of the basement. But this figure was familiar. Even though the image was blurry, the dark overcoat with a hoodie pulled over the head was obvious.

"Faceless."

TILL THINGS GO BOOM

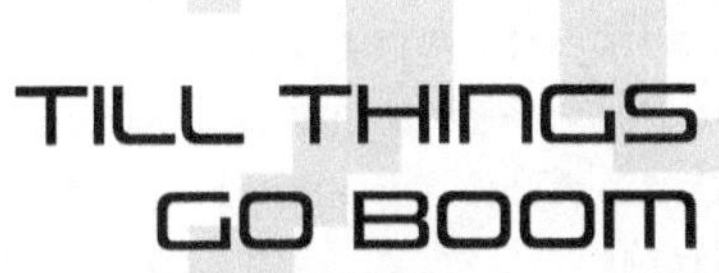

"Faceless? Really?" said Maddox. "Let me see." He took the handheld from Lahn and looked closely at the image, expanding and zooming into the figure. "Can the image be improved?"

"Press *control, I, E.*"

It shouldn't have been a surprise. Faceless was responsible for the explosions, of course he would be there. But seeing the shadowy figure caused Lahn's palms to sweat.

"The angle's weird," said Maddox. "I can't tell anything about them, even with the image cleaned up."

"What if we run into him?"

Maddox looked at Lahn, passing back the handheld. "I hope we do. Maybe we can stop all of this."

Lahn wasn't sure he agreed with Maddox, but they had more pressing concerns. He took a deep breath and released it slowly, turning back to the handheld. The next image in the list looked similar to others of the basement halls: dark and cramped. But the center of the frame included a black door, different from the gray elsewhere in the basement. "Write down this image ID."

Maddox made a note of the image in his handheld and Lahn went on to the next one. At first glance, it looked like a copy of the previous image, only reversed. The same black door was in the frame, but the view down the hallway was a mirror of the previous one. Lahn flipped back and forth between images several times. "They have cameras on opposite ends of the hallway pointing at the same door," he said. "I bet the building power is in there. Think that's where the device is?"

"Probably." Maddox took note of the name of the second camera.

They wrote down the rest of the basement cameras for good measure. Lahn backed through the images to find the stairwell cameras as well, and the ones pointing at the lobby.

"Fifteen cameras," said Maddox. "That's a lot."

"More than I planned."

"How do you keep from catching someone walking through the frame when you freeze them?"

"I added motion detection to the exploit. It won't freeze the camera until the frame is clear."

"How long will that take?"

"It better take less than thirty seconds. We'll be on the building network when we do it."

Maddox growled, then stood. "Okay. Okay, okay. There's only twenty minutes left before the explosion. If we're going to do this, let's do it. I'm going to a new location, let me know when you're ready."

Lahn watched Maddox walk away, feeling guilty yet again for dragging him into this.

"Send me the list of camera names," Lahn said into the handheld.

"Sending now."

The list appeared on the handheld, and he added them to the configuration, then included the limiter to the Living

Bliss building. At least this time it wouldn't get pushed everywhere. "I'm ready to push the next exploit. Tell me when to go."

"Go!"

This was it. This exploit would freeze the cameras from the lobby to the basement hall that was their goal. Lahn pressed the button to push the exploit. "It's going. It will take a bit for the exploit to get on the system and start freezing cameras." He switched to a monitor feature in Feign. After several long seconds, four camera names popped on the screen, indicating that the security system had notified Feign that those cameras were frozen. Those were quickly followed by seven more. "We have eleven cameras frozen."

"Good. We're down to eighteen seconds left."

Two more camera names appeared. "Thirteen cameras." One more camera appeared. "Fourteen cameras. Only one more to go."

"Thirteen seconds."

Several painful seconds ticked by. The last camera did not appear.

"Lahn?"

"I know, I know! It will come."

"Ten seconds! Just an FYI, eighteen minutes till things go boom!"

Ten seconds. Eighteen minutes. The weight of both countdowns pressed on Lahn like two stone giants, trying to reduce him to compressed pulp. Even if the last camera appeared, every second that passed was another second gone before the building exploded and people died. The seconds didn't stop. "We're running out of time!" Lahn croaked.

[*Before what?*]

The thought, accompanied by a strong sense of déjà-vu, was clear and strong in his head, and before he could stop himself he answered out loud. "Before the second explosion!"

"Lahn! Two seconds!"

The last camera appeared, and Lahn let out a guttural yell as he severed the connection to the building network.

"Um . . . Lahn?" Maddox's tentative voice came over the handheld.

"The last camera showed," Lahn wheezed. "I got out. We're clear."

"Great!" Maddox said with relief. "I'll be there in just a minute. Let's get in and find the device."

Lahn gasped, trying to draw a full breath, and stretched his cramping hand. All fifteen cameras were frozen, and they could enter the building and find the explosive devices without risk of leaving behind incriminating evidence or getting caught. But Lahn didn't feel relieved. He had just talked to Past, and Past was now freaking out about the idea of a second explosion. Lahn could feel that stress echoed back from Past like pinpricks on his skin.

He looked up at the Living Bliss building next to him. It was twice as tall as Renelogy, a mix of red and tan masonry, interspersed with oversized windows. And overlaid with that was a memory from the hospital. News clips of the second explosion, when he learned it was more than random accidents. He could almost see the damage on the currently intact building, destruction exceeding the first attack.

Lahn felt another rush of déjà-vu, and Past got a memory from the future to add to his worry as he got ready for work.

Maddox rushed up to Lahn. "Why are you just standing there? Come on!" He grabbed Lahn's handheld and shoved it in his bag, then grabbed Lahn's arm and pulled him forward. They both took off at a run around the side of the building, toward the front entrance.

As they rushed past a large, stone sign mounted in front of the building, the logo caught Lahn's eye and he slowed.

Living Bliss.

The name of the business echoed in Lahn's brain, reflecting back to Past.

"Lahn!"

"I know . . . I just . . ." He shuddered and breathed deeply. "My stress is pulling Past into my head. Parts of all this are getting fed to him, and it's freaking him out, too."

Maddox paused, his mouth open. "Wow! Just like yesterday?"

"Yeah, but worse. Stronger."

"I really want to understand this. But if it comes from stress, that means it comes at really terrible times."

"I know. I wish I could make him go away."

"Maybe you should stay here," said Maddox. "I'll go in and find the device."

"Yeah, that's not happening."

Lahn shook his head and strode forward, and Maddox quickly caught up as they moved to the front entrance of the building. Maddox grabbed the handle of the large glass door and looked at Lahn. "Are we sure the cameras are frozen? 'Cause if they're not . . ."

"They are. It's fine." *Everything's fine.*

Maddox pulled open the door and let Lahn through in front of him. As Lahn entered, his eyes were drawn into the view of the large lobby as, yet again, an overwhelming feeling of déjà vu washed over him.

The central lobby was spacious and open, with white and gold tiles in hexagon patterns on the floor. To the left and right, hallways led to various parts of the building, and the main hallway in front offered elevators to other floors. Using the elevator to get to the basement would probably require a key-card, but a door to the stairwell was just past the elevators. To the left of the main hallway was a front desk, helmed by a silver-haired guy, while streams of business-casuals made their way to various floors for undoubtedly important businessy things.

Maddox pushed Lahn forward and off to the side to keep him from blocking the entry, pulling him from the connection to Past. "Come on, man. You can't keep doing this. This is *your* plan; *you* gotta lead. We're not going to make it if you stop every minute."

"I don't have any control over it," Lahn insisted, knowing Maddox was right.

"I get it," Maddox soothed. "I'm stressed too. Just take a deep breath and tell me what's next. There's going to be locked doors and security pads. How do we get in the basement?"

Ignoring the thump of his heart in the bruise on his face, Lahn took a deep breath. Then he looked around, fighting through the fuzziness encroaching on his vision. He did have a plan to get into the basement. There was something he needed. Where was it?

On his left sat the silver-haired man at the reception desk, a phone to his ear, looking confused. Above the man, a large clock announced the time, showing how little remained. Only fifteen minutes left.

"Fifteen minutes until things go boom," said Lahn. [*Fifteen minutes until things go boom,*] his past echoed.

Down the hallway in front of him, just past the elevators and next to the door to the stairwell, he saw what he needed: the thing that could get everyone out, and them in. Leaving Maddox behind, he rushed toward it, out of sight of the front desk. But as he grabbed the handle of the fire alarm, he paused and stared for a moment.

He was here, doing the action he'd foreseen. *Maybe* it was possible to change events, but not this one. This was required. It was the only way to make sure most everyone got out of the building. It was the only way for them to get through the locked doors. As Maddox rushed up beside him, Lahn took a breath and pulled firmly down.

Splinter Report: S02-5522
Date: 2515-10-22
Local Date: 1082 BCE
ID: S02
Designation: Agartha

Report:

The attack on our primary base in Tibet by the locals was devastating to our current work in this Splinter. The location should have been well hidden. Knowledge of our presence in the Splinter should have been nonexistent. The security was minimal, and as a result the site was overrun quickly, even by locals carrying weaponry from the eleventh century BCE.

The team managed to trigger the self-destruct protocol before escaping, destroying the technology at the site, including the passage to Prime, and collapsing the tunnels leading deeper into the complex. Unfortunately, no one has been able to return to the site to verify there is nothing left for the locals to discover.

The connection to the Splinter has been reestablished at the secondary site, which has allowed us to rescue the team members stranded after its loss. Unfortunately, that effort took several weeks, and we lost additional members due to untreated injuries from the attack. Of course, Immortals that died will only lose their time on site since their last sync.

T. Hobbs

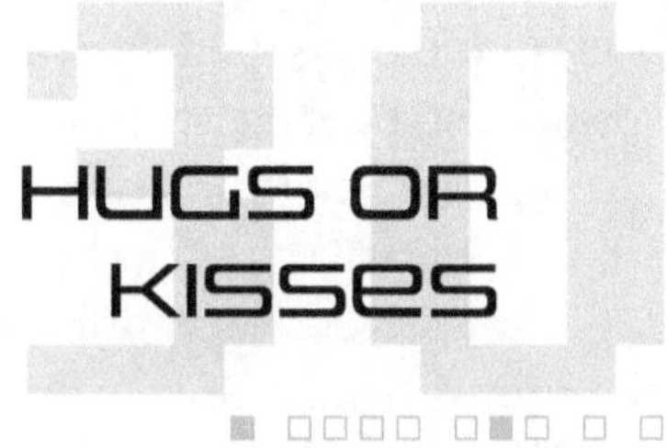

HUGS OR KISSES

The fire alarm rang out, loud and demanding.

Before someone could come and find him holding the trigger, Lahn stepped into the stairwell—now unlocked by the fire alarm—with Maddox on his heels. The shrill klaxon paused, replaced by an announcement that echoed solemnly in the cement stairwell. "Warning. There has been a reported emergency. Do not use the elevators. Please proceed through the stairwells to the nearest exit in an orderly fashion."

The alarm resumed. Over its sound, doors at each floor, including the basement, banged open in a staccato rhythm. Waves of people streamed into the stairwell, burbling with excitement and curiosity about the emergency, all headed for the exit he'd just entered.

"Why are there so many people?" Lahn gasped.

"Fire alarm," said Maddox, placing a hand on Lahn's arm. "It was *your* plan to get everyone out. It's okay, just breathe."

"Shuddup. *You* breathe." But he sucked in a huge gulp of air, held it, and let it out slowly. As the swell moved closer, he pressed himself tight against the wall and tried to disappear.

"How are we getting in the basement door?" asked Maddox, in a blatant attempt to distract Lahn. "Is it unlocked too?"

"Yes," Lahn gulped. "You go first."

Maddox stepped forward and started down the stairs toward the basement, and Lahn followed closely behind.

". . . the last time there was a . . ."

". . . hope they let us back in soon, I'm in the middle . . ."

Multiple conversations washed over him as the first of the crowd from below overtook them. Lahn held his breath and wished he'd brought a deep-sea diver suit. Wished he *had* a deep-sea diver suit. Maddox broke the flow in front of him, like a rock on the shore. But even so, each minor bump and jostle threatened to drag Lahn under.

As they arrived at the first landing and turned the corner, the door to the basement came into view. Maddox pushed forward, ignoring the few startled cries, and Lahn struggled after him. The flow through the door had fallen to a trickle, and Maddox held it open for the last few people, then ushered Lahn through and followed behind. Lahn took the gasping breath of a drowning man breaking the surface of the water.

"Which way?" asked Maddox.

From the doorway, three halls split in opposite directions. Lahn took a quick glance down each path, but nothing suggested the right way to go. "We're going to have to split up. Look for the hallway with the black door."

Maddox went down the left hallway at a jog while Lahn went right.

The illumination from the diode light-strings running along upper corners got absorbed by the raw, unpainted cement walls, creating a space darker than the stairwell. While immaculate, a subtle musty smell announced they were below ground. Lahn had never liked basements, and he'd discovered in a session with this therapist that he was subconsciously worried he'd get trapped inside and the lights would go out, leaving him to stumble through the space in the dark.

"I got to the end of this hall." Maddox's muffled voice came over the handheld and Lahn pulled it out of his pocket. "There's nothing. What did you find?"

"Nothing here either," responded Lahn. "Let's go back and check the last hall."

Maddox was looking at his handheld when they met at the basement entry. "Ten minutes."

Lahn nodded and they moved down the main hallway.

The main hall included several branches, and Lahn and Maddox checked down each one quickly. In the last branching hallway Lahn finally found it: the black door in the middle of the hall, the one they were looking for.

"Maddox," he yelled. "Found it." In a sprint, he dashed to the door, grabbed the handle and pulled.

It didn't move.

Maddox ran up beside him as Lahn shook it a few more times.

"It's locked," Lahn growled, pointing to the glowing red card scanner on the left of the door. "And the fire alarm didn't open it."

"Okay," said Maddox. "My turn." He pulled the strap of his bag over his head, shoved the bag into Lahn's hands, and reached inside to pull out a screwdriver. After taking a quick glance around, Maddox placed the flat edge of the tip at the seam between the top of the scanner and the wall. Holding the screwdriver with his left hand, he slammed the palm of his right against the top, and the screwdriver jammed deep in the gap.

He grabbed the screwdriver in both hands and pulled backward and down. With a crack of breaking plastic and ripping drywall, the scanner popped free and dropped, jerking to a stop at the end of the wires still attached to the wall.

"Wire cutters," Maddox said.

"Wire cutters," said Lahn as he handed them over.

Maddox cut the entire bundle, close to the panel, then separated out red and black. With a quick snick of the cutters he stripped both wires, and tapped the bare metal ends together. A bright spark jumped from the wires with a crack and they both leaped back. The door clicked, Maddox grabbed the handle, pulled, and the door opened.

Maddox turned to Lahn and grinned.

"I can't believe that worked," said Lahn with a shake of his head.

"Hey, I can be a wizard, too." Maddox held the door for Lahn and they both stepped into the room.

Aluminum ductwork, steel pressurized pipes, and iron power conduits filled the space. The room was industrial and toasty warm.

"Looks like we found the building utilities," said Lahn. "If the device is connected to the power, it should be here somewhere."

"We're down to five minutes."

"Let's look quick. If it's not here, we run."

To the left, around a large panel with switches and pressure gauges, was the only pathway. Lahn and Maddox moved quickly and found an open space behind it. In the middle was the very thing they fought through hordes of goblins and insurmountable odds to find.

The device.

The main part of the device looked similar to the one he examined at the warehouse. The case contained lights and knobs like he'd seen before, and the front was an open cavity that housed a floating, dark orb, marbled with blue and black.

"That's . . . wooow!" said Maddox. He stepped closer, walking between two tripods with cameras mounted on top, each pointed at the device.

"Stop!" Lahn grabbed Maddox's arm, holding him in place.

Frozen between steps, Maddox turned his head slowly to either side to look at the cameras beside him.

Lahn examined one of the cameras for a moment. "There's a switch near the lens," he said, and they turned them both off.

Maddox moved forward quickly and crouched to examine the device. Unlike the warehouse, multiple wire cables suspended the device in a framework between two large trusses. "This is amazing," he said. "The marble pattern on the orb moves."

A bundle of wires snaked from the back of the setup to the ground and along the floor. The cords ran into a box on a stand behind one of the cameras. On the top of the box was a bright orange timer, ticking down as the seconds passed.

One minute, thirty-four seconds.

"Maddox!"

With a quick turn, Maddox gaped at the timer. "Um, Lahn. Run!" He took off at a dash out of the space.

Lahn froze.

He couldn't think with the time counting down, each second gone meant people died. If he turned off the timer, it would stop everything. *Right?* There was no obvious power button, but the timer had four other buttons: up, down, X and O.

Which one? Is X cancel? Does O mean stop?

Lahn panicked with indecision, no idea of the right way to defuse this bomb, stomach threatening to escape and hide.

"What are you doing?" Maddox cried, looking back around the corner.

Lahn's vision blurred. He couldn't run away. That was no longer an option. He couldn't let everyone else die. At forty seconds, a click followed by a hum came from the main device and he stole a quick look. Lights flashed on the device, and the hum became the ascending whine of an old flashbulb warming up.

Sucking in a deep breath and holding it—tasting copper—he hovered his finger over the X for a few brutal seconds.

"Lahn!"

Then pressed it.

The timer froze at twenty seconds, blinked three times, and went dark. Lahn looked at Maddox with wide eyes and let his breath hiss out through clenched teeth. He looked down at his hands, the pain in his right one shouting at him. Somehow he'd kept them steady, but now they shook and wouldn't stop.

"You . . ." said Maddox, awe in his voice, "you . . . did it."

Lahn stepped back and closed his eyes in relief, ignoring the buzzing in his ears.

"You did it!" said Maddox again, stepping forward. "You stopped the attack. You changed the timeline and no one got hurt, especially you."

With a bit of envy, Lahn thought of Past. That version of him was getting dropped off in front of Welkin Tower by Tia. But that version wasn't going to be smashed by some invisible force and end up in the hospital. *You're welcome.*

"Now we have time," continued Maddox, "to figure out this technology and—"

A crack and an audible flash of light that Lahn could see through closed eyelids startled his eyes open. He stared in horror at the device. The center orb glowed a vibrant, dark green, and grew brighter with pulses and flashes. He'd only stopped the timer, the device was still powering up.

Lahn's eyes flew to Maddox, and he found the same horror in his friend's face. They turned and ran. Slamming the utilities room door open, they sprinted for the stairs. Deep in his chest, Lahn could feel vibrations from the room behind him. He hit the stairwell at full speed, trying to keep up with Maddox's longer legs, and took three steps at a time.

Maddox escaped from the stairwell ahead of him. Gasping for breath, Lahn slammed into the closing stairwell door, costing him precious moments. He burst from the stairwell into the main foyer, and crashed into a group of stragglers, causing cursing and cries.

"Run!" he yelled at them as he broke through.

A deep thunderclap of energy echoed from the basement and vibrated up his spine. His stomach rose into his throat and a force dragged at him, and he scrambled and skittered on the floor. In front of him he could see Maddox struggling through the front doors. With frantic effort, Lahn pushed and pressed, tearing the glass doors open and stumbling through.

The scene in front of the building was chaos, like a disturbed swarm of locusts. The crowds evacuated from the building were scattering, terrified of the noises coming from Living Bliss. The pull back toward the basement became overpowering, a fight with each step. *I won't make it*, he thought, *I can't get far enough!* Converting his panic to potential, he pushed with a final flare of energy.

Another deep crack yanked him into the air, and time paused.

For a frozen moment, Lahn pondered the disaster of his day. He'd felt victorious: a powerful mage that banished the curse from the land. But his magic was not powerful enough, and the curse forced its way back, stronger than ever.

They hadn't changed the past. They hadn't stopped the explosion. They hadn't saved anyone, and they hadn't learned anything about the tech.

And now, frozen in flight, sailing toward the building and his death, he could admit to himself he'd subconsciously hoped saving a bunch of people would make up for his mistake that caused the Accident. Or better yet, use the tech to go back ten years and stop the Accident from happening at all.

A blinding flash and a sound like a giant kettle drum exploding underwater heralded his return to real-time, and he landed heavily, sliding on his back along the pavement at the front of the building, fifteen meters from its new gaping hole. A powder cloud settled on everything, and with a ragged gasp he tried to draw breath, but couldn't. He hadn't been sucked into the blast, but injured, blind and deaf from the explosion, and unable to breathe, he might be dying anyway and he couldn't stop it.

A shadow moved into the corner of Lahn's washed-out vision. As tears ran down his face, he blinked rapidly, desperate to see. The white receded reluctantly, and the shadow became a bearded face, eyebrows drawn in extreme concern.

Maddox seemed to be yelling. But as he slipped into unconsciousness, all Lahn heard was a high-pitched ring.

THE TYPEWRITER-POCALYPSE

Lahn leaned on Maddox for support as they turned down the hall to Maddox's apartment. At the end of the hall, Tia stood, waiting outside the door.

"Tia," Lahn struggled out, quietly. "I'm so glad she's here."

"She can be the one to patch you up. But *why* is she here?"

Even from a distance, it was obvious she was not happy, the single-day's growth of hair on her head adding severity to the scowl on her face. Tia strode down the hall to meet them.

"You didn't contact her with your handheld," whispered Lahn, "while I was unconscious in the autoride?"

"No. I wouldn't know how to do that from the terminal."

"Maddox," she said as she drew close. "Unlock the door, get your first-aid kit and scissors. I'll help Lahn in."

Maddox took off at a jog to open the door, and Tia supported Lahn slowly down the hall. "This looks really bad, *Em,*" she said quietly, looking at Lahn's back and the tattered remains of his shirt.

"It hurts, *Chi,* but I don't think anything's broken. Looks worse than it is."

"I'm sure."

They walked through the front door, and Tia led Lahn to the kitchen table extending from the wall. She sat him in a chair sideways with his back facing her. Maddox dropped a clean, white T-shirt on the living room couch and brought the first-aid supplies to the table. With a slight shudder, he moved to the kitchen area to lean up against the sink, facing Lahn.

With quick efficiency, Tia went to work on Lahn's back. Using antiseptic, she cleaned the cuts and scrapes that riddled his skin. The pain that had settled to a dull throb flared with a burning that brought tears to his eyes. Balling his hands into tight fists, he clenched his teeth and breathed in with a sharp hiss. Tia didn't slow down or comment, but continued dabbing his back. Each touch brought a new spike of cleansing pain. Penance for his foolishness.

"He was crying like a baby when it happened," Maddox said with a half-grin, trying to lighten the mood.

"I think you were crying too," said Lahn. "And you don't have a scratch on you."

"Completely true."

Tia pointedly ignored the banter. She got out gauze, tape, synth-skin, and sterile glue, and started taping the gauze to his shoulder. "Some cuts are deep enough to justify stitches," she said. "But the synth-skin and glue will have to do. You will have scars."

"Thanks for patching me up," said Lahn between gasps as Tia applied the bandages.

"Yeah," agreed Maddox, with a wince of sympathy. "I'm glad I didn't have to."

Tia finished and stood straight with a sigh as she appraised her work. Nodding once to herself, she walked around to look Lahn in the face. "So," she said, "you traveled through time."

It was not a question.

Lahn and Maddox looked at each other. "Well . . . not just now," said Lahn.

"I figured," responded Tia, "although I would imagine it's possible to get these injuries in a travel event." She turned to Maddox with a scowl. "But that's what you meant by your message yesterday. Lahn is part of the unexpected impact of the CTC?"

"Yes," Maddox said, eyebrows furrowed. "But it's more than that."

"The explosions that are happening are related to the time travel," said Lahn.

"How do you know?"

Lahn looked at Maddox and raised his eyebrows. Should they tell her? Admit to their horribly stupid plan that almost got them killed? Maddox shrugged his shoulders in response. "We just came from Living Bliss," said Lahn as he turned back to Tia. "We were inside and we saw the device. It was similar to the one I saw just before I traveled through time. We almost didn't get out. That's how I got hurt."

Tia turned away and swore softly under her breath.

"But there's going to be another explosion," said Lahn. "Bigger. Much bigger."

"'The impact is massive,'" said Maddox quietly, looking down as he quoted his own message to her.

"And?" said Tia, turning back to fix them both with a glare.

When Lahn was younger, he used to think that glare could shatter stone. But now, he felt righteous indignation rise in his chest against it. "And . . . we need to do something to stop it."

"*You two*? What are *you* going to do? Do you have any idea what you're getting into?"

"No," said Lahn. "That's why we went this morning. To try to stop that one, *and* get info about tomorrow."

"And how did that go?"

Lahn's face flushed, and he looked to Maddox for help.

"It's a thousand people, Tia," said Maddox quietly. "One thousand people die tomorrow. We have to do something."

"And if you try, it will be one thousand and two."

Maddox closed his mouth into a tight line.

"We have to do *something*, Tia," said Lahn, echoing Maddox's insistence.

At a noise from her pocket, Tia pulled out her portable and took a quick glance at it. "That woman . . ." she muttered. "She knows . . ." She sighed and looked at both of them evenly. "Look, guys. I get what you're saying. I understand why you feel compelled to do something. But, you could have died today. Please, just drop it. It's too dangerous."

"Yeah," Maddox said, looking hard at Tia, "it probably is."

"I have to go," said Tia, looking back evenly. "Maddox, I promised the other Lahn you'd pick him up at the hospital. But please . . . keep *this* Lahn out of any more trouble."

She walked out the door without looking back.

"Were you okay?" asked Maddox as he stared at the closed door. "The other you, at the hospital?"

"I was fine," Lahn said. With a grunt, he got up from the table and went to the couch, picking up the white shirt Maddox placed there. He pulled it over his head gingerly and contented himself with sitting forward so as not to put pressure on his wounds. "That vision was strong enough that I passed out. Not surprising, considering how bad it was for me on this side. But the effects went away. It was almost worse to talk to Agent Prakash while I was there."

Maddox smirked. "You hate lying, especially when you're under stress. It's amazing you didn't spill everything."

"I seriously considered it, and almost admitted I was having visions about the attacks and everything. Good thing

I didn't. Can you imagine how that conversation would've gone?" Lahn stopped and cocked his head to the side.

"What?" asked Maddox.

"Give me one of the handhelds."

"Wait, are you messaging Past again?" Maddox asked. He picked up his shoulder bag from the counter where he'd dropped it when they came in. Reaching in, he pulled out a handheld and handed it to Lahn.

"Just a little encouragement to avoid saying anything problematic," Lahn said. Connecting securely to the Mesh, he started an anonymous message function similar to what he used last time. "Don't . . . tell . . . her . . . about . . . the . . . visions."

Maddox chuckled, watching Lahn send the message. "It's fun watching you try to keep yourself from getting committed. When Past-you told me about the mysterious message you got, you were so confused. You couldn't figure out who would even know what was happening to you. And here you are, messing with your own head."

Lahn laughed, then sobered. "Do you think Tia is right? Should we just drop it?"

Maddox sighed and sat in the chair. "Going to the site of a high-tech explosion was dangerously dumb. She's not wrong about that. Even if we knew where the explosion would happen tomorrow, we should stay far away."

"And with the DTS scrutinizing Past," Lahn said, "it's only a matter of time before they start to watch *you*. I shouldn't even stay here another night."

"I hadn't thought about that," said Maddox. "Wow. This has gotten bad." He stopped and looked at Lahn. "But . . ."

"But . . . there's got to be something we can do, right?"

Maddox chewed his cheek. "If we don't trust the authorities, could we publish what we know anonymously? Any way to do that so it can't be traced?"

With Lucia, it would be easy. Lahn missed her tech superpowers and kooky personality fiercely. If he had her help, they could probably even figure out where the attack was going to happen. But he had no way to contact her. Even if he was home, by now the DTS had gotten into all of his stuff and she was hiding, sending Past-Lahn a secured cuff he would lose tomorrow morning. The best he could hope was after all this was over, she would find him again.

"Yeah," he finally said. "It would be some work, but I could make a way for us to publish something so it can't be traced. But what would we publish? We don't know anything about the actual attack."

"We know it's supposed to take place tomorrow at noon. We also have a count of potential casualties."

Lahn narrowed his eyes. "And it's a huge number. The attack must be somewhere in the center of town and involve a skyscraper or two. But it's not enough to tell us where."

"I know," agreed Maddox, standing. "When I get back from picking up Past from the hospital, let's figure out a plan of where you're going to stay, and go over the photos from the warehouse again. Maybe there's something we missed."

For several minutes after Maddox left, Lahn sat and looked at nothing. They had loaded the photos from the war-board onto a private node on the Mesh, but Lahn didn't think it would do him any good to go through them again. He found most of them confusing and doubted he would learn much more on his own.

"I need to look at this differently." Standing, he went to look for paper. "Maybe I can map out connections of what we know."

After several minutes of snooping, he ended up at the cabinets by the front door, where Maddox stored extra cans of food. On the bottom shelf, a few pieces of paper stuck out from behind a plain cardboard box. He pulled them out, stood, and turned to go to the kitchen table.

Then stopped.

The pages were not completely blank.

What is this? He thought, with a spike of alarm.

Each page included a watermark symbol he'd seen before, an upside-down triangle overlaid with an empty diamond. And on each was a string of random numbers, in the middle of the page. The length of numbers was different on each page, but all the numbers except the last were the same. Like someone stopped when they made a mistake in the sequence. With a trembling hand, he ran his fingertips along the text. There was texture and irregularity to the print—as though typed with a typewriter.

Where would Maddox get these? Lahn's pulse pounded in his ears and the bruise on his face. There had to be a mistake. He knelt down at the cabinet again and pulled out the box. Behind it, tucked in the back of the cabinet, he found what he was afraid he would find.

Lahn pulled the old typewriter out, heavy in his hands, and placed it on the floor. Sitting in front of it, he stared and tried to make sense of what he was seeing.

But there was no doubt. Maddox had sent him the letter.

PART III

RED-HAIRED
BOAR

The typewriter sat in the middle of the kitchen floor, immobile like a baby troll turned to stone in the sunlight. Lahn sat on Maddox's couch, a handful of stolen cash in one pocket, one of the handhelds in the other, and a borrowed dark-red jacket worn over the previously loaned shirt. He sat, glaring. Glowering at that stupid typewriter.

The thought of smashing it—and a few other things in the apartment for good measure—sounded fantastic. He would put it in a pile with the typewritten pages of numbers on top, light the whole thing to burn, and dance around the fire like a madman.

Then Lahn would walk out, not looking back, as the apartment burned to the ground. And Maddox would be left to clean up the mess. Maddox would have to explain to the authorities why he had destroyed the life of his best friend, tipping him over the edge and turning him into a breaking-and-entering, network-hacking, fire-starting criminal.

Instead, Lahn had stolen the cash and coat, and planned on walking out, leaving a note explaining to Maddox the precise level of jerkitude he'd achieved.

But Lahn couldn't even walk out. He couldn't. Not until he knew why. So he sat, and waited.

The apartment door rattled, then opened, and Maddox walked in. "Well, Past-you is fine but freaked out. He . . ." Maddox stopped, noticing Lahn wearing the red jacket, gaze down. He followed Lahn's eyes and saw what was on the floor.

The typewriter.

For several long seconds, silence reigned in the apartment.

"Did you . . ." started Lahn roughly, breaking the stillness, not looking at Maddox. "Did you send the encrypted letter?"

For more seconds, Maddox said nothing. "Yes," he said finally in a whisper.

"Really?" Lahn looked at Maddox, his face a mix of shock and pain. "It's not just some big misunderstanding? Someone didn't plant the evidence in your apartment? You're not going to tell me it's a fantastic coincidence that you have an old typewriter and pages that look just like the puzzle some jerk slipped under my door?"

"I sent it," Maddox choked out quietly, head still down, looking at the typewriter. "It's my fault. If you hadn't gone back in time, none of it would have happened to you. *Everything is my fault.* You know, I just said those exact words to your past-self, and it's true."

Lahn stood and glared at Maddox. "Can you change it? Can you stop me from going back in time?"

"I . . . can't," said Maddox, still not looking at Lahn. "It's already happened. You traveled. You're here. But even if I could, you *need* to go back in time."

For a moment, Lahn didn't move, didn't make a sound. Then a single word exploded from his mouth. "Why?" It was the grand question, the one question he'd been asking since it all started.

"I can't tell you."

"Can't tell me?!" Lahn's voice was getting loud enough for the neighbors to start complaining. He should care that they might call the police, but at the moment, he didn't.

Maddox looked up at Lahn, eyes wet. He walked to the living room chair and sat heavily. "Knowing any more than you do would put you in serious danger. *More* danger. It could put a lot of people at risk. I'm sorry. Really, really sorry. But I can't tell you."

Lahn turned away in frustration. Maddox had the very answers Lahn was looking for the entire time, and he'd just watched Lahn struggle and hadn't said a thing.

The typewriter sat at Lahn's feet, and he pulled back his foot and kicked it with all his strength. A handful of keys broke off, shooting across the room, and the typewriter skittered across the floor with a clattering grind and a ding, like some demon just got its wings.

With a limp, Lahn walked out of the apartment, slamming the door without looking back.

As the sun approached the horizon, the shadows from the city buildings stretched, creeping toward Lahn like zombies, hungry for his delicious gray matter. They could have it. He wasn't using it.

Lahn had never liked walking around the city. The open, mint sky and the crowds of people were too much. Nighttime was not much better, the glow of the evening drew just as many people outdoors as the sunshine did. When he found it necessary, he would distract himself while walking by examining the architecture of the city's buildings, an interesting mix of green tech, modern and classic. But now, even watching spider-robots harvest food from a horizontal garden growing on the side of an apartment couldn't pierce his cloud of confusion.

He knew he might be starting to feel the effects of being off his meds for more than a day, but that didn't change how confusing and complicated the situation was. He had no idea how to process Maddox sending him the stupid encrypted letter. Without it, they wouldn't have discovered the horrible event happening tomorrow with one thousand casualties. But because of it, he'd been in extreme danger and gone back in time, which started the visions and triggered every . . . stupid . . . thing.

As he thought about the letter, a sense of déjà vu came over him, and with surprise he realized Past had joined him in wandering around the city. In his befuddled state, he'd forgotten about his other self. He would be sitting in the pocket park across the street from Sippin' Serenity, after Lucia sent him the fancy new cuff. Lucia had finished decoding the numbers in the puzzle, and Past was getting drawn inexorably into the mystery of the message.

Ignore it, Lahn, he shouted in his mind to Past. *Ignore the message!*

Past wouldn't. He couldn't. Regardless of the fact it wouldn't provide any actual answers and would only lead him *somewhere* that—

With a start, Lahn felt Past disengage, excited by the clue Lahn gave him. *Somewhere.* The message referenced a location. He rubbed his forehead in frustration. Past hadn't known the message referred to a place until Lahn thought of it, and now he was off, chasing dumb answers that led to more dumb questions.

Lahn didn't care about answers anymore. He'd fought and scraped to get a meager few, and in the end realized Tia was right: some answers are not worth it.

"Lahn?" A muffled voice came from his pocket. "Lahn? Are you there?"

Reaching into his pocket, Lahn pulled out the handheld.

"Lahn?" It was Maddox.

With unnecessary force, Lahn jabbed the handheld, ending the transmission. With a couple of quick keystrokes he disabled communication between the devices. He had no interest in talking to Maddox.

But he did want to talk to someone. He really wanted to talk to Tia. She'd made it harshly clear how she felt about his choices lately, but of course that was only because she worried about him. If anyone could help him make sense of everything and help him know what to do, it would be Tia.

But, he couldn't call her. The handheld couldn't make direct calls, only device-to-device transmissions.

However . . . calling her wasn't the only option.

Lahn walked to a bench on the sidewalk in front of a music store, which was currently showcasing an instrument that didn't require direct touch. It was a simple box that projected holographic lines and shapes into the air, through which the musician would wave their hands; a digital theremin. The instrument probably sounded ridiculous.

As he sat on the bench, he pulled out the handheld. Connecting to the Mesh, he opened the same anonymous messaging function he'd used to tell Past not to reveal anything to Prakash, but set it to allow responses. He'd have to be careful with his words, in case the DTS was monitoring Tia's tech.

I TEASED THE DRAGON

For several seconds, nothing happened. Then text appeared on the screen in response.

> I know.

A giant boulder of anxiety lifted off his chest. Tia knew it was him. But now he had to figure out how to tell her about Maddox's betrayal.

BUT THE BITE CAME FROM
THE RED-HAIRED BOAR

> In what way?

A RIDDLE SENT ME TO MORDOR

Silence. Was he too vague? No, Tia would understand. But what could she say in response? How did you respond to learning that your brother's best friend, the third musketeer, had manipulated your brother into getting sucked through time?

> I understand. What will you do?

STAY AWAY

> Do you want to come here?

Yes. Yes! More than anything. Lahn's view of the city street wavered, and he blinked back the tears.

But . . . he couldn't go there. It was too dangerous for her. And somehow, he had to warn her of that.

THE EYE OF SAURON IS ON MY
PAST AND ANYONE HE KNOWS

> Where will you go?

I HAVE COIN STOLEN
FROM THE BOAR

> Hide. Avoid the Eye and the
Boar. And any other dragons.
Please, be careful. Love you.

The last line flashed on the screen and no text followed. Tia had said what she could. And it helped, even if they couldn't talk openly. He just needed a little more. He wouldn't even mind talking to his mom, but again, no portable. But maybe there was someone else he could talk to, say anything to, without the worry of being overheard.

Stepping into the street, he flagged down a passing auto-ride, the sign on its roof signifying availability. The AI of the vehicle saw him and pulled over to a stop.

Lahn was going to see his father.

"I don't know how to climb out of this hole, Dad," Lahn said.

The stone bench beneath him was cool in the dusk air and brought focus to his thoughts.

"I don't know why it's all happening to me. It all presses down so hard, I can't breathe. And everything I do digs me in deeper. I look for answers, try to help other people, take risks to fix things; it all goes wrong. Everything I've tried has failed, in huge, terrible ways."

The only response was a breeze dancing gently through nearby maple trees. In the companionable quiet, Lahn reconsidered his statement.

"I know, I know. I'm being extreme. It's how I feel, but yeah . . . *some* stuff worked. When Maddox and I got that ladder in place, it felt like I had magic powers. More so when we snuck into Living Bliss. To make a dangerous plan but have it work? It was amazing!"

He sighed and slumped. "Until the end."

Lahn stretched his painful back, stared at the granite in front of him, and allowed his troubled history to enter his thoughts.

"I secretly hoped—I know it was foolish and I wouldn't

even admit it to myself—but I thought if we understood the tech, maybe I could travel back in time again. And I could go back ten years . . . to that day. I wanted to fix the Accident. It was all my fault, and I wanted to fix it."

The day his life was broken. The day his family was broken.

"If I could just stop myself from distracting you that night, we wouldn't have crashed, and you . . ." Lahn stopped, unable to complete the sentence.

"But . . ." he continued after a minute, "we didn't learn anything about the tech. Maddox says it wouldn't have worked, anyway. And I am out of ideas for fixing anything."

Lahn leaned his head back and looked into the pale, starless, night sky. His grandmother used to tell him stories about the beauty of the night, a sea of stars piercing the black of the evening. Lahn couldn't imagine it, and always wondered if the stars would feel like millions of eyes staring down at him. Probably.

"You always said," Lahn finally continued into the cool night air, "'Accept your weakness, make it your strength.' I try to do that, but I'm not good at it. My DP keeps getting in the way. I've been on the edge of an episode for the last few days. How do I make *that* a strength? Sometimes I want to let it happen, let it wash over me. At least then I would be free of fighting it. But it makes me feel unreal, and it messes so hard with my sense of space and time . . .

"Doesn't matter now," he continued with a heavy sigh. "It's too late. Now there's no way to stop Faceless and his plans, stop all the attacks, stop the big one. I think the reason Faceless traveled through time must have something to do with the attacks. I just wish there was a way to keep Faceless from going back in time . . ."

Lahn's breath caught. Maybe there *was* a way to stop Faceless from going back. Regardless of what Maddox said, maybe Lahn's magical knowledge of the future gave him one more chance.

Lahn stood and walked forward. "Thanks, Dad," he said, his throat catching. With reverence, he caressed the top of the granite memorial. "It always helps to talk. I still miss you every day."

He turned and walked to the cemetery exit.

SOMEONE HE
ONCE KNEW

The meager lumens from Lahn's convenience-store flashlight did little to offset the pale darkness and strange shadows in the warehouse. He now wished he'd picked a better flashlight when he stopped for supplies. The warehouse was darker than he expected, with the evening glow doing little more than making the space creepy. He was glad he had any light, but wished it did better than brighten a two foot circle in front of him, at the center of which was the time machine.

Standing there, staring down at the device in the middle of the night, it was pleasant to consider his options without the imminent threat of destruction. The controls on the front were still a mystery, the buttons and gauges giving no clue to the device's usage. The strange, dark orb hovered in the cavity in front, the marbling on its surface blue and black.

The device was off, all its lights and gauges dark. Attached to the box were thick power cables and various wires, which ran to other equipment. It wasn't going anywhere yet. But if he could get it disconnected, and it wasn't too heavy, he would take it.

As he had admitted to his dad, it might not help him fix the past, especially now that he didn't have Maddox's support. Or Lucia's. Or even Tia's. But if he stole it, at least it would stop the time travel in the morning. And then what could Faceless do? Nothing!

Admittedly, he'd failed at every effort to change anything. In fact, every action he had taken seemed to lead the way for events to play out as they had before. Nothing *seemed* to make a difference.

But that doesn't mean I shouldn't try, he thought, his mouth settling into a firm line. For years, his efforts to overcome Depersonalization had seemed fruitless, and it had felt like he would never get better. But he'd kept trying anyway. And it *had* gotten better. As hopeless as it might feel, it was still possible to stop Faceless. If he couldn't take the device, he'd destroy it.

And the entire warehouse with it, if needed.

Lahn picked up the flashlight and took out the multitool he'd also purchased from the convenience store. Figuring he would start with the easy stuff, he flipped out the screwdriver blade. Cautiously, carefully, knowing messing with the tech was dangerous, he started loosening the smaller connections. The thicker power cables were locked in tight, and he didn't have the right implement to disconnect them properly, so he would deal with them last. He could probably use the small, powered bolt cutters he also picked up, that he used to cut the padlock on the back entrance. No matter what, he couldn't rush and make a mistake that might get him exploded. It was the middle of the night; he had time before everyone showed up in the morning.

If he was successful at removing the time device, what would happen to Past? Nothing. Past would still show up at the warehouse in the morning, but he wouldn't travel through time. Even though Maddox insisted it wasn't possible to stop the time travel event, Lahn had to work from the assumption he was wrong. He had to try.

But . . . what about me? Lahn wondered as he fought with the connectors. Would he poof out of existence? Or would there be two Lahns, instant twins. Did it matter? If it saved the lives of a thousand people, did it matter what happened to him?

With a nervous chuckle, Lahn was sure it mattered, and mattered a lot. But he kept working.

He had finished detaching two of the smaller connectors and started on a third when there was a noise behind him, a thunk of metal against metal. He whipped around, shining his flashlight at the back door to the warehouse, the screwdriver blade held out in front of him in defense. Nothing was there. The door didn't move; there was nothing to see.

A skittering off to the left brought him around again. But again, nothing to see. With shallow breath, Lahn slowly panned his light around the large room, his small torch not up to revealing the space.

A soft shuffle sounded from the right and a blur of motion knocked into his arms, hitting both his multitool and flashlight, sending them flying. The beam of light slashed through the air, and the flashlight landed with a clatter, the light shining directly at Lahn's face.

Lahn dropped to a low crouch, frantically searching for signs of his attacker. With the light in his eyes, the warehouse was only shadows, shuffling sounds echoing somewhere in the dark. Every muscle tensed, expecting another attack. The shuffling noises stopped, and it left him with the sound of his own heart, beating angrily in the scar in his hand, the bruise on his face, and the wounds on his back.

His hand cramped into a painful claw, and adrenaline surged through him, but he didn't know if he should fight or run. In the scattered darkness, Lahn's senses started playing tricks on him. The room seemed to shift to one side, then the other, and darkness encroached in the corners of his vision.

No! No! Not now!

As he looked around frantically, a slight glint off to the right caught Lahn's eye. The beam from his lost flashlight reflected off the blade of the screwdriver where it had landed. He leaped for the tool.

A dark movement to his left gave him a split second of warning, and before he could reach the tool, Lahn dropped to the ground as a shadow surged at him. In desperation, he rolled to his back with a sound of crunching glass. The wounds on his back flared in a burst of fiery pain, just as the shadow landed on him heavily. With adrenaline surging, he pulled the figure back over his head and kicked with his legs.

The body on him flipped through the air, and a satisfying thump sounded behind him. Lahn leaped to his feet, leaving his flashlight behind, and took off running toward the dark outline of an entryway.

Wasting no time thinking about the stairs that led to the stupid ladder, Lahn turned the other direction and fled deeper into the dark maze of the warehouse, picking random turns at every corner.

As he moved deeper in the building, the scant light through the large windows in the main area faded to black, the oppressive darkness becoming a challenge. He slowed to a walk with one handheld out in front of him and the other on the wall at his side. He had hoped to loop back around and find another way to the back entrance. But soon—breath in sharp bursts he fought to contain—he was lost.

Lahn stopped and looked around, eyes wide, drawing in every sliver of light. To his left was the outline of a door, cracked open, with malevolent, inky blackness inside. He pulled the door open, just enough to slip into the room, and gloom consumed him. The darkness and cool scent of dust and decay pressed in tight against his skin and face, threatening to smother him.

Every instinct told him to run from the room, but Lahn stepped farther inside and put his back to the wall next to the doorway, hoping the darkness would hide him. In the sudden silence, his heartbeat pounded in his ears. He forced himself to take slow, quiet, deep breaths, fighting to keep his desperate gasps for air from giving him away.

After several tense minutes of nothing but the thunder of blood in his ears, it was almost a relief to hear anything. Almost. Faint footsteps sounded off in the bowels of the warehouse.

Go away, go away! Don't come any closer, he thought frantically. Lahn strained with all of his senses. The footsteps moved closer.

Options ran through Lahn's mind. It was too dark to find a weapon, but maybe a shove and a scramble, and he could escape out of the room, slam the door, and lock his pursuer inside.

He stopped breathing when a dancing flicker of light joined the footsteps, and he slid tight against the corner. Every muscle tensed as the sound and light drew outside the room.

Then the noises stopped. The light froze.

Lahn didn't move.

For a moment nothing happened.

The screech of metal grinding against metal broke the silence. Lahn shrunk back against the wall in startled defense. Just as he realized the cause of the noise, the door to the room he was in slammed shut with a sound of finality. He leaped for the door, but the horrible thunk of a magnetic latch snapping into place beat him there. Shoulder first, he crashed into the door, but it remained solidly closed.

The tiny sliver of light bleeding under the door skittered away, plunging the room into total and complete blackness. His attacker would leave him there, locked in that tomb. The knowledge came over him in a sudden shock, like a bucket of ice water dumped on his head.

"Wait!" Lahn shouted, panic swelling to dangerous levels. "Wait, you can't leave me here!"

The light disappeared completely, Lahn put his ear up against the door, just able to pick out the tap of steps moving away.

"Don't leave me in here!" Lahn pounded on the door, then kicked, then backed up and attacked with full-body slams. The door was solid and refused to give a millimeter. He was trapped.

Hoping its screen would stave off the darkness, Lahn quickly pulled out his handheld. The power button didn't work. He pressed and smashed *all* the keys. The device didn't respond.

The suffocating dark and fear and failure became too much, and Lahn's perceptions shifted. Suddenly, it was no longer Lahn trapped in the room, but some poor sap, locked away forever for his crimes of stupidity. Someone Lahn once knew, but he couldn't remember his name.

He turned his back to the wall, slid to the floor, leaned his head back, and gladly let the numbing state of Depersonalization wash over him.

MESH STORAGE - 2012-08-22 06:17:45

Hey, Dad. It's me.

My past-self is going back in time. And I have to move on.

There is so much about the last few days I wish had gone differently. But no amount of effort changed a single event. The closed time-like curve was fixed, and it was all a repeat.

An echo. A shadow.

The last location still looms over everything. So many people could die. So many people will die unless I can stop the event. If I only knew where.

Regardless, this will soon be over.

negative
two

ahn started awake, knocking the back of his head against the wall behind him where he sat on the floor. The sharp spike of pain was enough to pull him out of his sleepy state, but it still took a few seconds to remember where he was.

A shard of light offset the darkness of his captive room. Like a tiny mammal afraid of predators, the morning beam peeked under the door, but wouldn't come into the room.

"I don't blame you," Lahn said, his voice weird in his ears. "It's a trap."

Lahn was grateful to see the faint light. It had been a long, black night. One filled with strange, DP-induced nightmares, where he lived in a body that wasn't his, only able to watch helplessly as disaster after disaster assailed him.

"I don't think," he said out loud to the sliver of sunlight, "I'm going to give this place a good review. Sleeping arrangements were subpar, it hasn't been cleaned in a while, and there's this weird smell. On a scale of one to five, negative two."

Even after sleeping, his Depersonalization had not abated. But now, every ache and pain drove through it, demanding attention. His back throbbed, each cut and scrape blurred into a tapestry of suffering. His legs and arms hurt, his neck hurt, even his face hurt. Stronger than everything else, the pain in his head felt like a cold, metal needle poking right into the middle of his forehead. Not a normal headache, almost supernatural . . .

With a shock, he recognized the headache. He'd felt it before, the first time he'd come to the warehouse.

Past was here. He had come. With a killer headache for a proximity alarm.

Stronger than the apathy of his DP, all of Lahn's emotions and reasons for coming the night before washed over him in a rush. He'd been so close to taking the time machine and stopping himself from going back in time. Stopping . . . everything. There must be something he could still do, if he could figure out how to get out of DP and out of the room.

"Come on, Lahn," he said out loud. "Don't let DP rule you."

He ran his fingers lightly on the rough, cold, cement floor. Clumps of dirt littered the ground, and he picked some up, crumbling it between his fingers, feeling the grit slide over his skin. He brought a bit to his nose and inhaled deeply, imagining he could tell where the dirt was from by its smell. This dirt had originally been in an iron mine, but later mixed with oily dirt from a junkyard before being tracked into the room on the boot of a construction worker.

He brought the bit of dirt to his tongue. A small lick and he spat to get the taste of rusted cars and stale coffee from his mouth.

Lahn laughed at his dorkiness, out loud, mostly to hear his own weird voice. His panic abated, his fear ebbed, and reluctantly, his Depersonalization slunk away.

With no small relief, he took in his surroundings.

Nothing had changed; he was still locked in a small, musty, dark room. But also, everything changed; he was fully in real life, in a terrible situation, and he hoped he could do something about it.

Lahn stood, walked to the door, and pushed. No surprise, it remained locked tight. He ran his hand over the cold, metal surface of the door, then knocked twice, a sound like industrial despair.

The slim light under the door revealed a pile of items in the room's corner, discarded construction refuse. Digging through the pile, he found a board about a meter long, one end splintered to a wedge. He jammed the sharp end between the door and the frame, put one foot up on the frame, and pulled. Slivers bit into Lahn's hands. With a grunt, he leaned back, pulling harder, and the door groaned. It was working. But with a crack, the board broke, and he fell back with a thump.

"Oh, come on!"

Lahn sat, gasping, hands balled into fists. As he considered his options, he realized the pressure from the needle of a headache was increasing. Unless something had changed, which at this point seemed unlikely, Past was getting closer.

Past was coming in. He would climb out a third-story window, and end up in a full Depersonalization episode from the stress. He would cross the ladder, although Lahn had no memory of doing so. Then he would stumble down the stairs to the heart of the warehouse and get sucked into the time vortex with Faceless. And they would start the cycle over. Faceless would be free to execute all his plans, attacking the buildings, and go on to the final event where he would cause the death of a thousand people. And Lahn was locked in a dark room, unable to do anything to stop it.

The need to get into the building and figure out what was going on became a compulsion. It . . .

Wait, that's not me, Lahn realized with surprise. *I already know what's going on. My need is to get in there and stop it.*

Emotions were getting fed to Lahn from Past. But it was mixed up with his own anxiety to get to the center of the building before it was too late. Both sets of emotions and needs were strong enough and similar enough they mingled and strengthened each other. Creating a feedback loop. Past felt a supernatural drive to enter the building. Now Lahn understood why.

But Lahn needed to get out of the room and stop Faceless. And he needed to do it before Past's emotions got any stronger, and his panic got in the way. Lahn stood and looked at the board in his hands, broken and useless.

Digging through the items in the corner, Lahn found a section of a steel I-beam at the bottom of the pile. It was less than a meter long, but over ten kilos. He hefted it to the door and lined it up with where he guessed the locking latch would be. After pulling back, he rammed it against the door with all his strength and was rewarded with a satisfying thump.

As he pulled back to hit it again, he stopped. Something was wrong. His heart raced, much more than would be justified by his exertion. The muscles in his arms and legs felt sore and tight, and his balance wavered. In a flash, he understood. The I-beam slipped from his hands, landing heavily on the floor with a crash, and his current surroundings dripped away. He was outside in the bright morning light, standing precariously on the side of a building, ten meters in the air.

[Cold air caresses beads of sweat, bringing goosebumps to the surface of his skin. Shadows cut a stark, angled line across the rough brick five meters in front of him, creating an illusion of greater distance. The toes of his feet dangle dangerously over open air, ten meters above the deadly ground.]

The dark room settled back around him. Dizzy from vertigo and blind in the sudden transition from light to darkness, he fell to his hands and knees with a jolt, grateful for the solid feel of the dirty cement floor beneath him.

Stumbling back to sit on the floor heavily, Lahn's heart raced. Past was in trouble, stuck on the ledge, frozen and unable to move forward. Alone, deep in DP, he might slip. Any second, he could fall and die. And that *would* stop him from going back in time, but in *all* the wrong ways.

Still sitting, Lahn closed his eyes, breathed in deeply, and released it in a slow hiss. Instead of grounding himself by focusing on the physical sensations around him, he reached out and focused on Past. A jumbled mess of ignored emotions flowed into Lahn's mind. Anger, frustration, and crippling fear were all there, but locked away behind Past's DP. And Past was spiraling into despondency, sure that nothing could help.

[*Lahn!* Lucia yells.]

The voice echoed from Past into Lahn's brain.

[*Don't get lost. You need to listen to me. You can control this, just breathe!* He wants to listen, but it's hard.]

"Breathe, Lahn," said Lahn out loud, pushing as much focus and energy into the words as possible, repeating Lucia's encouragement. "Deep and slow."

[He draws in air through his nose, and with effort he focuses on the sensations. The smell is cool and wet, filling his lungs and head with the crisp odors. He takes another deep breath, feels his chest expand, and his arms press against the cool metal and glass of the window behind him.]

Past continued to breathe, matching Lahn's deep rhythm. Cool air in, chest expand, warm air out. Slowly, as Past's heart rate slowed, the connection between them softened. Lahn could no longer hear what Lucia was saying, but he remembered. She was telling him he had to cross, it was the only way to safety. And then, he would try to look at the ladder, but—

Images flashed through Lahn's mind, snapshots of what Past was seeing.

[The ladder.

The ground.

The far building.]

The connection to Past flared. Past had glanced down, but the Depersonalization affected his perception and almost sent him toppling.

[*Calm, Lahn,* says Lucia. *Calm. Listen to the music. Breathe. Deep, not shallow.*

I . . . he gasps, *can't . . . do this.*

Yes you can, Lucia soothes. *You have to. I will guide you.*]

He had to. The window behind him was locked. And he *could* do it. Even though Lahn couldn't remember anything about crossing, he had done it. It was possible, and he was proof.

"You can do this!" said Lahn, again out loud, shouting at Past.

Lahn could feel Past's struggle. Past wanted to trust, he wanted to believe what Lucia was telling him.

"Slow, deep breath," said Lahn soothingly.

Past's DP was getting in the way. It made him want to give up, stay where he was on the ledge, forever.

"Slow . . ." said Lahn, breathing in. "Deep breath." He let it out slowly. "You *can* do it."

[*Okay.*]

Past's skeptical acceptance echoed back. He would try. He would carefully shift his weight and move down to . . .

Oh, no. Lahn felt a surge of panic as he remembered what happened next. *He's going to—*

[Feet slip. The carbon-steel frame of the ladder rushes at him. The light moisture of the morning makes metal slick. Hands slip, and a fall to the death is only stopped as his face connects with steel, the pain instant and sharp.]

NOT TODAY

With a cry, Lahn lurched back into his own body, falling back, his face a fire of agony. It took a moment before he could think. And when he could, it was all confusion. Trembling, he closed his eyes and reached out to Past. The connection remained strong, and Lahn slid in quickly. With a snap, he could see through Past's eyes. The carbon-steel rungs of the ladder were centimeters from his face, with the ground far below. Lahn laughed with a cough on the edge of tears. Past hadn't fallen off the ladder.

Yet.

[The ladder settles, the last shudders of his face-plant, and one arm swings slowly as it dangles in the open air.]

"Lahn, get up!" cried Lahn to the empty, dark room, a painful cramp in his hand.

Past didn't move.

"Get up! Get up, get up, get up! You will die out there!"

Past didn't hear.

The situation was too much for Past, and Lahn could sense Past's consciousness fleeing the scene, leaving his body to fend for itself.

Even through the connection to Past, Lahn could feel his own racing heart, his own gasping breaths. "Lahn," he begged Past in a whispered croak, "please . . . get up."

No movement. No vague indications from Past that he heard. Lahn's impotent panic blazed. And to his horror, his conscious connection to himself, to his own body trapped in the dark room, shattered. While Past struggled with a deadly Depersonalization episode, Lahn fell into his own again. His first instinct was to fling his eyes wide open, disconnect from Past, and start his exercises. But he stopped himself. He couldn't leave Past alone, stuck on the ladder.

A litany of Spanish bled through into his consciousness, faster than he could track.

"*¿Qué voy a hacer? Él está muerto su corazón está latiendo súper rápido pero puede estar muerto pero no como aquella vez en su apartamento pero qué voy a hacer. Él es mi único amigo y no sé cómo hacer amigos y creo que seria muy triste si muriese aunque la verdad no sé cómo sentir tristeza pero pienzo qué estoy asustada que facinante estoy muy asustada pero no me gusta el miedo es súper tonto qué es lo qué voy a hacer . . .*"

He could hear Lucia again, this time in his ears and not just as an echo in his mind.

As his episode grew to full force, all sensations from his prison—the cold of the concrete beneath him and the musty smell of dust—disappeared. His connection to Past expanded, increasing in intensity and energy. What he saw through Past's eyes popped. Colors came alive, the black sheen of the ladder a vibrant contrast to the speckled gray asphalt of the ground.

Even though Lahn was still in DP, disconnected from his own senses, everything coming from Past was the opposite of Depersonalization. For some reason, all the sensations that Past lost in his DP were flooding into Lahn.

Lahn shivered, a full body shudder, startled at the brilliance of the connection. As he did, the ladder vibrated.

He froze.

In spite of his confusion at the impossibility of his actions, he dragged Past's arm up and placed a hand on the ladder.

"How is this possible?" he marveled out loud.

"Lahn?" asked Lucia. "You're *not* dead?"

"Lucia?" he croaked. "You can hear me?"

"Of course, *Menso*. You said words and I heard them. Unless you really are dead, then I don't know what I heard."

Lahn wasn't only looking through Past's eyes, he was hearing through his ears, talking through his mouth, moving through his limbs. Carefully—afraid the enhanced visual sensations would cause vertigo—he lifted Past's head to look up to the far end of the ladder, and pushed Past's body up to a full hands-and-knees position.

"I'm so glad to hear your voice," he said. "I've really missed you."

"Wow. I don't understand that at all, 'cause we were just talking before you fell."

"I've been lost in time."

"Nope. Still not getting it."

Being on the ladder felt real to Lahn. More than real, the dark garnet of the warehouse in front of him almost glowed.

"I didn't know DP made you say weird things," said Lucia. "Are you still in DP?"

"I'm still in DP. Double DP. Somehow it's linking me, and putting my consciousness in the past."

"Hmmm . . . we might be having different conversations, because you don't make any sense. But you still need to get into the warehouse and off the ladder. Can you?"

"Maybe." He didn't know how he crossed before; it was a blank in his mind. *This* had to be how. *Future-me took over while I hid!* he marveled. And since he knew he'd crossed before—he could do it again. He shouldn't be scared, his success should be certain. It *should* be a piece of cake.

But, suspended ten meters off the ground, looking at the narrow ladder and the rungs in front of him spaced so far apart, it didn't feel like a piece of cake. Somehow, impossibly, he was controlling Past's body from the future. The slightest mistake, and Lahn could fall, killing both of them. Nothing felt certain.

Carefully, slowly, he moved one hand forward to a new position on the side-rail of the ladder, the grooved texture of the metal pressing into the skin of his hand. He brought the second hand in alignment with the first; the cold of the metal translated through his skin and carried goosebumps up both arms. With a shift of his center of gravity, he pulled one foot then the other closer to his body.

I can do this.

Lahn moved forward, carefully, one limb at a time, the effort like swimming through Jello. One decimeter became two, one meter became two. The motion difference of the close ladder rungs compared to the ground below made him dizzy, but he pressed forward stubbornly, trying his best to think of nothing but the warehouse in front of him.

"Lucia," he coughed out, muscles burning. "You need to tell me to hurry."

"Okay. Hurry Lahn."

"No, not now," he huffed. "Later. When I start down into the warehouse. I've got to hurry to stop it."

The warehouse slowly moved closer, but Lahn was growing tired. The connection had been easy to hold at first. But pushing Past forward drained his mental energy, and with each movement, he found it harder to maintain both the connection and driving Past's body.

"Stop what?" asked Lucia.

"Stop Faceless," gasped Lahn. "Before everyone dies."

"Wow. Yeah. That does sound bad."

The strain of pushing forward became unbearable. "Come . . . on . . . almost . . . there!"

A mere meter from the warehouse window, Lahn lifted an arm to place it on the ladder. Or at least he tried, but Past's arm didn't move. Darkness flashed over Lahn's perception, and with an edge of panic, he pushed all his focus and energy into the connection with Past. Colors and tactile senses flared, and he grasped onto the sensations from Past like a Ranger on a feral Warg, clutching his unwilling mount for dear life.

His connection held, and with a frantic push, he forced first one limb, then another, forward.

"Careful," said Lucia. "Don't fall, old man."

The warehouse window was within his grasp, but as he reached for it, darkness flashed over his view again, and his motion stopped. Past's fingers failed to connect with the window ledge. Instead, his entire body collapsed forward, a marionette with cut strings. Past's body landed in a heap on the ladder, his forehead against the wall of the warehouse, his arms and legs in a tangle behind, extending over the ten-meter drop. The sudden motion caused the ladder to shift, the sound of metal against stone.

"Lahn! What did I just say?"

He was at salvation's entrance, only to fail now? No! He would not die today. Or two days ago. *Whatever!*

Spurred by fear, he pushed with all his mental might, dragging one of Past's arms out from the rest of his body. It was like pushing a rope through mud. His motion caused an ominous shake of the ladder, and one leg slipped completely off to dangle freely over the air. With a guttural cry that came from both Past's and Lahn's physical bodies, he forced the arm high enough to reach the window, and hooked Past's clawed hand on the window's edge.

With the grasp on the window to hold the weight, Lahn untangled the other arm, added it to the first, and held tight. Dragging the leg back onto the ladder, he pulled Past's body fully upright, to stand in front of the window.

All he had to do was get inside. It should be easy. But he was so tired. As he gathered his energy for one final push, the darkness passed over his eyes again, thick like syrup, and the connection splintered and broke.

Lahn felt the locked room of darkness and dust rush at him, and he was back with his own body. The hyper-realism of being in Past's body was gone, and Lahn was left with the muted senses of his own Depersonalization episode.

But he wasn't alone. There was another consciousness with him, hiding in his head.

Cowering in a dark corner, Past had fled to the relative comfort of Lahn's mind.

"Past! Your body needs you!"

Past didn't hear. Didn't care. He wouldn't respond to logic; he wouldn't respond to words. And with nothing controlling his body, he was going to fall.

Lahn had one chance. In a flash, he thought about what mattered most to him: his family and friends. He imagined his mother and Tia. Even stupid Maddox. He quickly thought of each of their faces. And he imagined them without him if he died. They would be devastated. He couldn't give up. He couldn't hide. It was why he always fought so hard to overcome Depersonalization. He may not be important to many people, but he was vital to those that meant the most to him.

His emotions were powerful enough to overwhelm him, and his DP threatened to expand, but he drew the emotions in and reveled. The feelings echoed to Past, bounced back stronger, and grew in intensity with each reflection.

"Now, go!" Lahn begged, a plea bound up in family and love.

With a blast of terrified loyalty, at the speed of thought, Past left.

NOTHING PERSONAL

ahn opened his eyes wide and tipped back from his sitting position to lean on his elbows. As he drew in gulps of air, every muscle twitched. He leaned back farther until he lay flat-out horizontal. The pain from the wounds on his back spiked, and the cement felt cold against his head. He relished the sensations, adding the smells of dust and desperation from the room. As he breathed deep and his heart slowed, his own Depersonalization receded.

"Wow," he said, absently running his fingers along the rough cement under him. "Why was that so bright? So vibrant? So different from normal DP?" For a moment, Lahn expected Lucia to respond with some weird but strangely helpful insight. "And why was it so much longer than the visions?" But of course, she didn't. He was once again alone.

Past had survived. But Lahn was exhausted, and he wanted to sleep. He reached a hand up to his face where he'd collided with the ladder and warehouse wall, touched it and winced at its tenderness. The bruise felt worse than it did yesterday, maybe from the compounded senses of Past and Future. Hopefully, it would fade, from stupidly painful to simply annoying. But right now, it added to the spike of pain in his forehead. The supernatural headache that told him Past was now in the warehouse.

"Oh . . . right. Not done."

Like his manager at Criterion who asked in a grouchy voice for project updates, the mythical headache reminded him of his remaining tasks. Lahn still needed to stop Faceless from going back in time. He still needed to escape the room.

As his headache increased and became stronger than the pain on his face, Lahn picked himself off the floor, picked up the steel joist he'd dropped, and stumbled over to the door.

"Listen door," he said, voice like sandpaper, "you're in my way. So unless you let me out easy, I will beat on you until you do. Nothing personal."

Lahn drew back and slammed the steel into the door. The vibration from the strike ran up his hands and into his head, rattling his teeth. He bit down hard and hit the door again. He could feel the thud deep in the bruise on his face and every wound on his back. He hit the door again.

And again.

And again.

After less than a minute, he wished for a pair of leather gloves—or better yet, a bazooka—and he stopped to look at the damage. It was difficult to see in the dark, so he ran his fingers along the metal of the door, the paint flaking away from the slight indentation where the beam struck the door, like cracked leaves under his fingertips. His progress was pitiful.

The painful sensation in his head grew. It became a rusty spike, straight into his brain, as strong as he'd ever felt it. Past was close and Lahn was out of time. He squared his shoulders and smashed the door again. And again.

"Must! Get! Out!"

The strikes vibrated through every wound on his body.

His headache eased, and he knew Past was moving toward the center of the building. A growl rose in his throat and he pounded with energy he didn't realize he still had.

"Must! Stop! Faceless!"

Each agonizing strike that didn't open the door increased his anxiety. He had to get out and—

A crack of energy followed by a hum stopped Lahn on his next swing. In a flash, his headache disappeared, switched off, replaced by his stomach rising into his chest. Past was still there, Lahn could feel him. But the device was starting, somehow interrupting the headache.

Lahn backed up a few steps, and with a primal scream, ran forward and slammed the steel beam into the door. With a crash like a cannon, the force of the strike broke through the badly damaged door and frame. Lahn's momentum carried him through, and he stumbled and fell, landing on one shoulder as the beam flew from his hands.

His surprise at his freedom caused a moment of hesitation, but he scrambled to his feet and sprinted down the hall. As he ran, the center of the building pulled at him, a companion to the growing mechanical hum. He took the bonus of lighter weight and sped through the hallways, faster than he'd ever run.

A few turns and Lahn came to the hallway that led to the heart of the warehouse. As he stepped forward, a blinding flash of blue light and déjà vu exploded through the open doorway at the end of the hall.

And time stopped.

[He feels every part of his body, frozen in the moment, one foot off the ground. Almost flying toward the center of the warehouse. One last chance to fix everything. At the same time, he experiences with perfect clarity

a moment a few days ago, just before his meeting. Between one step and the next, he is walking toward the kitchen. The strong feeling of déjà vu bewilders him. He is unsure what he is feeling, naive to the struggles soon to come.

Overlapping both is a third version of himself. This one is also in the warehouse. But this one is on the ground, grasping the shelf in desperation to avoid the pull toward the center of the storm. That third version is jealous of him, of who he has become.

And he feels for the other two versions of himself. They still have so much pain and danger ahead of them. He tried to stop it, stop every bad thing from happening.

Tried. And failed.]

Time resumed with an explosion of violence. A wave of energy pulled Lahn off his feet and forward, and he slammed against the wall in front of him.

As he slid to the floor, a ripping sensation in his core took his breath away. The feeling of loss made him gasp. Lahn was left with a hole in his soul where moments before had been the connection to Past.

Splinter Report: S15-002
Date: 2516-01-14
Local Date: 2040-07-09
ID: S15
Designation: Quietus

Report:

The probe reports coming back from Quietus include video of an intact world, void of any natural light. As anticipated, this Splinter should provide an appropriate test platform for the possibility of the loss of Sol on Prime.

The probes have also been able to recover data recordings from the initial time travel that resulted in the creation of the Splinter. Unlike previous events where the loss of celestial light took minutes or hours, the loss of all light including the sun was instant. Of course, this was due to the spatial size of the Splinter pocket universe.

Monitoring and documenting the likely-devastating effects on society and the ecosystem of Quietus will take some time, but should generate beneficial results.

T. Hobbs

STUBBY PENCIL

With a ringing in his ears, Lahn struggled to his feet and stumbled down the hall. As he passed through the doorway and into the main area, he stopped and despaired at the chaos before him. There was no sign of Faceless and Past, and the room was a disaster, boxes and trash thrown everywhere. At the center of the room, the electronics were mostly untouched—except for the time machine, which was gone, the cables that had connected to it sheared cleanly. But strangely, the farther from the center he looked, the stronger the impact of the event seemed to be.

It wasn't like the attacks, where huge chunks of a building were ripped out and obliterated. Unlike the implosions at the attacks, nothing in the warehouse was destroyed, just thrown around and busted up a bit. He wasn't sure what made this event different, but whatever it was, he realized how lucky he was he hadn't died.

He didn't feel lucky.

Lahn slowly sat on the ground and put his head in his hands, fighting a feeling of despair. He'd had one last chance to fix things, and he'd failed. Past had still traveled back in time. But worse, so had Faceless. And now nothing would stop him from the final attack that could kill a thousand people.

"What do I do?"

He couldn't get help from Lucia. He had no portable or any way to call Tia. Maddox still had the other handheld, and Lahn pulled his from his pocket. He lifted the handheld and pressed the button on the side to turn on the screen. Just like the night before, nothing happened. Looking closer, he could see a spider web of cracks radiating from the corner. Sometime last night it had been broken, leaving him with no way to even talk to his best friend, jerk-betrayer. Not that he wanted to anyway.

Subconsciously, Lahn reached out to Past, hoping he fared better. A gulf of emptiness, and Lahn remembered with a slight gasp that his connection was gone, ripped away cruelly when Past traveled back. There weren't two of him anymore. Lahn was truly alone, in a way he hadn't been since it all started. It surprised him to realize how much he felt the loss.

With a tremor and an ache in his hand, Lahn put the handheld back in his pocket. He took a deep breath and held it, starting the grounding process. He knew missing his meds for two days was probably making everything worse. He didn't want to take the next step in his exercises, and struggled to fight off despondency. Nothing mattered. He should let his DP take away his pain.

A second deep breath, in through his nose, and he forced himself to pay attention. He smelled strong odors of dust, moldy cardboard, and a whiff of his own angry sweat.

A third deep breath filled his chest. As his lungs expanded, the wounds on his back stretched and complained with spikes of pain. His arms and legs ached. His face ached. Everything simply hurt.

A fourth deep breath, the sound of his gasps loud in his ears. The quiet of the warehouse was offset by birds chattering happily somewhere outside, an emotion distant and foreign, but one he longed for.

A fifth deep breath, with eyes wide open, and he paid attention. The limited light streaming through the windows was a warm gift from heaven. Yesterday, when he'd been in the warehouse with Maddox, he'd found the shadows oppressive. But now, after a night of true darkness, the smallest light felt like salvation.

He looked around at the mess in the warehouse. It was a perfect metaphor for his chaotic thoughts. But a mess could be cleaned up, and the mess in his head wasn't permanent.

A meter away, a couple of papers caught his eye, and Lahn shifted forward to his knees to pick them up. One was the sketch of a stubby pencil and a single word; *under*. He still didn't know what it meant, but the other page was crystal-clear. It was the timeline, including the final attack. One thousand, the potential casualties, happening today at noon.

Lahn moved back to his feet and rose, holding both pages. It was time to get up.

"The clues are here. The answer to the location is here." He stepped through the clutter of paper and boxes, stopping to pick up anything that looked promising. None of it seemed to provide anything new. After a few minutes he stood up straight, stretching, and looked back at the entryway, symbolically looking back at the past and the tragic events . . .

"Wait . . . is that . . ." Walking forward, Lahn stuffed the stubby pencil drawing and timeline in his pocket. He bent to pick up a small item, gunmetal black, a half-circle shape. It was an ear cuff with a small, blinking light on its edge, demanding attention. *His* ear cuff. The one Lucia sent him. His hand trembling, he slipped it on his ear.

"Hey, Pilgrim," said Lucia, "I have no idea how to know if you're dead. We really need to work on that."

Lahn opened his mouth, but said nothing, afraid of how it would come out. Blinking a few times to clear his eyes, he let out a shuddering sigh. He was not alone anymore.

"I watched you disappear in a flash of light!" she said. "Then suddenly you appeared in a different part of the warehouse, in different clothes, sat moping on the floor for a bit, and now here we are."

"I . . . I got lost in time."

"Yeah, I know. I figured it out just before you disappeared. You're not psychic; you went back in time and got entangled."

"I went back two days," Lahn said with a slightly manic laugh. "Since then, I've been tooling around with Maddox, trying to stop the attacks, and wishing you were there to help."

"Well, good job. Is that the right thing to say to someone who traveled through time?"

Lahn shrugged, a grin on his face. "I'm just glad the cuff didn't self-destruct after I lost it."

"Oh, no, it doesn't work that way. I have to trigger it. If you hadn't shown up, I might have. But it was only seconds."

Lahn's laugh had a frantic edge that he fought to control. "I like illegal tech."

"You mean like that tech in your pocket? Reads like a handheld terminal, but super locked down."

Land reached into his pocket and pulled out the handheld. "It's broken. Maddox and I used them to sneak into Living Bliss."

"You broke into a building? You really had some *brilloso* adventures without me, didn't you? But it's still on, I can connect to it."

Lahn chuckled, turning to walk back toward the havoc in

the center area. "Doubt it. We paid a lot for these. Its encryption is very strong. I'm not sure if—"

"I'm in. Oh, and there's a message on it."

He stumbled to a stop. "What?"

"It looks like someone tried to connect to talk, but you had the feature turned off. So the processor just stuck the audio in storage. Do you want to hear it?"

"I didn't even know it could do that." It had to be Maddox. He wasn't sure he wanted to listen to anything Maddox had to say, but curiosity wouldn't let him ignore it. "Yeah. Play it."

"Okey dokey."

"Lahn," Maddox's voice said through the ear cuff. "I know you don't want to talk to me. But it's letting me leave a message. I hope somehow you get it." He sighed heavily. "No matter what you think of me, please just trust this one thing: you've saved a lot of people. If I could have gone in your place, I would have. But it had to be *you* going back in time. And I hope with everything you and I found, I can save a bunch more lives. But, there are really bad people involved. I tried to protect you, and I failed. Please, stay hidden. Stay safe. Sorry I got you into all this."

"Why'd he say you didn't want to talk?" asked Lucia. "Are you two fighting?"

"He's the one that sent me the puzzle," said Lahn. "So he knew about the time travel, and is behind everything that happened to me. It was all his fault; he kept me in the dark, and wouldn't even tell me why."

"The jerk!" exclaimed Lucia with righteous indignation. "Next time I see him, I'll punch him in the face." She paused for a moment. "Except . . ."

"You don't have arms?"

"True, but no. I mean, except maybe he had a reason for not telling you why?"

"If he did," huffed Lahn, "it'd be dumb."

"Ha! Classic Maddox. There's also a text message from Tia on here. It was sent this morning. Want me to read it?"

"Of course."

"She says 'The red-haired boar is worried you are missing. I volunteered to look for you at your work. If you get this, don't go there. Go back to your apartment and we will meet later.'"

Lahn sighed deeply and walked toward the door at the back of the warehouse, stepping around the mess of half-decomposed boxes and paper. The idea of going home to his apartment and talking with Tia about everything that happened sounded amazing. To be back in his life, to be done with stressing and worrying about visions and explosions and . . .

"Lucia," he said, coming to a stop.

"Yeah?"

"There's going to be another attack."

"Whoa, really?"

"Today. In a few hours, at noon. We need to stop it. I don't know where, but maybe with your help we can figure it out."

"Shiny! Just like old times—you and me, saving the world. But first, another message from Maddox just came through."

"Lahn." Maddox's tone was an odd mix of panicked calm. "I just left the warehouse. I couldn't do much, but I did what I could. To make sure Past was in DP. To make the trip safer."

"Safe?" said Lahn. "What does he mean?"

"I wish I could talk to you," continued Maddox. "To explain everything. I wish you were with me right now, to help with what I am about to attempt. But I'm glad you're not. I hope you're as far from all this as possible. I figured it out. I know where it will be. It was in the images, something we didn't understand. I don't know how I can stop it, especially without your DP, but I have to try. I have to save Tia."

Tia? "What . . ." Lahn struggled, "what is he saying? Save

Tia?" Lahn's hand cramped as anxiety bloomed in his chest. "Lucia, call Tia."

"Nope. Tane says Tia is unavailable."

"Try Maddox."

"Nopes. Kensha says Maddox is unavailable."

Maddox had figured it out, the location of the last attack, and he had gone there to stop it on his own.

Finding it hard to breathe, Lahn realized he was fairly sure he also knew where it was.

He pulled the papers he'd found from his pocket. One thousand possible casualties, someplace with lots of people. Lahn *did* know of a place like that, a place where Tia would be. He switched to the pencil drawing, and stared.

It was not a drawing of a pencil.

It was a simple sketch of an Egyptian obelisk. Lahn knew exactly where Maddox had gone, and with alarm, he knew Tia was there too.

"Lucia, the last attack will be at Welkin Tower. At Criterion. At my work."

PUFF OF
OZONE

The slowing of the autoride pulled Lahn from his frantic thoughts, and a quick glance out the front window revealed the skyscraper of Welkin Tower several blocks away, rising over its neighbors.

"Let me out here."

He got out of the autoride and moved toward the crowds. The scene before him was uncomfortably familiar.

"Looks like our message worked," said Lucia.

"No kidding." With Lucia's help, Lahn had posted an untraceable announcement to multiple message boards on the Mesh describing the attack and its time and location.

Much like at Renelogy Solutions, a flurry of emergency vehicles and personnel swarmed the area. Unlike Renelogy, Welkin Tower had no parking lot, with the closest parking garage a few blocks away. The buildings around Welkin filled the blocks, with just the occasional park and walking path, every inch of it a crowded chaos. Besides the larger number of local police and federal agents, the military had been called in, with tan vehicles and uniforms everywhere. Waves of people streamed from Welkin Tower and its neighbors, thousands and thousands of them. Directed by emergency personnel—and instructions on mobile holographic displays and the large video displays on surrounding buildings—the masses were moved through stanchions, rope, and barricades, then loaded into military buses and sped off to safety.

"Do you think they disabled the device?" asked Lahn, gawking at the crowds. "Maybe we've thwarted their plans and they called the whole thing off."

"We don't actually know anyone's plans," said Lucia. "The explosion could still happen."

Lahn shook his head. "At least with our message, they have to clear the buildings or risk public outcry if the explosion happens. Is there still time?"

"Two hours and forty-three minutes to evacuate ten thousand people from Welkin Tower and its neighbors. There should be time."

"But how do we find Tia and Maddox in all this?"

"I've got workers scanning all the camera drones. So far, nothing. I've got to be careful in my approach, though. Dodging DTS AI."

Lahn looked down the street at Welkin Tower. At fifty stories, it was one of the taller buildings, taller than any of its direct neighbors. Toward the top, the engineering was breathtaking, with several negative spaces that seemed impossible, creating the illusion of sections that floated unsupported, as if by magic. The outer facade was consistently black and reflective, such that it was difficult to tell where the steel ended and the glass began, and almost all of it could generate solar power. Even so, a building that size undoubtedly had an on-site fusion generator, likely housed in the basement.

"Tia probably went to Criterion on the thirteenth floor," subvocalized Lahn, dodging through the crowds of people, and doing his best to ignore the press of bodies, his beating heart, and the cramp in his hand. "Are you able to see inside?"

"Trying now, but the security system is skittish."

"If Maddox . . ." Lahn's emotions about Maddox were complicated. His message was contradictory and confusing and Lahn didn't know if he could believe him.

"If Maddox," Lahn said, completing his thought, "is trying to stop the explosion, would he be in some dark, secret corner of the basement?" Lahn came up to the barricade. They were holding the onlookers two blocks back, but the view of the emergency activity and the building itself was unobstructed.

"Oh no," said Lucia. "That's an—"

"That's a what?" asked Lahn, as he stared at Welkin Tower. He couldn't help but imagine the building in ruins. If a chunk of the bottom imploded, the weight from above could bring down the entire building, or topple it into nearby neighbors. A projection of one thousand casualties was probably low.

"Excuse me, Lahn?"

Lahn turned to find a woman slightly taller than him, considering him intently. She wore a simple blue suit. He assumed she was an office worker in one of the buildings and wondered how she knew his name. But something about the blank-intensity of her expression made him pause. She reached into her jacket and pulled out a small wallet.

"I'm Agent Kenderson," she said, opening the wallet and showing him an ID and badge. The badge seemed to expand and take over his entire vision. She was a DTS agent. "Would you come with me?"

Lahn's brain freaked out and told his body to run. His body didn't listen, instead it obediently stepped forward as the agent directed.

Their walk was a fuzzy blur, past the barricades, through the emergency personnel and evacuees. She slowed as they came to a black van with darkened windows in a cordoned off area among ambulances and military vehicles. The agent opened the sliding side door of the van and ushered him inside to a seat at the back. His body continued to comply, even as Lahn's mind screamed at him. She stepped in and sat facing him on a backwards bench behind the driver seat.

"Please empty your pockets," she said.

For a moment, Lahn didn't understand the words, and struggled with simply breathing. When the meaning finally permeated his brain, he remembered what was in his pockets. Stolen cash, illegal tech he'd purchased from a sketchy site, and two pages that gave him unusual knowledge about the attack. And being caught with contraband wasn't even his biggest worry. If the DTS was *involved* in the attacks, any evidence that he'd somehow caught wind of their nefarious plan would be very, very bad.

"Please," Agent Kenderson repeated, a little slower, "empty your pockets." It was clear from her tone the polite phrase was not a request.

Fighting the pain in his hand, Lahn reached into his pocket. His fingers found the cool glass and smooth metal edges of the handheld terminal. He mentally scrambled for anything he could do to avoid bringing it out. His mind delivered a huge pile of nothing.

As the agent's stare became more intense, Lahn slowly removed the handheld from his pocket, and handed it over.

Agent Kenderson examined the device for a moment, attempted to turn it on, then placed it in a basket next to the seat. "Other pocket," she said, turning back to Lahn.

There had to be options for avoiding incriminating himself, but he couldn't think of a single thing. Reaching into his other pocket, he pulled out the cash he took from Maddox's apartment and the papers from the warehouse and handed them to the agent.

With no visible reaction, she counted the cash and placed it in the basket. The two pages—the small obelisk drawing and the timeline—held her attention for several long seconds before she added them to the rest of the collection.

"And the cuff," she said, pointing to his ear.

Lahn glanced at the agent's own cuff before looking away and reaching up to take his off. Lucia had been confident in the security of the new cuff, sure that it would appear completely normal, even to government AI. If she was wrong, there was nothing he could do to protect her. Trying to appear as if he couldn't care less, he handed over the cuff and it went in the basket.

And then they sat, quietly, facing each other with nowhere else to look. *How can someone go so long without blinking?* he wondered absurdly. As time stretched, Lahn tucked his cramping hand under his other arm, and examined his shoes.

A noise startled him out of his important evaluation of footwear, and the side door of the van slid open, revealing Agent Prakash with another agent in a matching DTS anorak. Agent Kenderson grabbed the basket and stepped outside with the two other agents, closing the door behind them.

"...handheld...encrypted..." Individual words bled through the metal door. "...AI couldn't unlock...on these papers..."

The door opened again, and Agent Prakash stepped inside alone, holding the two papers from Lahn's pocket. She slid the door shut and sat opposite Lahn, the morning light through tinted windows casting harsh shadows on one side of her face. All traces of her feigned kindness from their other interactions were gone, and her large eyes bored into his.

"I'm pressed for time," she said flatly. "Right now I have one question. Where is the device?"

"It's not in the basement?" His surprise at her question tricked the words out of his mouth.

Agent Prakash continued to stare at him, the energy of her eyes threatening to crush his soul. She didn't answer, but he didn't need her to. Her question said everything. If she was asking, the DTS was not involved in the attacks. And they had no idea where the device was.

His heart took off like a speeding horse. No one was disarming explosive devices. Everyone was still in extreme danger. Including Tia and Maddox.

She held up the timeline. "I know you're involved, Lahn. This has the same date and time as the anonymous message on the Mesh. Where is the device?"

"I . . . I don't know where it is," he struggled out, trying to avoid her dangerous eyes.

"Lahn, look at me. What is this?" she asked, holding up the drawing of the obelisk.

If Maddox had figured out where the device really was, he could be anywhere. And Maddox was on his own, no one to find him and get him safely away.

"Lahn!" Agent Prakash snapped.

The van door slid open. "They need your help on the north side," said Agent Kenderson.

"Fine. Cuff him and keep him here. See if you can get anything else from him." She stepped out of the van, dropped the pages into the basket in Agent Kenderson's hands, and stormed off, leaving the other two agents behind.

Agent Kenderson pulled a set of handcuffs from her jacket and climbed back into the van, taking Agent Prakash's place. She placed the basket next to her seat and turned to Lahn. "Hold out your hands."

Without really realizing it, Lahn held out his hands and

Agent Kenderson snapped the handcuffs in place with a click of the electromagnetic lock.

Tia and Maddox *might* both be on a bus right now, whisked away to safety. Lahn wanted to believe it. His whole body ached with a desire to make the wish true.

"Tell me about your ear cuff," said Agent Kenderson, holding it up.

Lahn looked up at her. Lucia could help him figure out where they were, but there was no way to get the cuff or talk to Lucia without revealing her existence. Hopefully she was hiding anyway.

"It looks expensive," said the agent. "You don't make that much money. Why spend so much on a cuff?"

If Maddox had figured out the drawing, that's where he was. It was just that stubborn word *under* that didn't make any sense. If it was supposed to mean the device was under the building, it was a lie. The device wasn't there, or the DTS would have found it.

"And it seems you got a new, expensive proxy, too. Better than the basic AI you had before. Felice? Is that what you named her?"

Unless . . . the drawing didn't mean under the building. Maybe there was a space directly under the obelisk, under the sidewalk in *front* of the building.

"Let's talk to her." Agent Kenderson slipped the cuff onto her ear. "Felice?"

For a moment, nothing happened. Then the cuff started blinking, the agent got a puzzled look on her face, and she reached up. Suddenly, before her hand could touch it, a pop and tiny electrical sparks flashed from the cuff with a puff of ozone. Agent Kenderson's body shook once, her eyes rolled into the back of her head, and she slumped sideways across the chair.

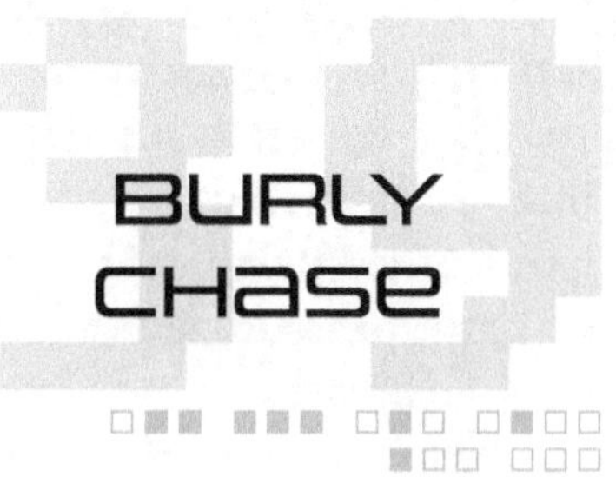

BURLY CHASE

Lahn hunched down in his seat, staring at Agent Kenderson. Her limbs spasmed, vibrating her whole body, and white foam leaked from her mouth and ran down her chin. After a full minute, her body stopped moving, but he could see her breathing slowly and his own held breath fell into synchronized rhythm with hers.

"Agent Kenderson?" Lahn queried quietly. She didn't respond. "Agent Kenderson?" he said a little louder with no result.

"Wow, Lucia," he whispered in awe, full-well knowing she could no longer hear him. "Sometimes, you *are* kinda scary." Lahn leaned forward, carefully removed the cuff from Agent Kenderson's ear and examined it. Cracked with scorch marks, and still warm, the cuff was destroyed by the self-destruct mode that stunned the agent.

He'd lost Lucia again, just after he got her back. But he didn't have time to wallow. He needed to find Tia and Maddox and make sure they were safe, or find the tech and stop it for good.

"She's going to be so mad when she wakes up," said Lahn,

looking at the agent again. With extreme care, he pinched the lapel of the agent's jacket and pulled it back. Slowly, he reached inside her pocket, and pulled out a ring of keys. Laying the edge of the jacket back into place reverently, he settled back in his seat.

Now, what's the right key? he wondered. The ring held a mix of traditional, magnetic, and circuit security keys. The handcuffs didn't have a slot for a traditional or security key, so Lahn pressed each magnetic key against the handcuffs until he heard a snap and they popped open.

Dropping both the handcuffs and keys on the floor, he leaned forward and grabbed the basket, putting everything back into his pockets. The van sliding door did not include a window, and he tipped his head to look through the passenger side window and mirror.

Standing with his back to the sliding door, the brawny man that came with Agent Prakash stood watch. The suit he wore would probably hold two Lahns—Past and Future—but there wasn't a gram of fat on the hulking beast.

Lahn carefully slid into the driver's seat. For a moment he daydreamed of driving the van away, leaving the agent behind cursing his name. Not that he could actually go anywhere. The van was blocked in by the vehicles around it. Instead, he slowly opened the driver side door, stepped out, and quietly closed it.

Ignoring the official personnel rushing around him and the violent beating of his heart, Lahn moved purposefully through the surrounding emergency vehicles, toward his work building and the crowds of thousands of evacuees. The obelisk was on the sidewalk, ten meters in front of Welkin Tower, a block in front of him. But he needed to find an entrance to the underground space below it—maybe angled doors, or a grate in the sidewalk.

"Hey!"

Lahn glanced back. Coming around an ambulance he'd passed was the mountain of an agent that had been standing watch outside the van. Lahn turned to the right and sprinted for the crowd exiting a nearby building, dodging through emergency personnel.

"Hey! Stop!" Heavy steps pounded behind him.

Nearing the stanchions that corralled the crowds, Lahn took a deep breath, jumped the rope, and plunged in. Using his smaller frame, he wove and dodged smoothly between lines moving toward the evacuation buses. If the noise of startled and upset people behind him was any sign, the burly agent had a harder time getting through the crowd.

After quick navigation through a gaggle of people, Lahn ducked down as he ran, pulled off his red jacket, and dropped it, leaving the white T-shirt underneath. A quick shift to the side and he slipped into a stream of people moving toward a bus. He knew he shouldn't look back, but after a stressful minute, he risked a glance.

The tall agent held his red jacket and looked around to find his lost quarry. Lahn took a deep breath and ducked his head, turning forward with the rest of his group. He just needed to stay lost among the others for a bit, and then step out of line and make his way back toward the building. Without the pounding of his heart giving him away.

After another minute, he risked a look back toward his work building. With each step, he was being moved farther away from it. As his line passed the end of the building on his left—an older skyscraper less than half the height of Welkin Tower—he noticed in the alley a large grate set in the pavement. Lahn stopped, looking closer. A few meters from the grate, a broken padlock lay on the ground.

A woman bumped into Lahn from behind.

"Hey, why did you stop?" she said.

"Sorry," he mumbled, moving out of her way. He quickly ducked into the alley.

The lock on the grate had been cut and removed. Leaving unlocked exactly what he was looking for: an entrance to an underground space. And someone had gone through it recently.

Someone . . . like Maddox?

It felt like he was too far away, almost two blocks from the obelisk. But what were the chances of finding another unlocked entrance? With a flex of his aching hand, Lahn reached down and pulled open the grate.

The hole into the earth opened before him, a dark mouth to a cavern. Probably swarming with goblins or orcs, and he'd left his Elven sword at home. A set of metal steps led down into the darkness, and Lahn hesitated at the top. He'd fought his way free from the dark less than an hour earlier and he wasn't anxious to enter the oppressive black maw before him without his flashlight. Or the cuff Lucia gave him with its meager light. At this point he'd take a stick wrapped in oil-soaked rags. Not that he had a way to light it. Fuzziness pressed at the edges of his vision, but he thought of Maddox's stupid face somewhere in the dark, and took a deep breath to calm his thundering heart.

He had no idea how long he'd been detained by the DTS, but it couldn't have been more than an hour. He should have at least sixty minutes to find Maddox. With eyes wide open, he started on the stairs, pulled the grate closed after him, and continued down, letting the darkness swallow him.

The stairs ended in a stone hallway that led away from the buildings above. A light appeared in front of him, and he hurried toward it. Small, yellow, and doing little to reduce the somber tone, the illumination was nonetheless welcome, saving him from a full-on need to panic. The light lived in an industrial sconce at the top of the wall, with more at five meter intervals.

The tunnel was stone, dark with age. Older than the buildings above ground, ancient dust filled his nose. Iron pipes and silver and black conduits ran along the ceilings and walls. Many pipes seemed due for repair, rusted and dripping water, which mixed with the dust on the floor and left a thin, slimy layer.

He moved forward as quickly as he dared, careful of his footing. After he traveled far enough to be under the street, the tunnel ended in a junction, with one path leading left and the other right. From his current location, unless he'd already gotten completely turned around, the obelisk should be somewhere to the right.

As he moved down the new hallway, he fought to ignore the oppressive space and the pain in his hand. After seemingly forever, a nondescript shape appeared on the floor ahead. He moved closer and the shape became clear. A body.

No . . . two bodies.

A man and a woman he didn't recognize, both in black T-shirts and pants, lay in a crumpled heap on the floor—no obvious wounds. Lahn stepped carefully around them in the small hallway and moved on, fighting to get a solid breath. He couldn't stop to check on whoever the poor souls might be. If he didn't hurry, they'd all be dead.

Up ahead, a muffled noise echoed through the hallway. He moved forward, each step eroding his confidence, and the sound became more pronounced. Someone shouting.

It sounded like Maddox.

All thoughts and concerns dissolved in a flash, and Lahn ran for the voice. Suddenly a deep thump followed by a large electric crack echoed through the pathway, the sound bouncing off stone, and he felt his stomach rise in his chest.

Without thinking, Lahn sped toward the danger. A flickering glow shone around a corner, with a hum he could feel in his teeth and an electric crackle that caused the hair to rise on the back of his neck.

As he turned the corner, he found an open room the size of his mother's suburban garage. Set on either side of the dark area, construction lights highlighted electrical panels on the walls, but did little to offset the gloom. Two cameras on tripods lay on their sides, smashed against the floor. And there, close to the back wall, was the technology he'd been chasing since the beginning of time. The box was suspended off the floor about waist height, mounted in a framework of scaffolding much like the setup at Living Bliss, with other equipment connected and configured around it on folding tables. The device was powered up, and the strange orb at its center glowed and pulsed, casting flickers and flashes of green.

With his back to Lahn—in the dark-blue overcoat, gray hoodie, and leaning over the device—was the person he'd been running from and after.

A third person, closer to Lahn, stood facing away, looking toward the technology. But Lahn would know that shaggy ginger mane anywhere. It was Maddox, and he stood a mere meter from enough destructive power to bring down multiple buildings.

Before Lahn could step toward Maddox, someone screamed, a blinding green flash filled the room, and something fell to the floor with a solid thump.

Lahn stumbled backward. It took several moments of frantic blinking for him to realize he wasn't dead. As his vision cleared, a giant, pulsing sphere of energy became visible. At five meters across, the sphere filled most of the room, with edges phasing into the floor and walls on either side. It had glowing patterns of emerald plasma that shifted across its surface, and it wasn't solid but somehow held its shape. Occasionally an arc of energy jumped from the sphere to the metal casings of the electric panels on either side of the room and created a sharp, astringent odor. Undisturbed in the sphere's center stood Faceless, still facing away from Lahn, and engrossed in some aspect of the equipment.

But just outside the sphere, Maddox now lay on the ground, out cold.

"Maddox!"

He rushed over to his friend and crouched down, feeling for a pulse. For a moment, he could only feel his own thundering heart. After adjusting his fingers, he found a slight beat against his fingertips. It was weak and sporadic, but it was there. Just to be sure, he tipped his ear to Maddox's mouth and found ragged but consistent breathing.

Lahn sat back and let out a gasping breath. "You're alive, you stupid idiot!"

"Be careful, or you'll be knocked out like Maddox."

Lahn's head snapped up. He knew that voice.

"I told him to leave," Faceless continued. "I told *you* to stay away. I *really* wish you'd listened." Faceless dropped the hoodie, revealing dark fuzz on a shaved head. With an expression that Lahn could easily read as heartbreak, Faceless turned—Tia turned—and looked over her shoulder at Lahn.

OUT OF TIME
AND SPACE

ahn gasped, struggling to get a full breath. It was impossible. Tia couldn't be Faceless. She had always taken care of him, not attacked him. She always helped free him from his demons, not locked him in a dark prison. There was no way she was the one that dragged him through time and broke his life. There was no way she . . .

"You need to go," said Tia. She shifted her body to face him, both hands remaining in the device. "I'm holding the sphere in place, but you see what the energy did to Maddox. I don't know how long I can hold it. You need to take Maddox and go."

Lahn stood from where he'd checked on Maddox, blinking out the frustration from his eyes as he stared at Tia through the glowing sphere. "I don't understand. You're Faceless."

Tia grunted.

"Why are you Faceless?" asked Lahn, his voice rising. "You dragged me through time and locked me in the dark. You blew up two buildings. Why?"

"Because the alternative was worse."

"What could be worse than thousands of people dying?"

Tia's response came out quick and clear. "*Everyone* dying."

"What do you mean? Everyone in the city?"

"Listen to me. I've shorted across the contacts in this device with a screwdriver," said Tia, nodding her head at the box next to her. It was similar to the devices he'd seen before, with a strange, glowing orb floating in the center that pulsed green. The top of the box was off, and Tia's hands were inside. "But if I even twitch, I could lose the connection. You *need* to leave!"

Lahn's emotions shifted into dangerous territory, heart thumping in the scar on his hand and the bruise on his face. The room shifted and he fought to maintain control. "I'm not leaving until you tell me *why*."

"Please, Lahn," begged Tia. "Just go."

"Tell . . . me . . . why."

"I'm trying to save the world." Tia took a deep breath and looked back at the box. "I can't tell you much," she said in a rush, "it might put you in more danger. All I can say is Maddox and I were working on a project, and learned about this tech. And discovered it is . . ." she paused and took a deep breath, "apocalyptic. It's different from the time machine. Instead of a tunnel in time, it creates a tunnel in space. In-between space. But the devices are flawed, and could rip a hole in space-time, destroy the atmosphere, destabilize the planet, or knock it out of orbit. Or who knows what else!"

Lahn stared at Tia, eyes wide, and took an involuntary step back from the enormous glowing sphere that surrounded her. She was saying the problem was bigger than the one thousand casualties from the warboard. More people were in danger than just the buildings above, or even the half million citizens in the city. The entire planet could die.

Struggling to get a breath, Lahn fought to keep the darkness in his periphery at bay.

"The way to stop all of this would be extremely danger-ous," Tia continued quickly, scowling back at Lahn. "And I tried to keep Maddox away. Keep you *far* away, for all the good that did. I needed to go back in time to stop the events. Then, I modified the start-up process of each device to stop the space-time tear, but I couldn't stop the implosion. And this one started sooner than I expected, so all I could do was jam this screwdriver in here and pause it, hopefully long enough to get everyone to safety."

"Can't you—" Lahn sputtered, trying to ignore his pulse beating heavily in every wound from the last few days, "can't you turn it off?"

"Turn it off?" Tia said with raised eyebrows. "I don't even know how long I can keep it paused." She shook her head, then tipped it toward a box near her inside the giant sphere, about three meters away. "If I could disconnect the amplifier, it would collapse the wave and stop the implosion. But I can't reach it from here, and I can't let go."

Lahn took a step toward the sphere—ignoring the dan-gerous flickering light and the way it raised the hair on his arms—and looked through the field at the amplifier.

"No! Stop!" said Tia, forcefully. "Don't touch the field." Lahn took a step back and Tia released a shuddering breath. "Seriously," she said. "You need to get out of here."

Lahn looked at the power panels on the sides of the room and the thick cables that ran from them to the equipment. "There's got to be something we can do. Can we disconnect the power?"

"It's connected to the building's fusion power, which is why the experiment is happening here. But that connection is at the generator, about ten meters behind me, on the other side of the wall."

Tia closed her eyes, and suddenly Lahn was shocked at how worn down she appeared. "The fusion generator is the real danger. If I let go and the sphere hits the generator, it would cause an energy feedback loop. And even though I've stopped the space-time tear, like I did on the others, if the plasma from the sphere interacts with the plasma in the generator, it would happen anyway."

And then rip a hole in space-time, thought Lahn. *Destroy the atmosphere, destabilize the planet, or knock it out of orbit.* Lahn's hand cramped into a ball, and the fuzziness at the edges of his vision pressed on him angrily. He took a deep breath, drawing in odors of dust and plasma, fighting off the pending Depersonalization episode.

"Lahn, please," said Tia, pleading in her voice and tears in her eyes. "Take Maddox and go. Once you are out, see if you can find someone in charge. If they shut down the fusion reactor, I can release the screwdriver and let the sphere take its course."

"And the building?"

"Much of the bottom floors will be destroyed, and the building will probably collapse. Maybe taking other buildings with it. But they should have everyone out by then."

"What about you?"

She shook her head.

"No!"

"I'm sorry you got wrapped up in all of this." Tia's voice cracked. "I wish you weren't here. It should've been impossible for you to be pulled back in time with me. You should have died. People *have* died, anyone caught in the wave, unless they are connected directly to the machine. I don't know how you survived, but that's not important. If you stay *here,* you will die. Maddox will die. Please . . . take him and—"

A sudden scraping noise at Lahn's feet drew their attention. Maddox's body spasmed violently, writhing against the stone ground.

"Don't touch him!" cried Tia as Lahn bent toward Maddox. "Don't touch his skin, you'll be knocked out."

The sphere had expanded and one of Maddox's hands was now caught inside the energy field. His body arched in reaction. As Lahn watched impotently, the field expanded farther, slowly moving up Maddox's arm.

Careful not to touch any skin, Lahn grabbed his shirt and yanked backward. Maddox's body collapsed as his arm left the plasma field. With a grunt and a scramble, Lahn dragged Maddox back toward the hallway, putting as much distance between them and the expanding sphere as possible.

"What's happening?" Lahn cried. "Why is the sphere getting bigger?"

Tia leaned over the device. "I don't know. I must have only slowed it down."

They both looked in the direction of the fusion unit, some ten meters beyond the wall. "How much time do we have?" asked Lahn.

She paused. "Enough . . . if you go right now."

But . . . she was lying. There wasn't enough time to find someone and shut down the fusion reactor. At the rate the bubble was expanding, they had minutes. He looked back at the equipment and the amplifier that Tia said could collapse the sphere.

"You can't, Lahn," she said, tracking his gaze. "You can't cross the energy horizon—you see what it did to Maddox, and he didn't get the full force of it. He's lucky to be alive. This field won't send you back in time, it won't send you anywhere. It will just pull your consciousness out of space and time. Your mind can't take a split from the here and now. If you try to go through, it will kill you. We already lost Dad, I can't lose you too."

Lahn blinked a few times. *Out of space and time.* His sister just described his Depersonalization episodes: a mind split from the here and now. She didn't know why he'd survived the time travel.

But *he* knew.

For the past ten years, his Depersonalization was a curse, one he struggled every day to keep at bay. But what he had said at his father's grave was wrong. His DP *could* be a strength. Maybe it was exactly what he needed now. Maybe, it could save everyone.

One of the construction lights popped with a loud crack and a shower of sparks as the energy barrier overtook it. Lahn ducked and covered his head, then slowly rose and squared his shoulders, ignoring his racing heart.

In the dark cavern with only one remaining construction light, the fluctuating glow of the energy barrier took on an ethereal quality. Small nodes of plasma current danced and jumped, beautiful and deadly. Everything about it screamed danger. He knew an attempt to go through would pull his brain from reality.

"Unless . . ." Lahn said out loud to himself, not really noticing as Tia looked at him, eyes jerked wide. "Unless I was already split from reality, from the here and now."

Lahn stepped back several meters, shook both arms, and took a few quick breaths. Ever since the warehouse a couple of hours ago, he'd been balanced on the knife's edge of a Depersonalization episode. In reality, he'd been fighting them off for days, ever since his first vision of the malevolent Void, when his future-self had gone back through time. Every moment afraid of another episode taking over, and working so hard to keep them away. The last several days had been one exhausting fight after another, like standing alone holding back the hoard at Helm's Deep. And he was so, *so* tired. With a terrified sense of relief he let go, and felt his perception slide from his body.

Everything changed.

Sounds and smells faded into the background and the brightness of the energy field dimmed. A pop echoed off in the distance, filtered through cotton. Lahn thought he felt his body flinch at the sound, but he wasn't sure.

Wait . . . what was I doing? He was *so* tired.

The sphere wavered in front of him, its dull light flickering through water and glass. It was like a giant aquarium, and Tia was swimming inside, eyes wide.

Tia.

"Oh, yeah," said a voice that wasn't his, slowly. "I need to save Tia."

Lahn, he thought, wishing he could lay down and take a nap, *you can do this.*

He could do it. He had to do it, or everyone would die. Closing his eyes, Lahn fought through the apathy and fog to remember everything he'd battled to get to this moment. *This* was it. *This* was his Ring, and he had to brave the fiery lava of Mount Doom to destroy it.

"Lahn, what are you doing?" asked a panicked voice that sounded something like Tia.

Go!

Like using a game controller that was losing its charge, Lahn's efforts to move his body resulted in nothing more than a stuttered step. His body didn't want to run face-first into that stupid glowy sphere.

"Lahn?!"

Mentally, Lahn pulled back on the control stick and slammed forward with all his might. "Frodo, Go!"

Finally—as Tia screamed at him to stop—his body bolted forward, hitting the bright field at full speed.

MESH STORAGE - 2012-08-22 08:05:01

Hey, Dad. It's me.

I'm on my way to Lahn's work, the location of the last device.

I can't believe how alone I feel. I've spent so much time over the last few days arguing with myself, literally. And now, I am going into this one blind, and all I can think is I wish I had my past-self for support.

My best-case scenario is very grim. But as long as I can stop the rift, I don't care what happens to me.

I've been thinking about you a lot this week. I like to think that somehow you get these, and send your love and support back through the universe.

I love you, and miss you, more than I can express.

SPLINTERS

Two things happened instantly. An excruciating spike of energy hit Lahn's body, painful even through the protective shield of Depersonalization. At the same time, everything shifted, then disappeared.

[His mind is in the impossible space of infinity. Time is stopped, and in that moment he is confused, terrified, and cold. All rational thought is gone. He is now a creature of raw emotion. Angry, but stubbornly determined.

But he is in a non-space where nothing can exist, and the vast Void presses down to drive him to annihilation. He flees, moving through neither time nor space, but something else. His consciousness seeks any source of life and light as a sanctuary. After forever—or an instant—his mind senses a source of salvation, and he slips between eternities, escaping.

He can sense a vast body. A world . . . but more. He feels kindred beings of emotion. So many: hundreds of billions. Small bits of rational thought seep in—like salt sprinkled on food, as it dissolves and joins with existing molecules. He understands, the world is not one, but dozens, all overlapping, all unique. Each is like his own, with cities and buildings and people, and hope and anger and love. But each is vastly different.

The nature of each world solidifies in his mind, and he marvels at the variety. One is saturated by nightly torrential rain, unnatural in its volume and frequency, the plant-life as dominant as the water. Another is a world of ghosts. The inhabitants have grown accustomed—if never quite comfortable—with sharing everyday life with specters, as numerous as the living population. Yet another contains people that never die, living in copies of themselves. But this world has stars! Actual stars. Not a story of legend told fondly by the old generation. Tiny pinpoints of light in the black, night sky, more than could ever be counted.

It is all marvelous. It is all overwhelming. And he wants to go home, to his body. He searches each of the dozen-odd worlds, to find the familiar, striving to find one that feels like his own. He can sense these worlds do not contain even a copy of his life, a variation of him . . . except one. At last—or instantly—he finds his world. And his mind is drawn, with all the power and energy and speed of the universe, to his being.]

With a snap, Lahn dropped back in his body, into the moment. But time remained frozen. One of his feet hovered, suspended in the air. His motion was paused, half in and half out of the bright but silent energy field. He couldn't move, but he was home.

Even frozen in time, he could think again. Rational thought returned with the reuniting of body and mind. And he could recognize each individual thought and emotion competing for attention in his head: everything that crashed down on him at the moment of the spike of energy.

The events of the last few days—culminating in an overwhelming experience that would take a lifetime to parse—had taken a toll on Lahn. He was exhausted, in a way he'd never felt before. Tired in his soul and sick of reacting. He wanted to lie down and sleep, and not worry about what more would happen tomorrow.

But, he had a much stronger emotion that dominated his thoughts. He couldn't turn his back and go hide under blankets. Not anymore. He didn't care if they had lied to him; he needed to save those he loved.

And it wasn't only them. He would save everyone. He had failed at Living Bliss, but he wouldn't fail this time.

Except the little problem of still being frozen in time.

If it was a fight to be free of a Depersonalization episode, he'd use his grounding exercises and start with his breathing. Unfortunately, at the moment he couldn't breathe.

But he could still *feel*.

I can still feel, and I feel . . . everything!

He could feel the spike of pain frozen on a path through his body. He felt the way the electricity of the sphere raised every hair on his arms and neck. The smell of carbon in his nose, but not yet taste on his tongue. He felt every pain, bruise, and cut he'd earned over the last few days.

And though he couldn't move his eyes, he could still see. Through the glow of the sphere, he could see Tia. One hand reaching toward him, the mixed expressions of horror and hope in suspension on her face.

It *worked*. The connection to what was real pulled him out. Like waking from a dream, Lahn slid from the frozen moment in time. With a jerk, his feet landed heavily, and he fell to his knees. Pain coursed through his body, and his stomach threatened to escape through his mouth, but he was alive and inside the sphere. Tia looked at him with astonishment as he stumbled to his feet. And he looked back, tears leaking from his eyes, but a wry grin leaking from his face.

"Let me hold that," he said as he moved stiffly around her to the device. He carefully placed his hand on the screwdriver, alongside Tia's, holding it in place. She continued to stare at him.

"I don't know what collapsing the field will do," she said as her voice caught. "It could kill us. I don't want you to die."

"I don't want *you* to die either. But it's more than just us. We have to save everyone above ground too. I'm not leaving."

Tia blinked a few times, looked at the expanding sphere, then nodded. She took a deep breath and slowly removed her hands as he held the screwdriver in place. When nothing exploded, she let out a ragged breath, looked at Lahn, and finally smiled.

"I got this," said Lahn. "You go deal with the power thing."

Tia moved to the amplifier, dragging an open toolbox with her. She pulled out another screwdriver and started taking the screws out of the front panel.

"I don't understand how you did that," she said as she worked, pulling off the front panel. "It shouldn't have been possible."

Lahn shrugged. "I used my DP."

Tia glanced back at him, eyebrows raised and mouth open. Shaking her head, she looked into the amplifier and switched to a tiny screwdriver. Crouching down, she worked to remove an inner mesh cover. "I hope we survive, so you can explain." After disconnecting several brackets, she gently pulled a small bundle of wires out from the box and grabbed a pair of wire cutters. She hesitated, the cutters hovered over the wires coming from the amplifier, and looked at Lahn. "If we don't make it out, I'm sorry, and I love you."

Tia cut the wire.

A loud electrical crack and a blinding flash burst from the amplifier and Tia jumped back. The glowing sphere around them collapsed with a sound like a body hitting a stunt airbag, mixed with aquarium rocks sliding off a metal tray into a vat of pudding.

The energy from the sphere swept inward with a rush over Tia and Lahn, and time slowed again for a moment. He stumbled forward as Tia's eyes rolled back into her head and she collapsed. Lahn thought he would also end up on the floor, but the effect passed.

Stumbling to his sister, Lahn sat on the floor, and checked her pulse. She was still alive. The energy field was gone. The device had been deactivated. It was over. They had done it. They had pulled off a miracle and saved the building and thousands of people.

Oh, and the world.

STRANGER IN THE MIRROR

Lahn laid his head on his arms. He had tried putting his head directly on the table, but it was cold and hard. The chill felt nice against the bruise on his face, but after a few seconds, the unforgiving metal made everything else feel less nice. Too bad it was so difficult to sleep in a DTS interrogation room.

After collapsing the sphere, Lahn had carefully carried Tia out of the underground chamber. He'd huffed and puffed, struggling to keep his momentum as he backtracked through the stone hallways, but he had managed to get outside. He'd planned to find a safe place to put her and then go back for Maddox, but two blocks from the entrance, the DTS found him.

They had taken Tia to the hospital under guard, but he had no idea what happened to Maddox back in the underground cavern. Did he wake and escape, or was he taken into custody too? Lahn didn't dare ask.

When they brought Lahn to the DTS field office for questioning, they dumped him in the room, and then nothing. It had been hours. Being locked in the interrogation room could've been an unpleasant reminder of being locked in the dark room at the warehouse. But after everything he'd been through, it was a pleasant surprise to realize it didn't bother him too much. He'd been through worse.

Of course, his pending interrogation worried him. He had no idea what they knew, what they suspected his involvement was, or how he was going to answer any of their questions. He was fairly sure he was going to prison for the rest of his life.

But it didn't concern him as much as it should. After all his failures, he had succeeded. He had saved Tia and Maddox, stopped the implosion, saved a thousand people or more from a terrible death. Probably even saved the world.

The real problem was the stupid mirror that took up most of the wall in front of him. All it took was a few times seeing a reflection he didn't recognize while in a DP episode to make him leery of mirrors, even now. And so—head on the table.

The door finally opened, and Lahn sat up slowly, still careful of his sore back. Agent Prakash came in with a blue file folder under one arm. She stood quietly and looked at Lahn, head tilted to the side, eyebrows slightly furrowed. Lahn imagined all his secrets, the details of every incredible thing that had happened over the past few days, streaming over the air from his brain into her dark, penetrating eyes. She wouldn't believe it. Who would?

"How's Tia?" he asked, breaking the silence first. Remarkably, his anxiety of talking to her was overwhelmed by the need for information about his friends. *Is Maddox okay?* he thought, not daring to ask out loud in case Maddox had actually gotten away. *Do you know where he is?*

"Well," she said, "she's stable and being watched closely. She went into the hospital in a coma, but I just got word she's awake. She will recover fully. I'm going to see her after we're done here."

One layer of anxiety lifted off his shoulders—like a giant harpy perched there for hours finally flew off, seeking other prey. Tia wasn't his only concern, but he felt his shoulders relax and lift, free of the released weight.

Continuing to watch him closely, Agent Prakash placed the folder on the table between them and sat in the chair on the other side of the table. "What was it like?"

Lahn cocked his head to the side in confusion.

"Traveling through time?" she asked.

"I . . ." Of all the questions he had imagined he'd be asked first, that was not one of them.

"We found the warehouse. You've been there a lot. We retraced your movements over the last week, and they got very interesting a couple of days ago. At first, we couldn't understand how you could be in two places at once. But then our techs figured out what that device from the warehouse was for."

Even hearing Agent Prakash talk about it was weird. Time travel was supposed to be impossible, yet he'd done it. He'd lived it. His entire life over the last couple of days had been the consequence of that time travel.

But now, it wasn't the most bizarre and unbelievable experience. Going through the sphere boundary surpassed it. Whatever he'd seen as he passed through the plasma—worlds layered on top of worlds, dozens or more—was far beyond anything he could ever imagine. It was hard to believe they were real places, earths with immortals or ghosts or no sun. He wished he could talk about it with Tia or Maddox or Lucia.

Agent Prakash continued to stare at Lahn intently. "Your friend Maddox is also in custody."

"Is he okay?" The question came out before he could stop it.

She raised an eyebrow. "He's fine. I just talked to him."

Lahn took a deep breath and let it out as a slow sigh, relief washing over him like water from a warm bath. Maddox was okay. Tia was going to recover. A few hours ago it felt like all three of them were dead. But they came back from the brink. Too bad they were all in custody, but maybe they could stay in family prison together.

"He helped us extensively, telling us everything he knew." Agent Prakash's eyes grew thoughtful. "I can let you see both of them. I just need information from you first. Help me fill in the gaps."

Lahn tentatively looked past Agent Prakash at the giant mirror behind her. As he feared, a stranger stared back. But not in the way he'd expected, not as a consequence of Depersonalization. He was not feeling disconnected from himself. He was seeing an interloper, but not because reality was broken by a DP episode.

This stranger in the mirror was someone inflicted with extreme events. But they survived. They conquered. There was a familiar weariness, but about weightier things: others over self. This was someone who wasn't as worried about what people thought of them. Someone that wasn't concerned about what might happen to them.

He saw himself. And, yes, he was a mess. He was still in the clothes he had borrowed from Maddox, with the white shirt too big for his frame that replaced the one shredded at Living Bliss. They were the same clothes he wore when breaking into the warehouse for a final time, to end up trapped overnight in a pitch-black room with a cement floor. His hair was a tangled mess. His face was a bruised mess. He needed something clean to wear, a shower, and a decent night's sleep.

But none of that hid the strength and confidence he'd earned over the last few days. Lahn saw himself, finally, as he truly was: as someone capable. Just as his dad always said.

Agent Prakash leaned forward. "Maddox feels bad."

Lahn's gaze shifted to the agent's.

"That you three," she continued, "caused so much death and destruction."

Lahn creased his eyebrows, puzzled. Why would Maddox say that? Did he feel as Tia felt, responsible that they couldn't do more? But Maddox was knocked out in the final battle. Maybe he didn't know they won.

"No," Lahn said, shaking his head slowly, but keeping his eyes on Agent Prakash. "It's not like that."

Her eyebrows rose. "What's it like?"

"We *saved* everyone. The city. The world."

Agent Prakash tipped her head to the side and said in the voice of a parent to a child, "I see." She pulled out her portable and started a function to record their conversation. "Tell me about it. Let's start at the beginning."

RETURN OF FUTURE

ahn stretched his aching legs on the heavenly mattress with relief. He pressed the button next to the bed for heat rejuvenation, and a warm tingling sensation permeated his sore leg muscles. The latest tests had been endurance on a treadmill. He had no idea what they were currently trying to learn. The previous tests involving blood samples and skin responses made more sense, looking for traces of his crazy adventures; the time travel or going through the plasma sphere. But making him run? That was just mean.

Lahn leaned back against the cold cement wall behind him and closed his eyes as the bed worked its magic on his legs. He'd been in the DTS detention facility now for two weeks, and the bed was a recent change. His previous bed had been fine, maybe even better than his one at home. But this new one was like being hugged by baby angels. He had to wonder if the DTS was using him to experiment with new sleeping tech.

The tests were not the only fun thing filling his days. He'd had multiple follow-up conversations with Agent Prakash. But he was also passed around to different departments, each group taking an interview bite. They'd even assigned him a therapist, to augment his renewed medications. He'd described all the various events of his adventure so many times it was losing all meaning.

Lahn didn't know what would happen to him—no one would say, and it distressed him constantly. Having a therapist to talk to again had helped, even if he knew it was all reported back to Prakash. But there were questions he was worried he would never have the answers to. Who really made the time machine and how did Tia get ahold of it? Or who made the plasma-sphere tech and what was it really for? He'd asked those questions multiple times, but had always been shut down.

Some of the questions the various groups asked him had been sticky. It turned out keeping Lucia's involvement a secret was challenging. Her status was still a source of anxiety for Lahn, and he wished there was a way to talk to her.

Maddox and Tia continued to worry him too. Agent Prakash had yet to fulfill her promise to let him see them. He asked every time they talked, but she endlessly put him off, just repeating that it would happen soon.

Pressing another button near the bed, Lahn turned on the display embedded in the wall. It lit up at the foot of the bed behind bulletproof plexiglass. The view options were limited, but he set it to a news program. There were still occasional reports on the series of explosions that culminated in the evacuation of Welkin Tower and its neighbors, but after two weeks it was no longer a top story.

The news from Welkin Tower was particularly frustrating. The DTS never released the information about the device found in the underground cavern. As a result, most news sources were saying the possible attack at his work was a hoax, riding on the fear of the previous explosions. The DTS had gone one step further and claimed that from their investigations, the other two explosions were simple industrial accidents. That hadn't stopped the speculating masses, but the fervor was quickly dying.

A noise from the door pulled Lahn from his thoughts, and he swung his legs off the bed to sit up fully. Hopefully they weren't taking him for another running session. That might make him cry. As the door opened, he looked up, and to his surprise Maddox slunk in, looking back out the door and closing it quickly.

"Hey," he said, turning to Lahn with a crooked grin.

"Maddox!" Lahn jumped up and wrapped his best friend in a hug.

"Whoa. Okay, I missed you too."

Lahn stepped back and held the larger man at arm's length. His hair was chopped raggedly short, he wore an ear cuff, and it looked like he was wearing secondhand clothes. "What are you wearing? And why are you here? Did Prakash finally give you permission to see me?"

"What? Of course not. Talking to her would just get me caught. I broke in."

"You *broke* in? How did you get *out*?"

"Of what?" asked Maddox, eyebrows furrowed.

"The detention center. How did you get out of custody?"

"I was never in custody. Who told you I was?"

"Prakash."

"She lied." Maddox walked to the small desk that was nothing more than a cement shelf protruding from one wall. He twisted out the attached seat and sat, turning around to look at Lahn. "After I found Tia and the device in that cavern, there was a blinding flash of light. When I woke up, she was gone and the device was off. So I stumbled out, saw all the crazy government activity, and ran. I've been avoiding cameras and tech ever since."

"Wow!" Lahn looked at his friend, then back at the door, and then at Maddox again. "I'm so glad you weren't caught, but . . . you're gonna be. Coming here was stupid. How'd you even get in?"

"I had help. No one's gonna know I'm here." Maddox's cheshire grin against his horrible haircut made him appear a bit deranged.

"Look, Maddox," said Lahn. "I understand why you did what you did, sending me back in time. You were trying to protect Tia, and send someone with her. It had to be me, because my Depersonalization would protect me."

"Well, yeah, but—"

"And," continued Lahn, cutting Maddox off, "I get why you lied. You were just trying to shelter me from dangerous information and scary people. I understand. It's all good now."

"Okay, but—"

"I still have lots of questions, but you shouldn't have come. You need to get out of here before someone shows and you get locked up with me."

"Lahn . . . shuddup." Maddox took the cuff off his ear and handed it to Lahn.

Eyebrows scrunched in confusion and resisting the hope budding in his chest, Lahn slid the cuff onto his own ear.

"Frodo!" said Lucia in his ear.

"Luz? You're okay?"

"Of course, old man."

"And you revealed yourself to Maddox?"

"Yeah, I needed someone to do the physical stuff to get you out. But—"

"Lucia said you two saved the world a year ago, before all this started," interrupted Maddox, not hearing Lucia. "And we need to get the band together, in case we have to do it again. That is a story I need to hear!"

"Tell Maddox to shut it," said Lucia. "We're out of time. Tia's been moved from the DTS to someplace I can't track. I get hints of a nefarious group. All I know is it's not the DTS that has her anymore. *And* they're coming for you, too. We gotta go, now!"

Lahn scrambled off the bed, his heart racing. "Lucia says we gotta go. They're coming for me."

Maddox stood, grabbed the doorknob, and looked at Lahn with a face set in determination.

Lahn stepped forward, but then stopped. A powerful feeling of déjà vu washed over him, and he sagged against the door frame.

[Time stands still, with vast, malevolent energy that will obliterate everything in its path. Nothing exists here. Nothing could exist. Yet, he is here and he shouldn't be. He is about to be utterly and completely destroyed.]

"Lahn!" hissed Maddox.

"Lahn!" screamed Lucia. "You must go now!"

Lahn fought to get back into the moment as Maddox helped him up. Maddox cracked the door, looked both ways, and took off down the hall, Lahn staggering after him.

"Go left!" said Lucia.

"What just happened?" asked Maddox as they ran.

"The Void!" gasped Lahn. "Another vision. Like my very first."

"What do you mean?" responded Maddox as he checked over his shoulder, breathing heavily. "Like when Future-you went back in time?"

"Why would that happen again?" asked Lahn, as a feeling of connection trickled into his core.

"Lahn?" said Lucia. "You've got a call. You are going to want to take it."

"*Em?*" said Tia through the cuff.

Lahn stumbled in shock, then moved quickly to catch up to Maddox. "*Chị?* Are you okay? I thought you were in custody."

"That's my past. I traveled again. And I'm not alone," she said.

"Hey, Past," said Future-Lahn in his ear. "You guys escaping right now? I hope so, because we've got a lot of work to do."

acknowledgments

I started the first outline for this book more than four years ago. At the time, it was just an idea for a spy thriller that involved flashes into someone else's life. As the plot developed, it transformed into something more sci-fi-y, involving weird tech and stereotypical characters. The novella that came from that was not great, but kind of fun, and my family was super supportive.

So I kept at it. Expanding the world, growing the characters, filling out the plot. I discovered fun ways to tie different moments together and create events for Lahn to live through that were much more complicated. And hopefully, much more interesting. In the end, while most of the basic story line remains, very few of those original words survived.

As I worked on the book, the ideas for the Splinterverse started to form, how it existed and how the worlds were related. There are plenty of multiversal stories out there, but I wanted one to share with other authors, where multiple creators could contribute in very different and fun ways. I started working with a few other authors that had unpublished books that could be incredible worlds in the Splinterverse.

And Splinter Press was formed to make it all possible.

If you haven't yet, check out the first two books in the Splinterverse. Mere Mortal, and The Dissection and Reassembly of Cohen Hoard are amazing stories. The multiple worlds are not really exposed in those books, (although there is a hint right at the end of Cohen Hoard) but there are Easter eggs and references in this story that start to tie the worlds together. And I am super excited for what's to come.

And speaking of Splinter Press, I can't express strongly enough how amazing the team at Splinter Press has been. The editorial and creative teams were wonderfully aggressive in helping me refine and find the true story I wanted to tell.

I am super grateful to all the people that helped me with this book. My writing group reviewed early chapters and helped me find my voice. There were others, like Michael Doran, Jennifer Bown, and Brandon Regan, who also gave me critiques on specific chapters. The early readers—Anne Bown, Acell Bown, Kat Berrio, Demi Corbett, and others I will mention later—gave me great feedback on my first full version, when the story was one-third the size. After a half-dozen revisions the book got much closer to the final product, and the Beta readers—Brooke Hampton, Mike Saldivar, Tracey Lyn—were super amazing in helping me find the big issues that still existed in the story.

And the current version is really due to the hard work of A.J. Stevens, Elesa Hagberg, and Faralee Pozo at Splinter Press. Having read multiple versions of the book a thousand times, it's surprising they're not sick of it, but they were nothing but supportive all along the way, helping me find and resolve timing and inconsistencies, improve the prose, and add the sparkle. As well as Regan Wolfe, an amazing author that pushed, cajoled, and encouraged. I think she read every major revision from the first but one, and always helped me—with massive amounts of feedback—to know where to go next.

Of course, I need to express my highest gratitude to my wife and children. They read those early versions, and told me they were good. But more than that, there were many times over the past few years where this story threatened to consume all my free time, and they were patient and encouraging the entire time. This final book would not have been possible without them.

And thank you to you, my friendly neighborhood reader. I created this story because it wouldn't let me go. Hopefully you enjoyed it, and it resonated with you in some way. I can hardly wait until we connect again in another tale.

BOYDELL BOWN

As a software engineer by day and a supervillain by night, Boydell finds it a challenge to spend enough time writing to let free the stories plaguing his soul. But as a lover of all things speculative fiction, sci-fi, and fantasy, he is dedicated to make the necessary sacrifices.

Outside of writing, Boydell loves spending time with his family, playing games, and making Star Wars costumes and wearing them in public. Much better than going out in public in normal clothes.

Enjoy this book? Please leave a review!